After Dad

Claire Shiells

The Book Guild Ltd

First published in Great Britain in 2022 by
The Book Guild Ltd
Unit E2 Airfield Business Park,
Harrison Road, Market Harborough,
Leicestershire. LE16 7UL
Tel: 0116 2792299
www.bookguild.co.uk
Email: info@bookguild.co.uk
Twitter: @bookguild

Typeset in 11pt Adobe Garamond Pro

Printed and bound in Great Britain by 4edge Limited

ISBN 978 1915122 940

British Library Cataloguing in Publication Data.
A catalogue record for this book is available from the British Library.

For Dad

'...a man is not dead while his name is still spoken.'

T. Pratchett

Chapter 1

'He'd get up on a cracked plate, that boy.'

Millie heard the brawny Belfast accent from the row behind.

'He said I was a big ride. Jesus, my cheeks were flying off me.'

The bullish snorts and shrieks brought a smile to Millie's tired face. She was going home.

As the plane rattled up through the sky, she glanced at the copy of the *Belfast Telegraph* she had picked up before boarding. Scanning the headlines, Millie wondered if her mother still had the paper delivered. She hoped not. But maybe it would be no bad thing? Any distraction to stop her picking away at Millie's life in London: '*What exactly is going on with Dom? Why are you coming back virtually unannounced?*'

She tucked the paper inside her bag just in case.

Once she had decided to go home, Millie was amazed how easy it had been. Her editor, Tom, was already in the office when she'd called just after seven that morning. She knew he liked her, he had told her so at the last staff drinks, said she had a nose for a story. But then he'd gone on to say how cute that nose was. Having a boss who thought your nose was cute was fraught with problems. She'd been there before.

Today, though, it suited her.

'Course you must go if she's sick. God knows I didn't see it coming with mine. Don't forget us, mind. If there's a celebrity hiding out there in Ballygobackwards, I want to know.' Tom had guffawed at his little joke and hung up.

She felt a twinge of guilt. Her mother *was* sick, but maybe not as sick as she'd implied. For now, though, she was glad to be free from filing celebrity drivel about reality stars with big egos and bigger arses.

'Well, look who it is!' A familiar voice caught Millie on her way to the toilet. 'We were just saying how you always meet someone you know on the flight.'

It was Mary McFadden.

'Home to see your mother? I hear she's not been well, poor thing. Especially with everything she's been through.'

She imagined Mary's face if she told her the real reason for her visit. 'Yep, home to help out.'

'Well, that's just lovely, I know you don't get back much. Eimear and your brother were only saying that the last time they had your mum up to stay.'

Millie felt the touch.

'Too busy hobnobbing with all those celebrities, eh? And I believe your man is only something else. Lives in Chelsea, eh?' She stopped, waiting for a reply. When none came, she went on. 'And I hear you're always gallivanting round the world with him too. What's his name again?'

'Dom.'

'That's right. Dom. Is that short for Dominic? A good Irish name, that. Is he Irish?'

God, her big brother Jamie was right. Mary McFadden was the nosiest woman in Belfast. She'd have to change the subject. 'Were you over shopping?'

'How did you guess?' asked Mary, laughing as she pointed at the bags stuffed under her seat. Millie's heart sank as she watched her lean down and lift a plastic glass of prosecco from her table tray.

Mary McFadden, her sister-in-law's best friend, was *very* BT9. She lived in Royal Park, the most expensive road in the city, and her house, according to Jamie, was enormous, with carpets as thick as champ. She and her friends loved coming to London, or the *Big Smoke*, as they called it. A chance to escape their privileged, but provincial, lives. Hair, nails, clothes would have been carefully considered, and they'd be showcasing every diamond they had ever bought from Scott and Sons. Birthday diamonds, push diamonds, sorry-I-had-an-affair diamonds, sold-the-business diamonds, I-can't-buy-you-a-house-in-Spain-but-here's-some-diamonds-instead diamonds.

'You should have looked me up,' said Millie, delighted that she hadn't.

They were standing by the emergency exit, and her hope of being told to move along by a hostess seemed unlikely given the commotion on the trolley run further down the aisle. She was going to have to make an excuse to get away.

'Look, it's lovely seeing you, but I need to get my head down. File copy,' she said, looking quickly at Mary's two friends in the row behind, one of whom was wearing a big red hat with the price tag still dangling from the rim. An impulse buy. Had to be.

'For the races,' the woman mouthed, pointing to her head enthusiastically.

Millie smiled and noticed all three women were now scanning her from head to toe.

'File copy?' Mary said, sniffing. 'You need to marry that millionaire of yours.'

The friends were now opening their second snipe of prosecco and howling with laughter. The one without the hat suddenly spoke. 'Take my advice, girl. Get a ring on your finger. Give your head some peace.'

Millie quickly walked on. Squeezing past the trolley, she realised the commotion was around a passenger who had been refused a drink. When she saw the man's face, she wasn't surprised; it was puce-red. The air around him reeked of whiskey.

'I just want a feckin' drink, darlin'. What's the harm in that?'

'I have to ask you again not to use that language with me, sir.' The hostess smiled professionally.

Oh God, thought Millie, wriggling past. *One more feck and he'll be in an armlock and we'll be diverted to Reykjavik.*

Clambering back into her seat, she saw a group of friends sneaking some duty-free vodka across the aisle. The girl with the bottle in her hand caught her eye and Millie raised her eyebrows, thinking she could do with a drink right now.

Trying to get comfortable, she wondered what the friends would think if they knew what she had done. Would they pity her? Or would they challenge her? Her head was heavy with tiredness and the glare of the overhead lights was making her squint.

She put on her headphones and closed her eyes.

Drifting off into a world of whys and what-ifs, she became aware of an infant's cry. She opened her eyes and through a gap in the seats saw a new mother struggling to cope with a thrashing baby.

As she tried to block out the noise, a familiar sensation started to come over her and she tensed, gripping the armrests. A metallic taste came into her mouth and she felt hot. She shook off her wrap violently and tugged at her headphones.

She sensed the eyes of other passengers on her, but she didn't care. She felt trapped, suffocated; she thought she was going to pass out. A feeling of deep shame crept over her. She tried to shut it out, but it was too strong. She grabbed the sick bag just in time.

***

THE NIGHT BEFORE

Water falls from her wet hair like saline from a drip. Staring into the bathroom mirror, Millie blankly follows one droplet sliding down her forehead to the end of her nose. Only when it tickles her nostrils does she flick it away. Touching her cheek gently, she decides her skin doesn't fit her face anymore. Like a long-forgotten balloon in the corner of a room, it is slowly losing life. In the dull light of the flat, she has the pallor of death.

Moving down the corridor, she carefully sits on the end of her bed. Another mirror. Letting the towel drop, she wraps her arms tightly around her shoulders. Once strong from yoga, they now feel weak. Cold after the bath, she pulls at the duvet and cocoons herself inside. The instant warmth is soothing, and she closes her eyes. Lifting her knees up to her chest, she turns on her side. A mistake. Her eyes widen as they fall on the box. Upturned, kicked over – its contents spewed out like the guts of a slaughtered animal.

To think this was once something that brought pleasure, each piece a reminder of a place she went when she wanted comfort from home. She jerks away, and the sound of her laptop hitting the wooden floor pierces the silence. She leans over in time to see a small crack spreading from the corner of the screen. Her toes curl in anger and she scrunches her eyes, hoping to stem the flow of more tears. But it's too late.

Finally, she sits up, sniffing hard while dragging the backs of her hands across her wet eyes. She kicks the box upright. She remembers buying it at B&Q when she moved into the flat years before, a faux suede cube used to hold all that was precious to her. Now, it has turned into her very own little box of horrors. She has been through it every day since her visit to the clinic. She knows she shouldn't, but like a child or a greedy addict, she can't resist. She wants to feel her chest tighten, her palms sweat, and the nausea of bile swill around her belly.

After what she did, she deserves to feel it all.

She lifts the crumpled black-and-white photograph and places it in her palm. Her baby's first scan. Studying the grainy picture, her shaking finger outlines the fetus. It was the size of a plum, that's what the leaflet in the clinic's waiting room said. A ripe, juicy plum, growing silently inside of her, innocently preparing to burst into life.

Until it was plucked. Sucked out. Neutralised into nothingness.

Placing the image gently back in the box, her fingers touch the large brown envelope she'd wedged in there months before. The one the police report came in. The one about her father's death. A surge of guilt runs through her and flushes her cold cheeks. She's only read it once since the day it arrived, unannounced. She promises herself she will look at it again. Just not now.

She draws the curtains and makes the bed. Pulling on jeans and a sweatshirt, she twists her wet hair up on top of her head with a clip. She hunkers down by the bed and starts to tidy the rest of her keepsakes: the photographs of her mother's seventieth at the golf club, when all seven of them had made it home; the last birthday card her father had ever signed; a small, framed painting of Ardmara, the family cottage in Donegal.

Sitting cross-legged on the floor, Millie lifts the faded watercolour, remembering the day her father paid a man to paint it. The sun had been splitting the trees for a week and her mother was so happy, she had brought the kitchen table outside so everyone could eat lunch under the big oak. The artist, Pat Rafferty from the village, sat with them, and her father had said it was all very continental. Millie smiles, remembering the older children playing waiters with tea towels over their arms – running around the table saying, 'Oui,' and, 'Merci.' They had kept it up at supper too, even though by then the table had been brought in because of the rain.

She found the picture the last time she was home, propped up against the scullery wall. It looked so sad, and she had wondered whether it was about to be thrown out, no longer needed in the new kitchen extension Jamie was planning for their mother.

Millie thinks about Ardmara. She hasn't visited the cottage in years, yet she'd been so happy there. They all had. Pulling herself up to sit on the bed, still clutching the picture, she makes a decision – the first real decision she's made in weeks. She will go home.

***

Millie loitered as far away from the carousel as possible in an attempt to avoid Mary McFadden and the Derby hat. Leaning against a pillar, she watched an army of Savile Row pinstripes mill around the arrivals lounge. Civil servants. No doubt over for another crisis talk at Stormont. Her mother would have had a field day. As the carousel started to move, she felt a heaviness settle on her bones.

In the new terminal, drivers with name boards were everywhere, picking up passengers in Yeezy sneakers, heading off to the new offices of Google or Amazon on the banks of the Lagan. She felt a stab of resentment.

Why couldn't it have been like this when I was growing up?

Outside at the pick-up point, her eyes caught the gleam of a white Range Rover. It stood out boldly against the greyness of the Belfast sky and the familiar *CH1K 3* number plate made her heave with relief. Sasha had come for her.

Straight away, her oldest friend's blonde curls came bouncing out of the driver's seat window, just like a puppet on strings. The horn was beeping repeatedly, and her face prickled as she walked towards the noise, smiling apologetically at an elderly couple who were scowling in the car's direction.

Sasha beamed as Millie pulled herself up into the passenger seat, and for a moment, the friends sat in excited silence, taking each other in. Millie couldn't help but notice her friend's tan. This time it was beyond Mediterranean and, teamed with her neon gym gear, reminded her of a ballroom dancer. Like the ones on the TV.

'Well?' asked Sasha, handing her a takeaway coffee. When Millie remained silent, she pushed again. '*Well?*'

Millie considered blurting out the truth, telling her friend everything, but quickly decided against it.

'It's Mummy. She's not great.'

'Your mum? Not Dom?'

'Look, she'll be fine. I just wanted to see her. You know how long it's been.' She was using her best let's-not-talk-about-it voice. 'Anyway, how's your own mum?'

'Oh, you know, up and down. It was Michael's anniversary last week. She always goes quiet on us then.'

Millie's smile dropped and for a moment the old friends were lost in a shared past. Millie's father and Sasha's brother: one shot, one blown up. Both gone forever.

A new melancholy had seeped into the car like stale air, and she tried to shift the mood. 'This place looks different every time I'm back.'

'Dave says we're the toast of Europe now.'

Millie laughed in her head. 'How is the grumpy git anyway? Mummy says he's taking over the town. Or his chickens are.'

'Oh, he's alright. But I sometimes think all he cares about are those bloody birds.'

'How many now?'

'Another factory and abattoir.'

'Christ, where does he get the workers from?'

'Still Portugal, Poland, Lithuania – but we try to stay away from the Liths. Honestly, Millie, they're lethal. Once they start drinking, they just can't stop. They'd stab their granny for a drink.' Sasha sipped her coffee. 'A bit like the way we used to be.'

They laughed in unison, even though Millie winced at her friend's bigotry.

'I know most of the town don't like what we're doing,' said Sasha, lowering her voice. 'But we treat them well. Not like others I could mention.' Then, as if she had said something wrong, she changed her tone. 'Did you manage to tell your mum about our wee detour?'

'Ballydunn? Wee detour?' Millie made her eyes big. 'Yes, I told her, but you can imagine she wasn't too pleased. Seriously, Sasha, I can't be too late, or I'm dead.'

Her friend pulled a sad clown face. 'I promise. I just really want you to see the house.'

Millie knew she shouldn't go. She should go home. Sit with her mother.

Leaving the airport at speed, Sasha glanced over. 'We've put in a hot tub, you know.' Then she added enthusiastically, 'I'll never see the children – it'll be great.'

Millie briefly wondered how her friend's tan and various extensions coped in the heat and froth of a hot tub. 'How do you ever look after five?' she asked, watching Sasha skilfully queue up a playlist with one hand, without engaging her long purple fingernails.

'Jesus, Millie, I don't know how it happened,' she said with a laugh. 'Do you think I'm a Catholic deep down?'

As Millie settled back into her heated seat, Ed Sheeran blaring from the speakers, her shoulders dropped. This was the life her mother so wanted for her: five children, a rich husband, and a hot tub.

During the journey, Sasha gushed about her new holiday house and its sea views. Millie felt a stab of irritation. Ballydunn was where she had holidayed as a child. Not Sasha. Something she had growing up her friend didn't. About the only thing.

But in truth, the family had stopped going to Ardmara after Dad. If anyone ever asked, her mother was always quick to point out she didn't have time to bless herself, let alone take the family to the seaside.

And now here they were. Driving to Donegal in a Range Rover with white leather interiors to see Sasha's new house. As she pushed back into her seat, she inhaled deeply. Only then did she pick up a distinct whiff of chicken feed in the car. Her body softened. Not everything in Sasha's life was perfect.

After ten minutes of talk about London and Millie's celebrity gossip from the paper, the conversation changed. Sasha talked about an old school friend who was getting divorced and another who had cancer. Driving through Mulloy they stopped talking altogether. When they passed the memorial garden the friends were once again lost in a terrible shared memory.

She had been staying with older cousins in London when the bomb went off. It was scorching hot and they were out shopping. A crowd had gathered around a TV shop window and when she saw what they were looking at, she had started to shake. Her mother and aunt Lizzie shopped in Mulloy every Saturday of summer.

She had been helped inside the shop and the kindly owner let her use his phone. Thankfully, her mother answered. She had a cold and wasn't well enough to go out that particular Saturday in August. Millie still remembered her mother's rasping, ugly sobs. It was the first, and only, time she heard her cry after Dad.

Millie moved around in her heated seat and closed her eyes tight, trying to forget about everything.

Chapter 2

Thirty minutes later, they had crossed the abandoned border into Donegal. When she got her first glimpse of the sea, Millie's mood lifted.

The county had always been popular with families from home. It was quick to get to and the beaches were sandy and empty, but when the Troubles started many Protestants stopped going there, or anywhere in the south, preferring to stay with their own on the coast of the north-west.

Sasha drove quickly, navigating the wild Atlantic coastline with confidence.

'What made you buy up here anyway?' asked Millie. 'I thought Portrush was more your style.'

'Well, if the truth be told, Dave hopes to set up factories here.' Her voice fell to a whisper. 'Get in early… you know… for when things change.'

Millie stared at Sasha. For the first time in her life, she realised the place she had grown up in, the place she still called home, could soon be changing forever.

Sasha slowed right down as she entered the village, and as she crawled through Main Street locals stopped and stared at the car. Turning up a lane opposite the harbour, Millie's jaw momentarily dropped.

After fighting with electric gates, Sasha brought the car into a large, cobbled courtyard with two ornate fountains. Sasha swung round to Millie, erupting with pride. 'I know. The first time I saw it without scaffolding, I was speechless too.'

Starting at the top, Sasha showed Millie every room in the turreted mansion, including en suites, a sauna, and a triple garage.

'It's amazing, Sasha. Really amazing.'

'You don't think the chandeliers are, like, over the top?'

'Not a bit,' said Millie, shaking her head firmly. 'Not a bit.'

Sasha's perfect teeth glistened in the late afternoon sunlight. 'I knew you'd like it. The decorator said it's "*very London*".'

Half an hour later, after Sasha had Zoomed the interior designer in Belfast with her lengthy snag list, she suggested they stop at the Fiddler's Inn on the way home. 'There might be music,' she said. 'It'll be good craic.'

Millie thought of her mother but agreed one quick glass wouldn't hurt anyone.

'What wine do you sell by the glass?' Millie shouted over the din of the pub.

'Depends.'

'On what?'

'What you want.'

'White. Dry if you have it?'

'Fussy, aren't you?' said the barman, finally lifting his eyes up from pulling a pint.

'Am I?'

'I can do white… or red.'

'Okay, white. Do you have small bottles?'

The barman didn't answer. He just stared at her then dropped his eyes to her chest. Millie bristled; she'd forgotten how indiscreet the locals here could be.

'If you want more than a glass, you'll have to buy a bottle.

Twenty Euro. If you're paying in sterling – it's still twenty.'

Millie thought for a moment. 'That's fine. Can I have two glasses? Oh, and do you have an ice bucket?'

The barman lifted his eyes to the ceiling.

'Jesus, Dermot, stop drooling over there and get us three more pints,' a voice boomed from across the bar. A roar of laughter went up and Millie felt her face burn.

Much to her annoyance, the barman, Dermot, did exactly what was asked of him. In all the years Millie had visited the Fiddler's Inn, things hadn't changed. Women were still served last.

The pub wasn't a total tourist trap like some in the village; there was no thatched roof or cartwheel props. It did, however, have one magnificent attraction: a huge turf fire that burned day and night. The smell was pungent and reminded Millie of summers past, playing in the bogs of Armagh with feral cousins. Tonight, however, the main attraction was decidedly sick, spluttering and smoking badly.

She was worried the chimney was on fire, but no one else, bar the American tourists who were fanning themselves with beer mats, seemed bothered.

Millie thought of the last time she had seen a real fire this size. Courchevel 1850. Skiing with Dom.

Waiting for Dermot to reappear with the wine, she glimpsed through cracks in the crowd trying to see where Sasha had gone.

A yelp made her jump. She peered down to see a black, scruffy dog staring at her, its lead weighted down tightly by a chalkboard menu, propped up against the bar.

Tuesday Specials: Fish Chowder – 8 Euro, Fish & Chips – 13 Euro, Traditional Irish Music & Craic.

Someone had chalked in the word bum before craic. Millie smiled and leaned down to pat the animal, but within seconds it was growling at her through gritted teeth. She stood up quickly, half expecting the owner to come over and apologise, but no one appeared.

Looking again for Sasha's blonde curls, she noticed how the locals were stooped over the bar, their heads deep in their pints. To one side, by the slot machines, a group of Goth teenagers were crowding over a mobile phone, sniggering. It was just after six, but the pub was already packed. Then she remembered it always was.

Dermot finally thumped a screw-top bottle of wine down in front of her.

'Nothing colder?' she asked, already knowing the answer.

'I'm a pub, not a feckin' wine bar,' he bellowed, throwing his arms up.

Millie slapped a twenty-pound note on the bar. 'Keep the change,' she said, grabbing the bottle by the neck. With glasses tucked under her arm, she began looking for a free table. When she couldn't see one, she gave up, deciding instead to return to the counter. Sasha could find her.

Just then, the front door swung open and a strong headwind was sucked into the bar. A group of men followed.

'Finn McFall. What feckin' time do you call this?' shouted Dermot.

'Wind your neck in, will you? We had to mend nets.'

'Just set up. They've been waiting ages,' said Dermot, jabbing his thumb over in the direction of some tourists.

Mend nets. A fisherman. Yet to Millie, Finn McFall could just have fallen out of a Guinness advert. He was tall and broad with dark eyes and even darker curly hair. Very Catholic-looking, her sister would have said.

'All right, lads? Better late than never, eh?' Dermot laughed at the group of stragglers tailing Finn towards the smoking fire.

As they trundled past, Millie spotted an array of Irish instruments: fiddles, pastoral pipes, and what looked like a Bodhran drum. One of the band members was clutching a well-fingered tin whistle. He was old and wiry and his hands were flaming red, as if they had just been scrubbed with bleach.

The pub was now full of expectation. Chairs were being scraped along the worn tile floor, making a semi-circle by the fire. At least three of the group were tuning up and one young lad, who couldn't have been more than fifteen, had to fight off the Americans as he handed out grubby lyric sheets.

Millie smiled; she hadn't been to a Ceilidh session in years.

Within minutes, the band was up and running. Looking at the hand-out, 'The Mason's Apron' kicked off the set, followed swiftly by the 'Exile's Jig' and 'Hangman's Reel'. The pub was pulsating with pleasure. People were foot tapping, finger drumming and table slapping. Some tourists were trying to dance in the crush, laughing as they tried to steady their drinks. Even the Goths had got involved: standing on chairs, their bat-like coats flapping to the beat of the Bodhran drum.

She had forgotten how Donegal was. Only fifteen minutes over the border from the starched north, it was a different world. Here, people weren't shackled by inhibition; they sang and danced and drank on any day of the week, not thinking about tomorrow.

'*Sure they never think about tomorrow, that's their problem in the south*,' her sister Karen had said when they last visited the pub together, many years before. '*Oh, they're all smiles now. Drinking, singing, and shouting, but most of them haven't got a stroke of work in them. It's their way.*'

Millie suddenly felt guilty about stopping at the pub. She looked for Sasha again and finally caught a glimpse of her friend waving her over. She was sitting at a far table between two men, maybe golfers, a drink already in her hand. Things hadn't changed. Sasha had always been easy around boys, and then men. Her friend didn't see them as different creatures the way she did. Millie thought about joining the table but couldn't face making small talk.

Happy to settle at the bar, she poured herself a large glass of wine.

Now leaning on the counter, Millie revelled in the roasted cheeks of the locals, the smell of Guinness and turf hanging in the air. This was the Ireland she loved, the Ireland she wished she had come from. But it wasn't. What happened to her father made sure of that.

Her family only went to Ballydunn because their father had been left a cottage there by his aunt Elsie (a nurse who married a Catholic). The couple had tried to live in the north but were eventually forced out, shunned by Protestants and Catholics alike for *marrying the other side*. They had moved to the village where no one knew their business and Elsie had lived as a Catholic. She never had children and Millie had always been told the cottage was left to her father because he was the only one in the family who employed Catholics.

Looking around, she thought of Dom's local in Chelsea and for a moment wondered if they had enough people to run the pub quiz that week.

The music stopped abruptly and she saw the fisherman, Finn McFall, stand up. He was wearing a roll-neck navy sweater with patches on the elbows and worn jeans. Moving with confidence, he took a swig of his pint and cleared his throat. Behind the bar, Dermot clanked a glass hard with a knife and the room quietened.

'"Mid-Term Break" by Seamus Heaney.' Finn spoke with a bold, almost theatrical air. Amused by the drama, Millie tried to place his accent. It wasn't local, but it wasn't Dublin or Belfast either. A mongrel. Just like her.

'...In the porch I met my father crying...'

'...As my mother held my hand in hers
and coughed out angry tearless sighs...'

'... Wearing a poppy bruise on his left temple...'

'No gaudy scars, the bumper knocked him clear...'

'... A four-foot box, a foot for every year...'

The reading was over and for a moment the pub stayed silent. Lost in the awful beauty of the words.

It took the crack of new logs burning in the fire to bring the audience back.

The mood of the bar changed as quickly as it had arrived. A cheer went up. People were whooping, clapping, and whistling.

'Finn McFall, you'll have us wailing like banshees,' shouted a purple-faced man from behind a pillar. Another cackle of laughter.

But Millie was not part of it. Her cheeks were wet with tears.

She needed to get away, but the front door was blocked by a fresh group of golfers, bulldozing their way into the pub.

She looked over to Sasha, but her friend was laughing with everyone else. She caught a sign for the toilets and, with her head down, scrummed through the crowd. Hurling herself into a cubicle, she leaned her head against the wall and kept the broken door shut with her foot.

In a flash she was a child again, nine, maybe ten, sitting at the feet of her father. It must have been winter as the fire was lit and she was wearing a new chunky sweater from Cuddys that itched. There was a clatter of dishes coming from the kitchen as her mother washed up the tea things and her brothers and sisters were scattered about the house, some studying, some skiving off their chores.

Her father had been reading out loud. She didn't know what it was at the time, but it was poetry, not a book. He did that after dinner sometimes. As he closed the tatty cover, she'd wanted more.

'*More, Daddy. One more,*' she had pleaded.

'*Sure, how could I resist that smile, Scamp?*' her father had said, using the nickname he'd given her years before.

As soon as Finn McFall spoke, she knew it was the same poem.

'*I don't understand what it means,*' she'd said, and her father had gently explained it was a true story about a wee brother getting knocked down outside his house but who was now in heaven.

She couldn't remember her father ever reading to her again.

Sitting on the toilet in the dingy cubicle, Millie felt a surge of anger. She realised she still hated the men who took her father away from her. And then hated herself for still hating.

She was now unable to hold back big, throaty sobs. Her arms were folded tightly around her chest, and with her foot still against the door, she rocked back and forth. Once again the frightened child she had so often been.

'Are you alright in there, sweetie?' an American accent whispered from the next-door cubicle. The interruption made her sit up straight.

'Oh, sorry, yes. Yes… I'm fine.'

'I could always go get someone for you.'

'No, really, I'm fine,' Millie said, biting her lip hard to try and stifle her tears.

When she knew she was alone, she went to the basin and threw ice-cold water on her face. Exhausted and worried about what had just come over her, she made her way back to the bar.

Just as she bent down to get tissues from her bag, Finn McFall appeared beside her. She immediately felt uncomfortable, too aware of his presence.

'How did I do?' Finn was looking directly at her. Smiling.

She couldn't decide if he was oblivious to her distress or just ignoring it.

'Well, the tourists loved it.'

'Sure, doesn't everybody love a bit of Heaney?'

'Are you a poet?'

'Don't you know it?'

The lines on his face crumpled into laughter and Millie flushed with warmth.

'Slainte,' said Finn, as he drained the rest of his pint.

'Slainte,' she replied, suddenly aware she had raised the bottle of wine.

'You know, we generally drink from glasses in these parts, but maybe you're not from round here?'

Millie couldn't fathom if he was making fun of her or flirting with her.

Just as she was about to speak, she heard the familiar first bars of 'Teenage Kicks' by The Undertones. The song was coming from the jukebox at the far side of the bar.

Even over the din, the music was loud and thumping, and the pub immediately started to react. The Goths, still on their chairs, had their arms outstretched. One had a bottle of cider in each hand, and all were singing at the top of their voices. Millie smiled in surprise. The Alacadoos at the bar were gaping over their shoulders; some were frowning, but most were nudging each other, grinning. The mood was infectious.

'The young pups have started early the night.'

The words made Millie spin round. Finn McFall was still there. Still smiling.

'Do you fancy a dance?' He held out his hand and Millie could see how weathered it was, just like her father's used to be at the end of the day. 'Go on now, you know you want to,' he continued, raising his eyebrows.

Then somehow her hand was in his. She felt powerless as his large fingers closed around hers and without speaking, he pulled her into the middle of the pub. There, in the midst of the golfers and tourists and the Goths and the band and the staff, who were singing to each other behind the bar as they pulled pints, Finn and Millie danced.

They were spinning around and then they were jiving, like people who didn't know how to. She was worried about falling into people and apologised with every twist and turn. But nobody cared. Everyone was laughing and smiling, slapping Finn on the back as he passed them by.

At one point, he pulled her close. She couldn't believe she was letting him do it. But she didn't stop him. She liked it. Some of the band had gathered around them; they were clapping in unison, wolf-whistling.

Millie felt like the bride at a raucous wedding.

Immediately after The Undertones, 'Lola' by The Kinks came on, and now it felt as if the whole pub was singing. Those who had room to move swayed to the music, drinks in hand, shouting out the lyrics. Many leaned into each other's hot faces, stamping their feet and pointing fingers in the air. Those sitting or standing at the bar were smacking their flat palms on the edge of their stools or the wooden counter in front.

Millie couldn't believe what she was doing. But she didn't want to stop doing it. She felt elated, alive. More than anything else, she felt this *was* the Ireland she belonged to.

When the song finished, she stood breathless as Finn waved his arms above his head towards the Goths. Behind the bar, Dermot was once again hitting a glass hard with a knife. 'Enough, lads, enough now. Time for a wee bit more culture,' he said, smirking.

As the crowds quietened and faded back to their smoky corners, a slow panic started to rise in Millie. Her cheeks were burning so hard it hurt and her breath was laboured. She had no idea how any of this had happened. As she searched for Sasha to save her, Finn lifted her hand and kissed it. He bowed theatrically and led her back to the bar.

'I have to go. I'm on,' he said, turning back towards the fire.

Just then another man appeared from nowhere and pulled the dog's lead roughly from under the chalkboard. He was unkempt, and as he headed for the door, he caught Millie's eye. She was sure he licked his lips and she squirmed, turning back to face the bar quickly.

'That'll be mulled wine if you don't drink it soon,' said Dermot, eyeing up her glass from behind the bar. Millie laughed, even though it was the very last thing she felt like doing.

Desperate to find Sasha, she watched the front door of the pub swing open and a gust of rain spit in at the drinkers on the nearest table. A whoop of laughter went up, and she saw her friend come back inside.

Just as the live music started up again, Sasha appeared by her side. 'Told you it would be fun,' she said, pulling her close. Millie knew she'd been smoking. Grabbing her bag, she was relieved Sasha hadn't seen her making a total spectacle of herself only minutes before.

Sasha looked at her watch. 'Better be getting back. I don't want to feel the wrath of your mother,' she said, making a horror face at Millie. 'Anyway, Dave goes spare when I'm late. Let's go.'

Millie wondered how much her friend had drunk but didn't say anything. She just wanted to get out of the pub. As they pushed through the crowd to leave, she couldn't stop herself glancing back. Finn McFall was once again standing in front of the fire, his booming voice reaching out across the bar. 'Ladies and gentlemen. Let me share with you, if I may, "The Lake Isle of Innisfree" by William Butler Yeats.'

As they climbed up into the Range Rover, Sasha spoke first. 'I'll go the back roads,' she said, spraying breath freshener deep into her throat and then all around her like perfume. Firing a quick spritz at Millie, she giggled. 'Need to be careful – it's not like the old days.'

The engine roared into life, and it was Adele's turn to blast from the speakers. Millie leaned her head back, breathing in the minty air. She now wanted to tell Sasha what had happened in the pub, but she hadn't the energy or the words. 'I've got to sleep,' she said, closing her eyes, fighting thoughts about the fishermen of Donegal.

Chapter 3

Portland Terrace was a developer's dream: five large stone houses, double-fronted with wide worn steps and pillared porches of black-and-white tiles. To Millie, the houses had always seemed too grand for the town and, even in their faded condition, she thought they were stately.

The Malones had lived at number three all her life, and Dr Henley, now retired, still lived to one side. The ever-growing surgery was to the other. The Elliots and Bells book-ended the row, and the nunnery still stood across the street.

The heavy door, which had always been on the latch when Millie was a child, was locked, and she instinctively felt around in the dark to find a key under the flowerpot.

Once inside, the darkness made her think her mother hadn't bothered to wait up. Feeling like an intruder, she walked past the dining room on the left and the drawing room on the right, following a light to the kitchen at the back of the house.

She opened the door and for a moment was disorientated.

It was the kitchen, but it was different, bigger. Millie hadn't been home since Jamie had organised the renovation, and her eyes were instantly drawn to big sliding doors leading out to the garden. A new sofa, just to the right of the door, replaced some units and to the left Millie was relieved to see the large refectory table where all nine of them, well, eight after Dad, had eaten at every day. The benches now had fancy long cushions. Blacks of Hill Street would have done well that day.

Her eyes finally settled on her mother, asleep in her rocking chair by the Aga. Her glasses had slipped to the end of her nose, the *Belfast Telegraph* had fallen to the floor and her head was slightly to one side. Her mouth was open and her breathing was slow. Millie was shocked how frail she was and knew the two years she'd stayed away had been too long.

Watching her, Millie was flooded with love. Forgetting any worries she'd had about her visit, she let her eyes linger. Her mother's hands were clasped, and her legs were covered in an old Native American rug, a present from Aunt Bertha not long after she'd emigrated to America, a lifetime ago.

Millie stepped back into the hall to hang up her coat and the door creaked. Her mother woke with a start.

'What? Is that you, Matilda?'

Millie appeared round the door and her mother's face lit up.

'Well, here she is. Finally. Home from the city,' said her mother, pushing her glasses up her nose. 'Come and give your old mother a hug.'

Millie went to her, grateful for the warmth of her welcome.

'What have you been doing to yourself, Mummy?'

'It's the steroids, my bones are as soft as putty. But it'll take more than a few fractures to put me in a box.'

Millie pulled back from her mother, not wanting to hurt her, and kissed the top of her head. 'It's good to be home, Mummy. Sorry I'm so late. It's Sasha. You know what she's like.'

'Never mind about that now. It's just good to have you home.' Her mother held her gaze and Millie gently stroked the side of her face.

She moved to the sofa, all the time taking in the new kitchen. 'Very smart,' she said, waving her hand around the room. '*Very London*, as Sasha would say,' and they laughed together.

'Aye, Jamie said he wanted the best. I said it didn't need changing, but he insisted. We went to Blacks.'

Millie wondered what the others thought of Jamie's big gesture. Plenty, no doubt. She'd hear all about it soon.

'So, child, what brings you home so suddenly? It's not your mother's health, I know that much.' Her mother stared at her, sipping from a mug of tea she had lifted from the edge of the Aga.

Christ. She'd forgotten the power of her mother's eyes. She changed the subject. 'Are the nuns still opposite?'

'I never see any about now. Never did, mind – only ever scuttling across to the chapel at all hours of the day and night.'

'Looks empty to me,' said Millie, scanning the room, trying to remember the old kitchen. 'It would make a great house or flats, don't you think? All those high ceilings and stained-glass windows.'

'I can't see the church ever letting go of that one. They'll keep it whatever.' Her mother smoothed the rug lying over her legs.

'Maybe they could use it for all those paedo priests. A halfway house or something.' Millie kicked her boots off and sighed as she lay full length on the sofa.

'Enough of that now, Matilda,' scoffed her mother. 'Some of them are very nice. That Father Paul was always preaching peace.' After a pause she went on. 'In his own way.'

Millie tried to remember Father Paul but couldn't place his face, just his black cassock swirling past the house to lift the Sinn Fein collection boxes from the chapel entrance.

'Do you remember the time the nuns rang over to the house?'

'How could I forget?'

'Was I really out on the ledge?'

'Yes, Matilda, you were,' said her mother, rocking in her chair slightly, her head back. 'Bold as brass – even then,' she added. 'Such a child. Your father called you Houdini. Did you know that? Always out of that cot. When you got up on that ledge… Well, I couldn't believe it.'

'Well, I actually can't believe you left me upstairs with an open window. You'd be up for neglect today.'

'Listen, my girl.' Her mother stopped rocking. 'In those days, a baby napped with an open window. I had you outside the front door in all weathers. There were six others to think about. I hadn't time to sneeze, let alone worry about you all.' She went back to rocking.

'What did you do when you got the call?'

'I said, "*Thank you very much*," then ran like billy-o upstairs and pulled you in. Never told your dad, mind,' she said, smiling over at Millie, who loved hearing the story again.

'I sent a pavlova over the next day. Fresh cream and a whole tin of fruit on top. Never got a thank you, mind. They can be a cold lot, those nuns.'

Millie laughed and decided she was feeling brave enough to suggest a drink. 'I think I'll have a glass of wine. Do you want one?'

'There's none cold,' her mother said firmly.

'Oh, don't worry. I'll use ice.'

Her mother pursed her lips.

Millie ignored the gesture. Too busy admiring the ice dispenser on the new fridge-freezer. She poured them both a large glass of white wine and her mother reached for hers eagerly.

'Did you see the Spar on your way past? Lizzie says it's gone all foreign.'

'It's not called the Spar anymore. Polinvina. Polish, I think.'

'What?'

'Is there anything to eat? I'm starving.'

'Lizzie brought stew. Lovely meat. From the factory shop.'

'Ugh,' said Millie. 'Where's that?'

'Next to the new abattoir.'

'Lovely.'

Heating up the stew, Millie breathed in the pungent smell from the Aga. She ran her fingers over the heavy lids and touched the old pans piled up at the back.

Growing up, this was the place to hover if you wanted to know what was going on in the house. And with so many of them, there was always plenty. Exam results, good and bad; sporting fetes, broken limbs, broken hearts were all discussed here.

The time the boys were hauled into the police station for running naked around the rugby club's pitch as a dare. Or the time after Dad, when her mother had gathered them around her and told them he had gone, and that there was no rhyme nor reason to this world, and they would just have to get on with it.

She remembered trying not to cry when her mother said they needed to be strong for each other, and Matilda and Kate, being the youngest, needed looking after and not tormenting all the time.

After her stew, Millie felt exhausted. Snapshots of the Fiddler's Inn were bouncing around in her head, making her uncomfortable, and when her mother yawned, she suggested they go to bed. Her mother seemed relieved. Linking arms, they crept up the deep stairs, stopping on the first-floor landing for her mother to catch her breath. Peering out the window into the darkness, Millie sensed the garden was different. Another gift from Jamie.

With her mother settled she went to her old room. It smelt the same and the Laura Ashley curtains that didn't quite meet in the middle were still up, as was the pink Chinese lantern shade she'd bought on Carnaby Street during a school trip to London decades before. The two single beds she and Kate, her little sister, had slept in all their lives were still covered in the pretty floral eiderdowns that had come from The Birches, her grandmother's old homestead. Underneath were fresh sheets and wool blankets with satin trims; duvets had never been considered in their house. Her favourite yellow and white towel, now frayed with age, and a fleece nightie of her mother's she'd enjoyed wearing the last time she was home, were folded neatly on her pillow.

Her mother had been busy since yesterday.

As she unpacked her case, she heard the familiar murmur of Radio Ulster from under her mother's door, and when she pulled back the tightly fitted sheets, an old, familiar smell came to her. She searched under the pillow and found a tiny lavender-filled pouch with her initials sewn on it. The one Granny Malone had stitched for her the Christmas after Dad.

Clutching the memento, she slipped into sleep staring at a patch on the wall where a poster of Marti Pellow from Wet Wet Wet had once hung.

The next morning, Millie brought her mother breakfast in bed.

'So are you saying you've broken up? When you called yesterday, I could smell trouble.' Her mother appeared worried. 'Have you done something to upset Dom?'

Millie stopped what she was doing and stared hard at her mother. Why did she always think it was her fault? It was the same with all the girls. Even when poor Karen said Colin wanted a divorce. 'Dom's not all he's cracked up to be,' she said, slumping down on the end of her mother's bed.

'What do you mean by that? Has he been over the side with someone else?'

'I just don't know if he's right. For me. Do you want more tea?'

'Not right? I'd say Dom Hamilton is as right as it gets. And at your age…' Her words trailed off. She then added gently, 'It's just, you're not getting any younger, Matilda, and I want you to be a mother.'

Millie's stomach knotted.

'Thanks, Mum, thanks a lot.' She lifted her mother's breakfast tray sharply and went downstairs to put the kettle on for the third time that morning.

Later that morning, Karen came to visit.

As soon as Millie entered the kitchen, her mother and eldest sister became quiet. Her mother went back to her paper and Karen cleared her throat. Millie hadn't seen her sister in two years; she felt it could have been twenty-two as Karen appeared to have aged so much.

'Jesus wept. What have you done to your eyes?' said Karen, turning to their mother in feigned shock. 'Is this what's they're doing in London now? You look like, well, I don't know what you look like.'

'Nice to see you too,' said Millie, touching her eyelash extensions – a cheer-me-up present to herself she was beginning to regret.

'I suppose you remember who I am?'

'How could I forget? You're my bossy big sister who never lets up telling me where I'm going wrong.'

'Well, someone has to, Millie. Left to your own devices, God help us all.'

She was about to retaliate but then remembered the divorce.

'Now, girls, mind your age,' their mother said as she took off her glasses. 'Shall we have a nice cup of tea? Karen brought some lovely fifteens.'

Millie wondered when her sister last ate a fifteen. She had always been slim, but today, even with her coat on, Millie could see how bony she was. She was wearing no make-up and her face was ashen. Feeling a rush of pity, Millie wished she had come home more often.

'How are things, Karen, you know…?'

'How are things? Well, I'll tell you how things are, Millie,' said Karen, pushing her unkempt hair back from her forehead. 'Just how you'd expect them to be when you're a laughing stock across the town. When the father of your children takes off with a foreign tart half his age.' Karen's voice was high and shrill, and Millie immediately regretted asking the question.

'What about the children?'

'Well, I'm still their taxi driver-cum-cook-cum-money bank, if that's what you mean?' Her voice lowered. 'They're worse since it all happened. You know, playing up on the divorce talk and all.'

Karen was now picking at bits of fluff on her worn sleeves. Her thin fingers were red and her nails newly bitten.

'I'm sorry.' Millie went to her sister, but when she tried to put her arms around her, Karen stepped back. Millie saw she was shaking.

'Well, that's life. Isn't it, Mummy?' Karen nodded over to her mother. 'No one ever said it was going to be easy. Isn't that right, Mummy?'

Her mother smiled gently. 'Let's have some tea. We'll all feel better after tea.'

'I mean, what does he see in her?' Karen had found her voice again. 'She's so tarty, and all that dyed blonde hair. You'd think with her teaching at the tech she'd be better-looking.' Karen paused, then, shaking her head, went on. 'She'll be pregnant next. Mark my words. Then he'll never be rid of her.' Millie could see her sister's jaw clench firmly.

Her mother was tutting. 'I'm amazed she's allowed to keep on working up at the tech.'

'God, Mummy, you can't get sacked for having an affair these days,' said Millie, throwing herself onto the sofa. 'What does she teach anyway?'

'Hairdressing.'

Millie tried to imagine plain, downtrodden Colin arm in arm with a hairdresser.

'Anyway, enough of that. I didn't come here to air my dirty laundry in front of you, but God knows, half the town is talking about it. I just know they are.'

Millie tried to cheer her sister up. 'Mary McFadden was on the flight. She didn't mention it.'

'Well, that's just because I gave Lady Muck a flea in her ear when she phoned me. Chewed my ear off, pretending she wanted to help. Wanted me to come up to Belfast and stay over in that big new house of hers and maybe go out for tea with some of her friends.'

Millie thought about the woman in the Derby hat.

'Imagine. All that petrol money to go up to Belfast to sit and tell them about my husband whoring around the countryside with some trollop. I don't think so. Thank you very much.'

'Is that not quite nice? You did work together for years,' said Millie, trying not to sound irritated.

'Now, Karen, don't start. You'll make yourself ill,' said her mother. 'It's nearly lunchtime. We could have a wee bowl of stew instead. There's lots of meat in it.'

'From the factory shop,' said Millie, cheerily.

Karen made a face.

After stew and a fifteen, Millie jumped at the chance of a walk. Even if it was with Karen.

'I'm like a poisoned pup,' her sister said, rubbing her flat stomach.

'Really?' Millie glanced over at her mother, who widened her eyes. Her short-hand, she remembered, for stop talking.

Grabbing her parka from the hook in the downstairs loo, she caught a glimpse of herself in the mirror. Touching her new lashes, she thought about what her sister had said. Maybe she was right. Maybe they were too much. For Dungrillen.

As they walked down Lough Road, out towards the graveyard, they passed a few groups of factory workers. All men. They were very polite and always stood back to let Karen and Millie by if there was no room on the pavement. Karen rolled her eyes dramatically every time they did this, and Millie was annoyed with her.

Getting closer to the first of the factories, more groups of workers appeared. Karen yanked Millie's arm and pulled her across the road. A voice from behind started shouting, and Millie turned to see what was going on. A man, maybe Portuguese, had left a group. He had crossed the road and was running towards them.

'What do you think he wants?' asked Millie, mostly to herself.

'Oh my God,' said Karen when she looked back. Without asking, she grabbed Millie by the arm again, pinching her in the process, making her walk twice as fast as before. 'Pretend you can't hear him. Don't look back,' she hissed, all the time pulling at Millie's arm.

'What are you doing? For God's sake, Karen, wise up.'

By the time they got to the graveyard, they were nearly running. Neither of them said anything and Karen quickly pushed Millie into the car park and rushed to close the gates.

Just then, the man came running around the corner. He was out of breath and was waving something in his hand. Karen screamed and stepped back. Millie soon realised it was her scarf in his hand. A Hermes square Dom had bought her in Portofino. It must have slipped out of her pocket when they were walking from the house. Mortified, she opened the gates and reclaimed the scarf, thanking the man over and over.

After he left, she turned to see Karen bent double, her hand over her mouth. As her sister stood up straight, she started to laugh, all the time making funny faces.

Millie didn't think there was anything to laugh about. 'Why did you make us run like that?'

'Listen, Millie, you've no idea who's who anymore in this town. You must have heard about those raids. Sixteen to a room. Sleeping in shifts. They said the smell would have made you boak.'

'That's awful. Poor men.'

'Poor men! Are you mad?' Karen stepped closer. 'When they went to arrest the boss man, guess where he lived?' Without waiting for a reply, she went on. 'Right up there beside Lady Muck herself in Belfast.' Karen's voice was high and incriminating, then it dropped so low, Millie had to lean in to hear what she was saying. 'I've heard stories that would make your hair curl. All those men living together. It's not natural. No wonder they're animals.'

Millie was about to ask her sister if she felt alright, but Karen stormed ahead and was now walking through the car park towards the graves. An elderly man was standing by his car, watching her as she passed. Karen tossed her head high. 'Show's over, folks,' she shouted, smiling sarcastically.

Millie walked on quickly with her head down and her hood up.

When she approached her father's grave, panic gripped Millie like a vice. She hadn't visited for years and as she read the inscription on his headstone, she felt her throat tighten.

> *'Greater Love Hath No Man Than He Lay Down His Life for His Friends.'*

The sting of shame moved up her neck and onto her cheeks, and her mind slipped back to a day over twenty years before. The day before she left for college…

***

It's hot and Millie is running down Irish Street, late for a hair appointment. She has just lied to her mother about where she is going. The Catholic end of town is out of bounds to her these days, but it's where Orla O'Neil has her salon, and everyone knows she is the best hairdresser in town.

As Millie runs, a poster in the window of the Sinn Fein office makes her stop. It features a young man, dead, lying inside a coffin lined with the Irish flag. He is wearing an IRA uniform and a machine gun nestles by his side. Confused and breathless, she stares hard at the poster. Walking to the window, she touches the glass with her finger, following the words printed underneath – repeating them several time. Only then does she accept the biblical quote is exactly the same as the one chiselled on her father's headstone.

The sound of her heart thumping is unnerving. Sweat is starting to run down her burning cheeks and she feels lightheaded. It's just so hot. She looks up and down the street to see if anyone is watching and then, with a shaking hand, presses the entry buzzer of the highly fortified office.

For a moment she thinks they won't let her in and, relieved, steps back on the pavement, wiping the sweat from her face with the hem of her T-shirt. But just as she turns to leave there's a loud click and the heavy bullet-proof door swings open. She thinks about running back up the street to the safety of the town square, but instead, her legs carry her forward and she steps through the bullet-proofed door, where stagnant air and darkness rain over her. When her eyes adjust to the dimness, they settle on a boy behind the old-fashioned wooden counter. Millie recognises the raven black curls; it's Donal Manus from Manus's sweet shop in Church Street. She clenches her jaw in annoyance; he is always so nice to her in the shop and she to him. Yet here he is in the Sinn Fein office stuffing envelopes with a picture of a dead IRA man. He has seen her – she senses his awkwardness. Willing him to meet her eyes, she's disappointed when he silently moves back into the shadows of the room like an injured animal.

It's an older man who comes to the counter. His smile is cold and he looks the way people think Irish men should look – with an Arran sweater and unruly beard. Millie starts to talk, stumbling over her opening words. When he finally speaks it is with a practised tone. Her father, he says, will have been killed because he was part of the British war machine, and unfortunately, war yields casualties. Just like his brother in the window who was killed on active duty.

Millie is filled with rage. She wants to say it's not the same. Not the same at all. She wants to say her father was killed trying to protect people from being blown up and shot on their way to work or out shopping and that his brother was killed because he had been going out to kill people on their way to work or out shopping. But instead she says nothing and stumbles out of the office, humiliated, her face drowning in tears.

She doesn't get her hair cut that day and later lies awake all night, desperate for the morning to come so the plane can take her to London, away from the horror of it all.

* * *

Standing at the grave, she was about to tell Karen about her visit to the Sinn Fein office all those years ago, but her sister spoke first.

'Well, Daddy, do you recognise this big girl?' Karen was talking directly to the gravestone.

Millie looked around, embarrassed.

'Yes, it *is* Millie. The prodigal daughter returns. Yes, Daddy, all the way from her big swanky life in London.'

'Don't, Karen,' she said, pulling her hood back sharply.

'I'm only reminding Daddy who you are.'

'Don't do that.'

They stood in uncomfortable silence until Millie became aware of a noise. Music. Dolly Parton. It was coming from loudspeakers at the entrance to the chicken factory next to the graveyard. She wanted to laugh but, watching her sister, didn't dare.

Turning her head, she glimpsed the chimney towers of the old hospital standing tall and dark against the open sky and her mind flooded with memories of the last time she had been there. She'd been at the morgue, with her mother: the day her father was killed.

The stapled gunshot wound on his cheek had horrified her young eyes. She had wanted to reach out and pull off the dark crusts of blood around his nostrils, the bits the nurses, or whoever it was that cleaned up his body, had missed. But as she reached her trembling hand out, her mother had grabbed her wrist so tightly she cried out in pain.

Now, standing at his grave, she wondered why, as a child, she had been allowed in the morgue in the first place. Or had she been? Was it a memory or something she had made up long ago? Staring at the headstone, she thought how the town was back then. Murder was everywhere. Even at that age, she understood it. In all the panic, she decided, yes, she could easily have been in the morgue with her mother.

She fished in her pockets for a tissue but found none, and wondered would the memory, real or imaginary, ever diminish? Her sister was ignoring her tears and Millie now wished she'd not come to the grave. Not with Karen.

'I bring Mummy down once a week, you know. I sometimes come on my own. He knows all about Colin and that trollop.' Karen leaned down and gently brushed imaginary leaves away from the manicured mound.

Millie was crying too much to speak.

Straight after Dad, she had gone to the grave every day. They all had. Despite what she had seen, despite the funeral, she believed her father was still alive, just not living in the house anymore. Then, as the mounds of fresh flowers and wreaths began to shrivel and die, so too did her hope of ever seeing him again. On her last visit before going back to boarding school, all the flowers had been dumped into a skip in the adjoining car park.

It was then she understood. Her father was never coming home.

When Karen finally acknowledged her tears, her voice was kinder. 'Don't cry.'

'Do the others come?'

'Jamie brings Mummy down the odd time. When she asks. But I know he doesn't like it. Reminds him of his old life. He's the big man now and the Troubles are a dirty word to him.'

Karen cleared her throat. 'I don't even think he read the inquiry report, you know. Not sure you or the others did either?' Her sister stared at Millie, ignoring her tears again, wanting a reply.

Millie felt ambushed. She wasn't ready for this conversation. Not here. Not at the grave.

'I did read it.'

'You never let on.'

'What was there to say?'

When the report arrived, Millie had innocently opened it on the tube. Floored by its content, she had missed her stop and then sat, shaken, on a bench as she texted Tom to say she would be late and someone else would have to cover the supermodel's interview.

She had found an empty cafe in Victoria and sat at a grimy table in the back, poring over the cold, hard facts of her father's murder.

Hours later, she'd called her mother, furious no one had bothered to tell her the report was coming. From what *wasn't* said on that call, she gathered the family was split about its publication. Some welcomed the fact that all the murders were finally being investigated; others thought it was only raking up the past.

Millie wasn't sure what she thought. There were days she wished she hadn't read a single word, but now, standing here at her father's grave, she dripped with shame.

'I'm sure Jamie didn't read it, you know.' Her sister was in her own world now, shaking her head slowly. 'Not interested in who killed Daddy. Imagine that.'

'They didn't mention names.'

'So caught up buying houses to rent to the likes of those ones.' Karen threw her hand towards the factories. 'Gave up that good job. All to be the big landlord.'

Millie's eyes drifted.

'He works a bit with David Shannon, you know.' Then, exaggerating a fake Texan accent, she went on. '"*The chicken billionaire*".'

Millie puffed out a small laugh.

'Mummy said Sasha picked you up yesterday.'

'We went to Ballydunn. To see the house.'

Karen made another face. 'Big as the Taj Mahal apparently. But she'll need it for all those children she's pushed out… You've a lot of catching up to do in that department, Millie.'

Her sister waited for a reaction.

When none came, she went on. 'God, she was man-mad, but she's landed on her feet with that one. He's still a sight, mind. So through-other.' Karen acted like a bad smell had floated under her nose. 'Swinging around town in matching white Range Rovers. I mean, who do they think they are? Drug dealers? They've even got their own plates.'

'I know, *CH1K 2* and *CH1K 3*. I was in 3 yesterday,' said Millie, determined to lighten the mood. When Karen started laughing loudly, a woman at another grave gave them both a dirty look. Her sister gave a better one back and Millie dropped her eyes.

After that, Karen was full of chat and Millie briefly wondered if her sister was on drugs. Not drugs like Dom. But pills. From the doctor.

Walking away from the grave, Karen linked her arm and she felt better for it.

'You can't deny Jamie's been very good to Mummy. That kitchen is something else,' said Millie.

'You know, he's learning Irish.'

'Sorry?'

'You heard.'

'Are you serious?'

'First it was the dancing with the girls. All that fiddly-dee nonsense. Now he's learning Irish. He'll be in Rome next.'

'What's that about?'

'It'll be Eimear making him, but sure they're all at it now,' said Karen, putting on a fake happy voice. 'It's the "*New Belfast*". *Blending cultures. Healing the past.* Blah, blah, bloody blah.' Her sister tried to force out a laugh, but only managed a splutter. She leaned in. 'He's got more Catholic friends than Protestant, I'd say. They're the ones with the money now and that's what Jamie's all about these days. Money.'

'Well, there's nothing wrong with that, is there?' asked Millie. 'I mean, having Catholic friends. That's a good thing, isn't it?' She was trying to keep annoyance out of her voice. 'He's married to a Catholic, remember?' Unable to stop herself, she went on. 'God, Karen, you're sounding so...' She trailed off, shaking her head.

Karen looked hurt. 'Well, I suppose it's okay. But I just don't want this whole Irish thing rammed down my throat, thank you very much. It's getting beyond a joke. Mummy wouldn't like it, so don't mention it. I only know because Nosy Parker McFadden mentioned it when she was asking me up for tea.'

Her sister was now picking imaginary fluff off her coat again. 'When she told me, of course, I pretended it was the most natural thing in the world to be doing.' Karen put on her fake happy voice again. '"*Oh, how lovely,*" I said. "*Isn't it great the way this place is moving on?*" I said.'

Karen stopped picking and stared Millie in the eye. 'You could have lit a match on me. Honest to God, I was raging, but I didn't let on. Wouldn't give her the satisfaction. Irish my ass.'

Millie briefly wondered how her sister managed to conceal her rage. She'd certainly seen no evidence of it so far this trip.

Walking past the last of the headstones towards the car park, Millie thought about graves she'd visited in Italy with Dom. Lovely graves surrounded by scented blossoms, where old people who had lived long and happy lives had come to rest. It was a world away from this grey, cold place, filled with so many who had not been ready to die.

The sky darkened in a way she only ever saw at home.

'Smells like rain,' said Karen. 'Best be getting back.'

A beep from Millie's bag made her jump. A message from Dom.

On the way back to the house, her older sister asked about life in London. Millie didn't mention the clinic, or the drugs, or the fact that she didn't think she loved Dom anymore. And in that moment, she happily enjoyed the charade.

Arms still linked, they chatted about the family: Kate in Belfast, climbing the ranks of the police; Andrew, Josie, and Robert, all in America. Doing well. Her sister's body tightened as they talked about the others, all making their own lives away from home. Millie always presumed Karen wanted to live in Dungrillen, as their mother and her mother had done before her. Enjoying the familiarity of everyone and everything that went on in the town. But Colin's affair had maybe put an end to all that.

Now certain that this was the reason her sister was so annoyed with her, she was sure she hadn't heard the last of it.

Chapter 4

Over the next few days, Millie did everything she could to try and be a good daughter. She took her mother to get her feet done, the hairdressers to get her hair done and to the surgery to get her bloods done.

They went to Tesco a lot. Millie held the basket while her mother shuffled around the store on her walking frame, studying the backs of ready meals in a scholarly fashion. She offered to buy her mother anything she wanted but was always rebutted, being told she needed to keep her money for herself now.

They went to the in-store cafe packed with factory workers and agreed they could be in Brazil or Portugal but without the weather. Her mother laughed. Millie was almost enjoying herself.

'How long are you staying?' her mother asked, sipping on a hot chocolate topped with mini marshmallows and Flake shavings.

Millie was taken by surprise. 'Oh, I'm not sure, Mummy. Maybe another week.'

Leaning across the table, her mother reached out for her hand. 'I'll ask the others for dinner on Sunday.'

Millie tried to smile.

Everyone was called there and then from her mother's new mobile. Another present from Jamie. Kate couldn't come. She was going to be away on a diversity course with work. This annoyed her mother, who said that's all the PSNI do now, go on courses. Karen and Jamie were free. Jamie said he'd leave the kids up in Belfast with Eimear and her mother seemed very pleased about that. He suggested going to the new restaurant in town. His treat. But her mother was having none of it.

'No, Matilda will cook us a roast,' she said proudly.

Millie overheard Karen say she'd only pencil it in as she knew what her little sister was like. Her mother had scolded her and Millie imagined her sister making faces into her phone.

Leaving her mother in the cafe, she went to buy wine.

'Never married? A lovely big girl like you?' Glydis Smyth stood by the meat counter, peering at her with abject curiosity.

'Well, no… not yet.'

'Me neither. I was a career girl too and I loved every minute of it. Your dad, God rest his soul, looked after me so well in that firm. When it happened, well, I don't mind telling you – I was devastated.' She looked at her shoes, embarrassed, it seemed, at her intimacy, and added quickly, 'We all were. Anyway, enough of that talk, how's your mum?'

'Oh, you know Mummy, she's a fighter.'

Mrs Smyth smiled kindly, her eyes disappearing under creases of skin. 'That she is. That she is. Tell her I said hello,' and with that she moved on up the World Food aisle to the check-outs.

Millie felt uneasy, unable to remember the last time she had openly discussed her father in such casual circumstances. Pondering the Clubcard wine offers, she recalled there had been chat about Glydis Smyth at her father's funeral. The very fitted Paul Costelloe suit and her open distress were both eagerly debated at the house afterwards, mostly by her mother's sisters. At least one of them had called her '*blousy*'.

Walking further up the drinks aisle, she considered buying champagne but knew her mother would question the extravagance.

So she settled on six bottles of Pinot Grigio, pretending to her mother she'd only bought three.

On Sunday morning, when her mother was still in bed, Millie set about the house. She opened all the windows downstairs to air the place and washed the kitchen floor. Searching for wine glasses, she finally found a set of Tyrone crystal goblets in the drawing room. As she washed and dried the heavy glasses, she felt calm. Happy to be home.

When her mother saw the glasses by the sink, she got cross, saying they were only for special occasions. When Millie suggested that having a family dinner – even just with the four of them – was a very special occasion, her mother had relented, but didn't appear happy about it.

In the afternoon, the two of them sat together at the big table in the kitchen, her mother making sage and onion stuffing, Millie arranging sprigs of flowers from the garden into any little pots and old jam jars she could find. When she dotted them all over the kitchen and living room her mother said it was like living in a flower shop.

Millie couldn't decide if this was meant to be a compliment or not.

The house was warm when the others arrived and everyone, even Karen, seemed relaxed.

As Millie poured wine, her sister again asked about all the famous people she had interviewed. She teased her too, about her eyelashes and her accent, and Millie let her.

Jamie kept butting in with all sorts of questions about Dom and his job, and she was able, once more, to pretend they were still very much an item, which seemed to make her mother happy.

She felt glad they had all got together; she was just about to say so when Karen started to recount a story she had read in the *News Letter* about the police being called to an argument in the Holylands. A student from Queens had been found in the middle of a self-induced abortion, brought on by tablets she'd bought online.

'It sounded horrific,' said Karen, taking a large swig of wine. 'The police were called by a flatmate. Imagine…' Then she added casually, 'A Catholic.'

Millie was sure Jamie shot Karen a look, but her sister chose to ignore it.

'The girl was bleeding, everything. The flatmate, the Catholic, wanted her arrested. Can you believe that?'

Millie's stomach hurt.

Her mother had closed her eyes. She wasn't asleep, as her chair was gently rocking, yet Millie sensed she was preoccupied.

'Well, the law's not long changed, Karen. Many still think it's murder,' said Jamie.

'Is that your wife talking again?' asked Karen, with a smile.

Some old black-and-white photographs Karen had found in their mother's attic were produced. The snaps were so small and faded they had to be held under a lamp for their mother to see them clearly.

One picture in particular caught the girls' eyes; they were both trying to ride their father like a pony, while Jamie was leading them, using their father's UDR tie as a harness. Everybody in the picture was laughing. Even though they couldn't have been more than six and eleven at the time, the sisters agreed they remembered the day well.

When Karen next spoke, it was in a deliberately concerned tone. 'Mummy, I forgot to say I had a call from the inquiry team. They wanted to know if we had any comments before they closed Daddy's file. Forever.'

Silence fell across the room, bar the low hum of Radio Ulster in the background.

'Well, I can't believe they called you and not me.'

'They thought you were dead.'

'*Dead?* What do you mean by that?'

'*Dead?*' said Millie in disbelief. '*Dead?*' she said again, trying not to laugh.

'Well, I'm glad you find the thought of your mother's death so funny.'

Millie stopped laughing and her face flushed.

'Just as it isn't funny that the men got for Dad are out. Under that bloody agreement.'

Her sister was in her element. 'Yes, well, there you go. If you'd bothered to read the report, Jamie, you'd have known that. Not funny now,' she went on. 'One of them living not fifteen miles from here.' Then she added brightly, 'Shall I put the carrots on, Mummy?'

'For your information I did read the report, Karen, but it didn't say anything about where the boys lived.'

'Well, Jamie. I did a bit of digging. Two phone calls. That's all it took.' The faintest of smiles crossed her sister's face. 'Colin's best man, Paul, works in the police archives now. Probably felt sorry for me.' Anyway…' Her voice darkened. 'Fifteen miles. Can you believe that?'

Millie looked at her sister and brushed through memories of other times she caused upset. When she told Josie, in front of everyone that her boyfriend Bugsy Best had been facing Sharon Creedy outside the cinema. Or when she came into the kitchen swinging Millie's first bra around her head like a lasso. Worst of all, the time she found out Kate had taken her first period and kept sniggering and nudging the youngest, until the boys asked what was going on.

She was about to tell her big sister what she thought of her when Jamie spoke. 'Karen, we all think of Dad, but some of us have tried to move on.'

'What do you mean by that?'

'Well…'

'Well, what?'

'With the divorce and all.' Jamie cleared his throat. 'I'm just saying if Colin and Nadia are going to be together, maybe it's best to just let them get on with it. Let it go. For the children's sake.'

'Nadia? Let it go? We were talking about the report, Jamie.'

'No, Karen. You were.'

Millie watched her sister, who somehow managed to appear both hurt and angry at the same time, walk to the table and lift all the photographs roughly, stuffing them into her handbag.

Determined to move the conversation on, Millie spoke. 'I heard there's a big new Sinn Fein office going up in town. Big glass doors. Very smart, apparently.' Everyone turned and looked at her.

'Where?' Her mother stopped rocking.

'I haven't seen it,' snapped Karen.

'Well, it's there. Still Irish Street. Sasha said so.'

'What a joke. You know, they're trying to get the factory workers to learn Irish.' Karen was talking directly to Jamie. 'They should be made to speak English. That's what we speak here. No one speaks Irish, except the Shinners. It's ridiculous,' she said, trying to make herself laugh. 'I've a good mind to go through those big glass doors and ask them if Dublin even wants them.'

Karen's outbursts were so charged, Millie was now convinced she was on drugs. From the doctor.

'Sixty Euro for a GP appointment. Who wants to pay that?'

No one answered her.

'I've got about this week, Jamie,' said Millie, continuing her diversion tactics. 'Sasha gave me the grand tour of the house in Ballydunn. It's ginormous. David's opening factories up there too.'

'Well, I hope they're happy up there on the hill with all that chicken money,' her mother said gruffly.

'David's got some business there all right,' said Jamie.

Millie helped herself to wine, pointedly ignoring her sister's outstretched glass. 'Talking of empires… How's yours, Jamie?'

'Oh, you know. Busy. Being a landlord is a dirty word around here.'

Karen sniffed. 'Maybe one of these days we'll actually get to see the inside one of these great houses.'

'Do all your tenants come from the factories?' Millie was feigning interest.

'No. Not anymore. A few are David's lads, but most of them are from the car washes.'

'Car washes? I didn't know you had those.'

'Aye, I've a couple around the place now. It's a great wee earner. I don't care what anyone says, my black lads are built for the job.'

Millie pulled her head back. 'You can't say that.'

'What, black?'

'You can, too,' interrupted their mother. 'I heard it on the radio. You must say black, not coloured.'

'That's not what I meant.'

'It's the same with suicide.' Her mother ignored Millie. 'You must say completed, not committed suicide. Committed suggests a crime.'

'Jesus wept. What next?' asked Karen, pouring herself more wine.

Her mother was trying to stifle a smile and Millie could feel the tension easing off in the room.

'Times have changed, all right. Just think about this town.' Her mother leaned forward in her chair. 'Dungrillen used to be a great place to live. We had a hospital. And you know what that meant?'

'Doctors…' Millie and Karen said in unison. Millie found herself smiling over at her sister, even though she didn't want to.

'Doctors,' said their mother. 'We had doctors. Consultants. It was a lovely place to live. Even with the Troubles, the parties your dad and I went to before…' She stumbled slightly. 'They were lovely.'

A small silence followed her words. Karen got up and donned an apron with a picture of the *Titanic* on it, with the words '*It was alright when it left Belfast*' printed underneath, Jamie was instructed to carve the chicken and Millie sorted out who wanted white or red. Much to Millie's surprise, her mother said she would try a bit of both as Jamie had bought such good stuff, and this seemed to cheer everyone up.

They teased Millie over drinking bottled water, and Jamie laughed when his 'thermostatically controlled' cellar was brought up. A glass was raised to absent family and Jamie said he would maybe try and FaceTime Josie after dinner.

'This chicken is great, Mum,' he said.

'Second-hand from the factory shop,' Millie said, and everyone laughed except their mother.

Karen started to clear the dishes before her mother had finished eating and the noise was grating on Millie. 'Relax, will you? Mummy's still eating.'

'Relax, she says. Well, I suppose you're not used to clearing up after yourself over there in swanky London. Not like some of us who have to cook, clean and clear up every night of the week,' said Karen, banging plates together.

'That's ridiculous, Karen.'

'Ridiculous? Says she who's got the man, the job, the money. No need to worry about anyone else, just yourself, thank you very much. Isn't that right, Mummy?'

'Karen. Don't start—'

'Excuse me?' Millie interrupted.

'Well, let's face it,' said Karen, dirty plates in both hands. 'You're not exactly around to help, are you?'

'Karen. Enough.' Her mother's voice was now sharp and impatient.

'What do you mean by that?'

'You heard. Over there swanning around like Lady Muck. You haven't been home for two years or more. Don't deny it.'

Millie searched the room for support. None came.

'That's unfair. You've no idea what's been going on with me.'

'Oh, let me guess.' Karen thumped the plates down on the table. 'What dress will I wear today? Which restaurant will we go to tonight?' She stood up straight. 'You have no idea you're living, my girl. You should try walking in my shoes for a day or two.'

'God, I'd forgotten just how nasty you can be, Karen. It's no bloody wonder—'

'Stop it now, both of you,' said their mother, using the table to help herself stand before moving back to her rocking chair.

'Just like old times, eh, Mummy?' said Jamie. 'With those two at each other's throats.'

'Well, thank God Mummy's got me. That's all I can say.'

'Hold on a minute,' said Jamie.

Karen slammed the new dishwasher shut and then grunted as she got down on her hands and knees and started furiously wiping the floor in front of it. 'Don't go there, Jamie.'

'Who bought Mummy this kitchen, eh? And let's not forget who helped you out when it all went belly up with Colin. Or have you forgotten that?'

Karen lifted her strained face. 'Look, I'm not saying you're not good to Mummy, Jamie, or us. You are, but you're on the batter all the time, you never seem to have time – and that's what Mummy needs. Time. Kate's the same. Always away with her *friend* Amanda or running bloody marathons for the RUC. Oh, sorry, PSNI, as it is now called, thank you very much.'

'Wait a minute. I do my bit like everyone else. I come down whenever I can. You know I do,' said Jamie in a wounded tone. 'I just don't bang on about it like you do.'

Still on all fours, Karen went on. 'Well, that's all right then. Now you've told me, I feel so much better about coming here every day, making sure Mummy's got food and company and hasn't fallen down the stairs.'

Millie couldn't believe they were talking about their mother as if she wasn't in the room.

'God Karen. Turn any greener and you'll be a shamrock,' said Jamie, sniggering.

Her sister stopped scrubbing. She got up off the floor and Millie could see her fists were clenched. 'Aw now, that's enough. Poor Mummy. She'll be ready for the hills if we keep this up.' Turning her back to rinse out the floor cloth, she spoke using her by-the-way tone again. 'Oh, Jamie, forgot to say – Mary McFadden mentioned you're at the tech, doing some night course or other. Is that right?'

Jamie shifted his shoulders.

'Oh, that's nice, Jamie. Is it Spanish you're learning? Like you wanted?' his mother asked absent-mindedly, rejoining the conversation, though her eyes were still shut and her chair still rocking.

'No, not Spanish.'

'What then?' asked Karen, turning around slowly, smiling sweetly. 'Don't be behind the door now.'

'Well, I'm actually studying Irish. It's a cultural class, Mummy… nothing political,' he added quickly.

The radio seemed louder than ever, and it was their mother who spoke first. 'What's that, son? Did you say Irish? You're learning Irish?' Their mother had stopped rocking and was leaning so far forward in her chair Millie was worried she might slip off.

'Yes. That's right. I meant to say to you,' said Jamie, swallowing hard. 'Eimear and I and the girls are all doing it.' He was faltering. 'It was her idea. But, you know, I'm enjoying it alright. It's a very mixed class. All sorts go. Eimear thinks it's important we show the girls both sides. Of our heritage, you know.'

Karen was standing at full tilt now, smiling triumphantly by the sink.

For a moment Millie imagined going up to her sister and slapping her across the face.

'Heritage?' she heard herself say to no one in particular.

Jamie began to fold the napkins, putting them all back inside their *Titanic* rings. He then said time was marching on and he'd better be getting back to Belfast, as Eimear didn't like going upstairs alone.

As he spoke, their mother got out of her chair, using the Aga to steady herself. She said she was tired and was going to bed. Millie went to help, but her mother quickly put up her right hand like a stop sign, saying she could manage.

On the way out, she paused, and without lifting her head she put her hand on Jamie's shoulder. 'It's all right, son. It's all right.'

Jamie didn't look up. 'It's Eimear, Mum. It's...'

'It's okay, son... I understand.' But Millie knew she didn't.

She thought Jamie was going to say something else, but he just put his hand on top of his mother's.

The three of them then watched her leave the room and close the door gently behind her. It was Millie who broke the silence. 'How could you, Karen?' Her voice was an angry whisper. 'You said not to say. How could you?' she repeated, her voice rising. 'You're a bitch. I'm glad Colin left you.'

Karen pursed her lips, breathing heavily through her nose.

'Stop that now. Jesus, Millie, you're just home, for God's sake,' said Jamie.

'Don't you start. Bloody Irish. Why would you do that to Mummy, Jamie? You are disgusting. Both of you.' She was almost spitting the words out.

Karen had squeezed her eyes shut and was holding her palms over her ears. Jamie remained silent, staring at her blankly.

Chapter 5

***

The smell comes first. A stifling mix of disinfectant and plug-in air freshener creep into her nostrils and suddenly she's there, behind a set of patterned plastic curtains in the clinic.

The pain is searing, stoking her insides; much worse than the period-type promised.

'You all right?' The nurse's face is close.

Eyes tightly shut, legs pulled up to her chest, Millie knows she is moaning but can't seem to stop. She just wants the pain to go away.

The nurse tries again. 'You just had termination; the pain will pass.'

A warm hand touches her clenched fist, and she opens her eyes wide.

The nurse is Filipino. Catholic. She won't like what she's done.

Millie turns away, scrunching her eyes tight. She doesn't want anyone looking at her, not now. Not ever.

When she is alone, she squints through a crack in the curtains. The first thing her sees is a waste bin. The old-fashioned type with a metal lid and hanging bag.

Her eyes widen as they fall on a latex glove that hasn't quite fallen into the bin completely. Two fingers of the glove are sticking out over the edge, clamped in place, just like the forceps had clamped her uterus open twenty minutes before. The blood on the glove is fresh. Is it hers? Or is it the blood of her dead baby? Fourteen weeks old. Too late to let the pills do the work. The life had to be sucked out of her.

Murder.

By the mother herself.

***

The howling wind outside Millie's bedroom window brought her back from a terrible place, just below wakefulness. She shivered and pulled the eiderdown close, thinking about the banshees her aunt Lizzie talked about so often.

Still fully dressed, she lifted her phone. It was just before one. Her lips felt rubbery and her eyes ached when she moved them. She wanted water but didn't dare leave the room. What if her mother was still awake? She'd have something to say about the shouting match earlier.

Staring at the ceiling, she remembered feeling her mother's presence in every corner of the clinic that day. Lying across the landing from her now, she was sure her mother knew what she had done. How could she not? Shame was written all over her. Her cheeks burned and she rolled onto her front, breathing deeply into her scented pillow. Unable to ignore her thirst, she decided her mother would surely be sleeping and crept downstairs.

The ground floor was pitch black and silent in a way her flat never was. In Battersea, there was always a shout, a bang, a car alarm going off, and then, just as light came, a plane – the overnight from Hong Kong Dom used so often.

Waiting for water to boil on the Aga, she thought about how Dom had finally admitted he didn't want a family. He'd said it on the phone – the coward's way: a late-night call from New York, two weeks after she told him she was pregnant.

He had his reasons, he said. The search for his birth mother had ended badly – nothing like the happy-ever-after stories you see on TV. He had been disgusted and appalled by what he had found. He had decided then that there were enough children in the world, too many actually, and he wasn't going to add to the problem. He had said he loved her. Hoped they'd spend the rest of their life together – but children were non-negotiable.

He hoped she'd understand.

She hadn't.

But her loneliness and despair over the following weeks, together with Dom's power of persuasion, the persuasion that earned him millions at the bank, wore her down.

The clinic was booked for when Dom was in Singapore. That suited him. When he returned home a week later with elaborate gifts from the East there was no mention of what she had done and there was no sign of the life ripped out of her.

She was sick with remorse. Told Tom at the paper she had a virus and didn't leave the flat for fear of people knowing her dirty little secret.

The bleeding eventually stopped, and Millie had mourned. Or so she thought.

Now sitting in her mother's rocking chair, her knees pulled up under her, she wondered how it had all come to this.

When she first met Dom, she had been unsure about him; his money and the life that went with it made her uneasy.

She hugged herself, remembering the first time she said she loved him, during a surprise trip to Jura. Dom had taken a house by the beach for the two of them. Well, the two of them, plus a chef. Over the weekend they had learned to fish, cooked what they caught and drank the best whiskies from the local distillery. They made love and talked about their pasts and then tentatively about their future. He had shown her another, more vulnerable side, which begged to be loved.

She had said the words when Dom was pointing out Oyster Catcher and Rabbit Island to her. He had immediately taken her face in his hands and said he loved her too, said they'd be together forever.

Lifting her feet up onto the Aga for warmth, she closed her eyes, and for the briefest moment allowed herself to remember how much she had loved him then.

But in turn he had made her a killer.

At thirty-eight, she had been party to violent death twice. She still found it almost impossible to believe she had taken a life, having had one snatched away from her, all those years ago.

She raged silently for weeks afterwards. This brilliant man she had finally allowed herself to love had broken her.

She opened her eyes. She knew the love had gone.

It died in the clinic, with their baby.

Millie crept upstairs for her phone.

Now standing by the big glass doors that lead out to the garden, with the light of the moon to guide her, she called Dom.

It was nearly two o'clock, but she knew he'd still be awake, following the Asian markets on his phone, Sky Sports muted in the background.

She could feel a hangover beginning to settle and her hands were shaking.

'Hello there, stranger.' Dom spoke quickly.

'Still up then?'

'Something's kicking off in Japan. You know me.'

Dom spoke without hesitation and Millie wondered if he had gone over what he would say to her. She imagined him at his house, spread out on the sofa, remains of a takeaway and God knows what else on the table.

'How's your mother?'

'All right. We had a dinner tonight.'

'How was it?'

'Jamie's learning Irish.' Millie closed her eyes, frustrated at her own friendliness. But she would have said anything to stall the conversation she was about to have.

'Is that bad? I mean, with everything that's going on over there, it might be a good idea.' He gave a careless little laugh.

A surge of anger flooded her.

Standing in the darkness she wanted to say speaking Irish was what Sinn Fein wanted, not what her mother wanted. She wanted to say her mother felt the people who spoke Irish didn't like her or want her about the place.

She wanted to say all this to him but somehow didn't want to have to explain any of it. Because then he might be kind and where would that leave her?

'When are you coming back, Millie?' His voice had changed. It was urgent, lower.

She wanted to say so much to him, but she could only say his name.

'You are coming back, aren't you? I'm sorry about the other night. I know I've said it before, but it won't happen again. I promise.'

She closed her eyes.

'I've not been drinking, did I say? And everything else… you know.'

She thought about the last morning she had spent with Dom, less than a week before. Not yet dawn, yet both awake, saying nothing. Dom's drug-fuelled behaviour from the night before lying between them.

When she stayed silent, he went on. 'I've had a terrible week. I hate not being able to get hold of you.'

Millie's eyes drifted into the darkness outside, where she could just see the faint outlines of trees and branches waving frantically in the wind. She thought about the banshees again.

'*Terrible week?*' Millie found her voice. '*Terrible week?* Have you any idea about the terrible time I've been having since the…' She trailed off. Then she quietly said the word she had never once uttered to him: '*Abortion.*'

As she waited for a reply she could hear her own breathing, heavy and fast, and wondered if Dom could hear it too. He didn't answer. 'Yes, Dom… the abortion. The one I had three months ago. Remember? The one you convinced me to have and then never mentioned.'

She let a silence hover.

'It wasn't like that,' he said finally. 'I didn't mention it because I thought it was better that way. I thought you were trying to forget. I thought we both were.'

Millie could hear Dom's voice finally falter.

'No, Dom, only you,' she said quietly, now almost mesmerised by the dancing silhouettes in the garden.

Leaning her forehead against the coolness of the glass, her long hair loosely hanging over her face, she shut her eyes. 'You don't know what I went through in that clinic. Even now, I'm not sure you realise what I did. Dom, I… *I killed our baby.*' Her voice was straining, but words kept coming. 'Listen, it's your past, it's affected you… I'm sorry… I can't go over it all now.'

Millie's throat was tight, and she was struggling to swallow. 'It's over, Dom, I'm sorry I'm telling you like this – but it *is* over. I'm not coming back. Not to you.' It was as if all the fractured thoughts and questions she had been asking herself over the past months had been squashed, distilled into this one moment.

'Millie, please.' Dom's voice was breaking. 'Think about what you're saying. I've told you I'll change. You just need time.'

'Time? It's nothing to do with time,' she said, sighing. 'But you know what, it doesn't matter. It all doesn't matter. You see, Dom… I don't love you anymore.'

She opened her eyes and lifted her head off the glass. Standing tall, something ran through her. Relief.

'What?'

'I don't love you anymore.'

It was only when she heard the tapping of rain on the new glass roof of the kitchen, she realised the line was dead. She had ended the call.

Moving back to the rocking chair, Millie turned off her phone. Shivering, she pulled her mother's blanket all around her and waited for the sky to turn inky grey.

Making tea later, she was called upstairs.

'Well?' her mother asked, trying to prop herself up in bed.

'Well, what?'

'I don't know who was worse, you or your sister.'

'And Jamie? Let's not forget about Jamie.'

'I've thought about that and it's not his fault.'

'Is that right?'

'You said some very harsh things, Matilda. Don't think I didn't hear you.' Using her arms she pushed herself further up the bed. 'By the end of the night it was the drink talking. Always is.' Her mother paused. 'Anyway, I know this much – you were up half the night. What is the matter with you?'

'It's nothing. I couldn't sleep. About last night… I… feel bad.'

She knew she was going to cry and folded her arms tightly around her body. Keeping her head down, she began to speak. 'Mummy, I've done something… something awful…'

'What are you on about, child?'

'Something evil.' She spat the words out and was now shifting about on her feet, too afraid to look up.

'Evil? What sort of word is that? You're many things, my girl, that's for sure. But not evil. Never that.' Her mother spoke softly. 'You're just home. We've lots of time to chat. Just you and me. But right now, what you need is a good walk.'

She stopped talking when Millie's whimpers began.

Half an hour later, Millie was lying beside her mother on the bed, a damp handkerchief with her initials on it crumpled in her hand. Her mother had listened as she told her about the abortion and Dom and the drugs, and how she had finally told him it was over in the middle of the night.

After a time, her mother spoke.

'Do you remember the time straight after Dad I went away with Lizzie?'

Millie studied her mother's face, trying to remember.

'God, you made a terrible fuss about me leaving. You all did.' Her mother paused. 'I've told no one this now, mind. Only Lizzie knows.' She smoothed out her sheets. 'I was pregnant. Not long, but pregnant nonetheless.'

'What?'

'Your dad had just been killed. I couldn't keep it.'

Millie heard the chapel bells ringing for mass.

'Seven children and a murdered husband. I couldn't cope with another.'

She tried to think of something to say.

'I was tormented, Matilda. I had to go on a boat to Liverpool. The weeks after – well, they were pure hell.'

'Mummy… I'm so sorry. I wasn't easy… back then. I know that now.'

'You'd just lost your father, child. In a funny way, having to get you all up and out the door every day saved me.'

Millie held her mother's hand and then curled up beside her, closer this time. The familiar smell of lavender filled her nose.

'I won't judge you, Matilda. In time, God will do that for both of us.'

'Will he understand?' she asked quietly, picking at the embroidery on her now-sodden handkerchief.

'He will, Matilda. He will.'

Her mother inhaled deeply and, not for the first time, Millie wondered if her mother believed her own words.

'It's hard, but it gets better. Just like your dad, it was in my shadow for years, but it fades.' Stroking Millie's hair gently, she went on. 'You know. I sometimes think… *What if?* You could have another wee brother or sister. Imagine that.' Her mother was almost cheery.

'Did you know what it was?'

'No. I didn't want to.'

'Mine,' said Millie, 'was a little girl. Cara. In my head, I called her Cara.'

Millie was now sobbing into her mother's arm.

'Cara. That's a nice name. Very nice. You know, someone told me once, I think it was Father Paul, that good people sometimes do bad things. Would he have been talking to me at the house after your dad? God, that would have been a terrible thing for him to say to me then. I should remember that, shouldn't I?'

Her mother slowly clasped her own hands, rolling one thumb over the other. 'So many people came to the house the day of your dad. People I didn't even want to see came.' Looking down at her, she added, 'Catholics came too. Good Catholics. That can't have been easy for them.'

Her mother lifted Millie's face. 'Everyone loved your dad.'

Millie wiped her wet face with the back of her hands.

'Anyway, he's right,' said her mother.

'Who?'

'Father Paul.'

'What do you mean?'

'Sometimes, good people do bad things. What I did was bad, but it had to be done.' Her mother sounded strong, almost defiant. 'Maybe you're the same. Bringing up a baby alone isn't easy. I can tell you that. If Dom wasn't going to stand by you, why should you ruin your life? Because that's what it would do. Mark my words.'

A silence lingered until her mother spoke again. 'I just know you will be a mother one day, when the time's right. I saw on the news some woman in Italy had a baby and she was fifty-four. God works in mysterious ways, child.'

After taking a cocktail of tablets, her mother closed her eyes and laid her head back on the pillow. She'd be snoozing soon.

When she was sure she was asleep, Millie lifted her mother's fingers. These once-strong hands that changed tyres and heaved sideboards and beds on their own, were now frail and limp, with skin as thin as parchment.

This time she cried silently. Not for Dom or what she had done at the clinic; not even for the wee brother or sister that never was. But for her mother and the life she never got to live.

After lunch, Millie said she was thinking about going up to the cottage for a few days. Being by the sea was maybe just what she needed to clear her head, plot her new life. Her mother wasn't as upset as she thought she might be. 'You might find some peace there right enough. But real peace, Matilda, is in the person not the place.'

They sat chatting for nearly an hour, her mother in her chair by the Aga, Millie on the new sofa. The hum of the radio in the background.

'I had to stop going to the cottage so much after your dad. It was too full of ghosts for me.' Her mother closed her eyes. 'Sometimes I liked that, mind, it made me feel close to him. But other times – I don't know, Matilda. It frightened me.'

As Millie served tea she heard how Kate sometimes used the cottage with her flatmate Amanda. 'Thick as thieves, those two are. Never apart.'

Millie made her eyes big like saucers, but her mother chose to ignore her.

'Jamie wants to sell. Says it's too far gone to rent. Says it's the view that will make the money.'

When Millie didn't respond, she went on. 'Thinks I'd be better off buying a small apartment in Spain. Something serviced. There's direct flights and I'd get rent.'

Millie pushed back into her seat. She didn't like the idea of her mother selling Donegal or buying a serviced apartment in Spain.

Her mother rang Mrs McClarnen to say Millie would pick up the keys to the cottage by six and could she or her son pop in and turn on the heating for a few hours?

Millie talked about getting the bus there but was secretly relieved when her mother insisted she took her car. She wasn't driving it at the moment because of her back and said it would be good to get it out on a run.

Before she left she caught her reflection in the mirror by the front door and decided her new eyelashes had to go. 'Are there any decent salons in town? I want to get my lashes off,' she shouted into the kitchen.

Her mother scolded, 'No one will be interested in your eyes up there, my girl. If you're that desperate to get rid of them, pull them out yourself.'

She made a Karen face in the mirror but didn't say anything and went up to her room to pack.

Chapter 6

Millie drove to Ballydunn in her mother's old Peugeot.

With the window down she could smell a sweetness in the air. The sound of a distant lawnmower made her smile; summer wasn't far away. She couldn't believe how free she felt, but as the journey went on and the light gently started to fade, her sense of release turned to guilt as she thought about what she had said to Dom.

She pictured him in his empty house, sad and alone. Wriggling in her seat to get comfortable, she tried to immerse herself in the patchwork of green fields whizzing past, but her mind kept going back to it. She thought about his past – the adoption, the disappointment with his birth mother. He was damaged, but so was she. Maybe if she called him, they could talk. Then she thought about the clinic and very quickly decided that would be no good to anyone.

Looking out at the thick hedgerows, entwined with expectant buds, she recalled a book she had read at college. An Irish writer, maybe Edna O'Brien, or was it Josephine Hart, who wrote about damaged people and how they always survived. Happy with this notion, she felt a little better. Everything would be alright; she just knew it.

As the old car bumped and banged its way up Black Mountain – the potholes being a sure sign you were in the south (according to her father), she saw the sky above her was big and the emptiness around her stark. Nearing the top of the mountain clouds were circling the higher peaks, like smoke rings from a hookah.

She wondered why no hacienda-style bungalows had arrived here like in the rest of Donegal, but when she saw the barren plains, she wasn't surprised. The wild bleakness could not compete with the comforting ocean views and village life just over the summit. Here, only the bones of old famine cottages remained, inhabited by herds of sheltering sheep. As she shifted gear to meet the incline of the road, she glimpsed clumps of matted wool clinging to rusty fencing – boundaries once used to divide farms and families in this part of Ireland all those years ago.

For a moment she wondered if souls of that awful time wandered here, unable to settle. She thought again about Aunt Lizzie's banshees and then shook her head sharply; she didn't want to think about that now. Feeling sleepy, she wound the window down completely and turned on the radio, twirling the knob to get a station that wasn't hissing at her. As she drove down the far side of the mountain into Ballydunn bay, she found herself tapping the steering wheel to the beat of a Bodhran drum.

Then there it was. The sea. Big and wild, the way she liked it. Instantly, she was with her brothers and sisters scouring out the windows of their father's old minibus – the only practical transport a family of nine could use back then.

They would have fallen silent as the bus slowly climbed the near side of the mountain – waiting, hoping, to be the first to shout, '*I can see the sea!*' She smiled, remembering how they would then argue for the rest of the journey about who had seen it first and who was fibbing.

The light was fading fast and the sky over the ocean was darker still. Winding up her window, she knew she was in for a downpour, so she picked up speed, determined to get to Mrs McClarnen's before it started to hammer down.

Finding the winding roads difficult to follow, Millie was relieved when she hit the edge of the village. Within minutes she was turning into their old cleaner's back yard, narrowly missing an abandoned tractor dumped at the side of the gate. As Millie got out of the car, she was surprised to see Mrs McClarnen already lurching towards her. Like a character from a Brothers Grimm fairy tale, she was dressed head to toe in black and it was difficult to see where she finished and the night began. She was hunched over a nobbled stick and as Millie hugged her, she was sad to see their once sprightly cleaner was now a crumpled old woman.

Ten more minutes and she had turned down Sea Lane. The night around her was now bat black and Millie inched the car along, worried she might end up in the deep sheugh she knew ran along the side of the road.

A light above the cottage door guided her through the gate. She stopped the car briefly, then, clutching the steering wheel, accelerated, driving right round the back of the cottage, pulling up on the far side – just like her father did when he pretended to be a racing driver on a track. Then they'd all make screeching noises as he came to a standstill. This time, Millie just gave the horn a quick beep to announce her own arrival. She turned off the engine and sat in silence, letting the wind and rain batter the car. Sitting in darkness, she knew the sea was directly in front of her. It would be angry tonight and she was desperate to go to it. But the rain had other ideas. When she saw no end to it, she decided to make a run for the door.

The cottage was cold and smelt strongly of damp. Mrs McClarnen had turned on the heating, but the old stone walls were going to need more than a few hours of warmth to get rid of the festering odour. For a brief moment Millie regretted coming to Ardmara. In the darkness she felt sad and alone and considered booking into the new hotel she had passed with Sasha, but then decided she was being spoilt. She took her phone out and made a shopping list.

She headed to the Spar in Main Street, which was attached to the only petrol station in town. It had been owned by Gerard Mohan and was the one place in the village which sold the *Belfast Telegraph*. Millie remembered her mother always saying what a nice Catholic Gerard Mohan was.

The new owner had spruced up the place and as Millie entered, she was pleased to see a selection of wines behind the counter. After picking up some provisions, including firelighters and sticks, she enjoyed browsing the aisles, searching out her favourite Irish brands: Veda bread, Tayto crisps and Punjana tea. There was jaunty traditional music playing from the speakers and the only smell here was of cooked chickens turning on a spit behind the hot food counter.

As she finally approached the till to pay Millie glimpsed a newsstand stuffed with copies of Sinn Féin's *An Phoblacht*. There wasn't a *Belfast Telegraph* in sight.

Emptying her basket, she recognised the man serving behind the counter. He was from the Fiddler's Inn: the creep with the dog. Very soon, she knew he was deliberately ignoring her. She coughed and as he turned round, she forced out a clown's smile. 'Could I have a bottle of Pinot Grigio, please?'

It was as if she hadn't spoken. Millie said it again, this time with a tone her mother liked to use when disgruntled.

Only then did he respond. Without speaking he pointed to a sign almost hidden by a picture postcard of the Virgin Mary that read *No alcohol sold after 6pm.* A name, his name, underneath: *Cathal Quinn.*

'Are you serious?' Millie tried to laugh.

'I am.'

'But you can buy it anywhere.'

'Well, away to anywhere,' he said with an empty smile. Millie became aware of how stained his teeth were and jerked away quickly. She wanted to say how stupid his rule was, how rude he was. But she had just arrived in the village and didn't need the upset.

As she lifted her box of groceries, she studied Cathal Quinn and decided there was something most unpleasant about him. She didn't try to pat his dog on the way out.

The cottage felt no warmer when she returned and it was no wonder, as the front door, which was warped and rotten along the bottom, opened straight into the living room. As she propped some cushions up against the door to hold back the wind, she was sure this was something her father talked about changing before he was killed.

Glad of her warm parka, she set about trying to light the fire. From memory, she carefully stacked firelighters in between a pile of small sticks, then used logs she found wrapped in old newspaper by the hearth to build it up. She wasn't hopeful.

As she fanned the smoking mound she looked around. There were too many seats and sofas in the room; there always had been – but they were needed for a family of nine. There was a TV set that was newish, Kate or Jamie must have bought it, and through the door into the kitchen, she could just see a microwave and a NutriBullet sitting on the worktop. That was definitely Kate. There was an empty space under the sink, just like their old kitchen in Dungrillen – for the dishwasher that never arrived. This made Millie smile, and as the fire began to spark, she felt a little happier about being there.

All three bedrooms smelt fusty, and the two children's rooms with their double sets of bunks were just as small and cramped as she remembered. Turning on a side light, she relived how they used to hurtle themselves through the front door to take ownership of their favourite bunk. Karen and Jamie, being the eldest, somehow always managed to wangle their spot – only ever giving it up if one of the others had a birthday that weekend.

The grown-up room was no less oppressive. Seeing it now, Millie couldn't believe two adults slept in a bed so small. She thought of Dom's four-poster in London. It was so big, Harrods was the only place they could find sheets to fit it.

Before Dad, they came to Ballydunn for Easter and then every weekend after. In July, they stayed for two full weeks over the Twelfth holiday when their father's timber yard was closed.

Right from the start Millie recalled her father fixing things. Planks of wood and sheets of metal would be tied to the top of their minibus and stored in the outside shed. To be nailed or hammered, whenever their father felt the notion.

Their mother would either be cooking, washing, or cleaning, and any child silly enough to stay indoors after breakfast was immediately commandeered to help her out.

But this was all before Dad.

Afterwards, the visits were less frequent. Her mother paid for a new roof and wiring over time, but that was about it. Then, when they did come, it was always on the Saturday, not the Friday night like before, and Millie's heart used to sink when she saw her mother pack up the bus straight after lunch on the Sunday. Before Dad, they always waited until the light was fading over the strand and the sea was dead and grey before leaving.

The new early departure saw the minibus silent. As they drove past the beaches, all of them, bar Jamie and maybe Karen, would stare out the windows, searching the strand for sightings of their weekend friends who stayed to the evening, determined to make the most of the lighter nights. By the time Millie was fifteen, she and Kate had hockey, the boy's rugby and Josie always had a boyfriend to see.

She wandered back into the living room to check on the fire and spotted the old record player in the corner. To the side, stacked up against a small table were a bunch of records. And as if it was yesterday, she pictured her mother and father, and maybe some friends like the Conlons, pushing back the sofas and dancing in the squashed-up space to Kenny Rodgers and Elvis Presley. Or laughing and singing along with the children to something really old like Val Doonican's 'O'Rafferty's Motor Car', the words of which were printed on a sheet inside the album cover.

If it wasn't too late, their father would give in and allow the younger ones to take turns standing on his feet as he swirled them around like ballroom dancers. Millie remembered he'd always say it was just like the first night he met their mother at the Rotary dance in Dungrillen.

As she stared at the fire, now unsure if it was going to live or die, she heard the wind pick up outside. Whistles of noise were rushing through the cottage from every direction and Millie could feel cold air all around her. She wondered if the cottage was even habitable and decided Jamie was right. It would be sold to a developer, for the site. More hacienda bungalows. More double-glazing.

Deciding to sleep in the double bed her parents had shared, she lay there thinking about everything again: Dom, the clinic, her father, her mother's secret. Under fresh sheets and a brand-new duvet from home her mother had never used, Millie knew she had to start thinking about her future, not the past. The open window brought in much-needed air, but with it came a cold, biting wind. She pulled the duvet up to her eyes and, with her feet dancing around two hot water bottles she'd found in the cupboard under the sink, sleep came easily.

Chapter 7

Millie woke early.

Once outside, she found herself counting her strides from the front door to the rickety wooden steps leading down to the sand. Today, it was only twelve. She was sure it had been more before. It now wasn't as sunny as she had thought. Some clouds had appeared and were being dragged across the sky like kites in the wind.

The strand under the cottage was empty. It had always been that way, being the furthest from the village. Enjoying the solitude, she took off her boots and socks, revelling in the sensation of cold, damp sand clumping under her feet.

She followed the crest of the beach round until she could go no further, stopping at a high jut of rocks the family had called the 'Lookout'. A place, weather permitting, they would sit forever with their father, sucking on a quarter of clove rock, searching for pirate ships with telescopes made from stuck-together toilet rolls. Clambering up the slimy rocks dotted with spongy red anemones, or bloodsuckers, as they all called them, she instinctively found the old footholds. Stretching for the summit, she sensed she was not alone. Gingerly pulling herself up, she saw a figure, a man, sitting on the far edge, a plateau of rocks her father christened the 'Throne'.

Millie panicked and, dropping her head, started to scramble back down towards the sand. Just as she neared the bottom, a tall shadow loomed overhead. She cranked her face upwards, but the sun was out again and all she could see was a hovering mass.

'Jesus,' she said, stumbling backwards, losing her footing in her panic.

'Steady there.' A strong hand moved from the shadow and grabbed her elbow.

Her mind raced. Should she scream? Would anyone hear?

The voice came again. 'Well, now, it's you. We mustn't keep meeting like this. There'll be talk.'

Millie recognised the dramatic delivery. It was Finn McFall. The man she'd danced with in the Fiddler's Inn.

She shook off his hand roughly and steadied herself.

'It's you,' she said, holding one arm up to shade her eyes, her cheeks hot with new and old embarrassment.

'It is.'

'What are you doing here?'

'What are *you* doing here?'

'I'm out for a walk,' said Millie, annoyed by her complacency.

'I'm out painting.'

Millie's eyes could just see the edge of a large notepad flapping manically in the wind. She coughed out a nervous laugh. 'Painting?'

'What's so funny about that?'

'Sorry. I didn't mean to… I need to go.'

'You've just arrived.'

'Well… I think it's going to rain,' she said, peering up at the sky, which was once again clear.

'No, it's not.'

'Is that right?'

'Doesn't smell like rain.'

'What does that even mean?' She was unable to hide her agitation.

Finn laughed. 'Are you alright? You seem a bit jittery?'

Millie didn't answer.

'I've a flask of tea. Do you want a drop?'

'Tea?'

'Do you always repeat everything?' he asked, stifling a smile, running his hands through his curly hair.

With his back to the sun, Millie thought his eyes were as dark as night.

'I need to be getting back.'

'So you keep saying.'

Millie sighed heavily. She didn't want to play this game.

She wanted to tell him to leave her alone, to stop making fun of her. But when she looked up, she felt an unexpected rush of warmth.

'I'm Finn, by the way.'

'Right.'

Finn raised his eyebrows. 'And you are?' His smile had grown into a grin and for the first time Millie noticed his teeth. White and straight. Expensive.

She hesitated, not wanting to give him her name, but decided it would be rude not to. 'Millie.'

'Mill-ie,' he said slowly, as if pronouncing the name of some exotic flower.

She glanced at him again, her forehead wrinkled.

'Goodbye, Mill-ie,' he said as she walked away, clutching her socks and boots.

Unable to resist turning back, she was surprised how unembarrassed he was when she discovered he was still watching her.

'Goodbye, Fi-nnn,' she said, allowing a small smile to creep across her lips.

Heading back to the cottage, she wondered if he was still watching. Determined not to turn around, she was both irritated and excited at how much this interested her.

After cleaning the kitchen while singing along to Val Doonican records, Millie crossed the dunes to the village. She passed the entrances to the two caravan sites that sat on the beach side of the road and was sure the showers and toilets were much bigger than before.

She stopped and had a good snoop at the new hotel, deciding it was just the old B&B with a large extension. She thought it very sparse in appearance and not like a beach hotel at all. Millie wondered who owned it and decided whoever it was hadn't made much effort with the exterior. The grey plastered walls were unfinished and cheap double-glazing had replaced the old sash windows. Briefly, she recalled the hanging lanterns and whitewashed shutters of the hotel Tresanton in Devon where Dom had brought her for her birthday the year before.

Passing the front door of the building she saw a small rusty digger sitting to the side, but she could see no sign of building work in progress.

She was glad to see the Fish Tail takeaway was still there and, although it was only May, O'Neils already had their buckets and spades dangling outside the front of their shop. She imagined the faces of children as they were taken in to buy a new crabbing net or beach ball, just as she had been all those years ago.

Further along Main Street and as the road rose up, the Fiddler's Inn and its unrivalled views of the Atlantic appeared high on the right. Seeing it in daylight, Millie was amazed the old wooden benches outside the pub had survived. This was the spot where she and the others were eventually shunted to when they were allowed to come to the pub with their father. A rugby international involving Ireland being the only guarantee of a definite invite.

Then, it seemed, the whole village would cram into the front bar to watch the drama unfold on the pitch. A small TV was perched high up behind the counter, surrounded by faded pictures of the Virgin Mary, postcards from Lourdes and, in pride of place, a signed photograph of Willie John McBride.

'*There's an extraness in the air, Margaret,*' her father would proclaim at the breakfast table on any day Ireland was playing and they'd all laugh at their father using such a silly word.

On these mornings, her father would fly out of the cottage to stake his stool at the pub's counter. Millie and the others would then sneak into the lounge bar after lunch, trying not to be seen. As the place filled up, they would eventually be shooed away by the Alacadoos and take refuge in a stall by the door. Here, they'd all have to pile in on top of each other, balancing a Fanta bottle with straw in one hand and a packet of Tayto in the other.

Finally, they would be told to go outside and play and, inevitably, this would mean sitting on the benches, trying to knock each other off. She remembered how every try or drop kick Ireland scored brought a lion's roar from inside the pub. Sometimes Mrs Murphy, who owned the bar with her three sons, would bring out another round of Fantas on a rust-edged Guinness tray with a picture of a pelican on it. Now rooted in memory, Millie could almost see her wild red hair blowing in the wind, looking out over the Atlantic. '*Next stop America, folks*,' she'd say in a cheesy American accent, dramatically throwing her arm out towards the ocean.

The line and her delivery of it became a family joke with the Malones. When they walked home after a match someone, usually Karen, who was great fun back then, would imitate Mrs Murphy's words and actions. Her father and mother would burst into fits of giggles – the type of laughing only a few pints, and in her mother's case, one gin, could induce.

But this was all before Dad. Mrs Murphy got sick not long after her father. Later, there was talk about two of her boys having to leave the village quickly. Something about gun running across the border. Her mother never wanted to talk about it, only ever saying that Mrs Murphy had a heart of corn and didn't deserve the sons she'd been given. The pub had gone through several owners since then and Millie wasn't sure who was in charge now.

Further on the right was the Spar and adjoining petrol station and then, just beyond that, with panoramic views, Sasha's new house. Two open-winged eagles had appeared either side of the electric gates and Millie couldn't stop herself taking a picture on her phone to show her mother. She wondered if her friend would be up at the weekend and made a mental note to text her.

Turning left to the harbour, looking out over the ocean, she felt glad she had come to Ballydunn. If she was going to decide what to do with the rest of her life – surely this was the place to do it.

McBrides cafe was still on the corner, as was the adjoining post office, which sold everything.

The cafe was very different from before. Outside, upturned milk churns, topped with hand-stitched cushions, were being used as seats. The windows were bigger and the words *Always Local… Always Seasonal* were scrawled across the entire frontage. Old Mrs McBride had long died, replaced, so Sasha had told her, by twin grandchildren from Dublin with nose rings.

Her favourite Irish stew and pavlova were still on the hand-written menu nailed to the side of the door, but so too were a protein bowl and energy balls. She ordered a cappuccino and took the window seat closest to the harbour. This was the table the family so often decamped to for lunch after a morning on the beach or running around the village, darting in and out of friend's caravans or holiday cottages.

Then they had to push two tables together to fit the family in and, religiously on each visit, every child was told to have the same thing – so as not to confuse Mrs McBride – who was old and deaf and didn't need the annoyance of twenty different orders, thank you very much.

Jugs of iced water were produced for Millie and the others, when what they really wanted was a Coke float or a Fanta, like the other children in the cafe. But their father always said those drinks would rot their teeth and were only for special occasions. Like the rugby.

After a protein bowl Millie decided to head back to the cottage. On her way she went into the post office that did indeed still sell everything. She bought a Magnum.

Standing outside in the sunshine she studied the harbour, again thinking little had changed. A few weekend boats, a small rescue tug that had seen better days and some fishing boats bobbed about in the gentle swell. To the right some fishing trawlers had just arrived at the pier.

Enjoying the view, Millie was faintly aware of someone behind her and, turning round, she saw Cathal Quinn. The man from the Spar. He strode past without acknowledging her and something in his gait convinced Millie he was angry. He didn't stop walking until he was almost on top of a fisherman who was off-loading lobster pots from one of the newly arrived trawlers. She could hardly see the man under his yellow waterproofs and red woolly hat, but from the colour of his hands she was certain he wasn't local.

Within minutes, a sea of coloured waterproofs were wrestling with lobster pots and nets on the pier. A rainbow had appeared behind the men and Millie thought it would make a great picture. Then, just as she grappled with her Magnum and phone, she saw Cathal push the fisherman he had been talking to.

She stopped for a moment, swivelling around quickly, to see if anybody else had seen what she had, but there was no one. Still watching, her eyes crinkled. Again, the fisherman was pushed, so much so he tripped over a lobster pot and landed hard on the ground.

Millie couldn't believe how passive the man was. He stayed on the ground, his head bowed. The other fishermen were completely ignoring the situation.

She wanted to walk down the pier, find out what was going on. But something about Cathal Quinn made her stop. Instead, holding the Magnum in her mouth, she took a picture with her phone then, as Cathal bent down and repeatedly stabbed the fisherman in the chest with his finger, she pressed the video button.

Years of working on the paper had taught her the power of live footage.

As the Magnum started to melt Millie set it down on the ground and continued to video what she was seeing. And still the fisherman did nothing.

Now, some of the other men had stopped unloading the boats and were watching her, watching them. She stuffed her phone in her bag and walked quickly back up past the post office, throwing the Magnum in a bin as she went.

Back on Main Street she felt flustered. Almost running, she cut through the dunes, sighing with relief when she saw Ardmara in the distance.

She had left all the windows of the cottage open and, although it was cold, the air inside felt fresh and beachy. Watching through the window, she could see rays of sunlight piercing the calm water in front of the cottage, making it glisten. It was so unexpected, so beautiful, Millie threw down her things and pulled one of the old armchairs over to the window.

Curling her legs up under her, she thought about what she had seen at the harbour. Maybe she was overreacting, but her gut told her not. She played the video over, allowing different scenarios to run through her head. As she stared out over the ocean following a seabird dive into the water, a lone figure with a long shadow walked away from the beach. It was Finn.

She leaned forward in her chair, not wanting to lose sight of him, intrigued by where he was heading.

Just then, her phone pinged. It was Tom from the paper.

'*How's your mother?*'

Millie's shoulders slumped. She knew what his text really meant. She'd been away just over a week now and hadn't bothered to make contact.

With her eyes back at the beach, watching the broad figure fade to a tiny speck, she made a decision. She was going to stay on in Ballydunn for a few more days. Something had caught her attention. Millie then settled back into the warmth of her armchair, happy to watch the sea fade into darkness.

Chapter 8

The smell of damp clung to Millie's nostrils.

She now regretted not buying plug-in air fresheners from the post office the day before; when she had sniffed them, thoughts of the clinic had filled her head and she'd bought a Magnum instead.

She washed quickly with the old handheld shower head, all the time trying to avoid the mouldy tiles and faded shower curtain. Wrapped in a towel, she ran to the kitchen. It was the only warm room in the cottage, as she'd kept the electric rings on low all night – a trick she'd learnt from her student days. Flipping her hair up into a high ponytail, she admired her handiwork in the shell-framed mirror by the door, and for the first time in months decided she felt more like her old self.

It was just after nine o'clock when she started walking over the dunes. The sand was still damp from the night before and droplets of dew from the tall grasses clung to her leather jeans. She brought her laptop and notebook – to help her with a feature idea she had started to think about.

The inside of the Beach Hotel was as disappointing as the outside. Heavy flock-velvet sofas lined the lobby like logs and the lighting was cold, even harsh. A cheap pine fireplace played house to a large vase of dusty fake sunflowers and Millie once more thought about the Hotel Tresanton.

The foyer was busy, mostly golfers getting ready for a day on the greens. Settling herself on a sofa near the fireplace that wasn't really a fireplace, she ordered a cappuccino. The internet connection was surprisingly fast, and she quickly sent an email to Tom at the paper.

She told him she was sorry for not being in touch, that her mother was a lot better – thank you for asking – and that she had a whiff of a story he might be interested in. She didn't go into any detail.

Buoyed by her email, she then texted Jamie and Karen, apologising to both for what she had said at dinner. When she thought about it, she wasn't really sorry at all, but she knew her efforts would please her mother.

The cappuccino she ordered was good and the two pieces of shortbread that came with it even better. As she sat in the now-quiet foyer, a sign for the Residents' Lounge caught her attention. Trying to act like a guest she sauntered through reception towards the back of the hotel. The lounge was empty, and she was happy to see a real fire burning in the grate. The same swirly sofas didn't appear quite so ugly here and there were two large windows offering natural light and sweeping views over the beach. She could see Ardmara to her left and, further on down the sand, the Lookout. Beyond that, there was a high ridge of dunes, which she knew ran down to a flat where the old fisherman's cottage was.

To the right, the rocks eventually curled round the shoreline and opened up onto the main beach of the village. Beyond that was the harbour and McBrides cafe, and above it all, sparkling in the sunlight like a fairytale castle, was Sasha's new house.

Millie ordered a second cappuccino.

Another ping. Thinking it might be a reply from her brother or sister she grabbed her phone. But it was Dom, asking her why she wasn't returning his calls.

She bit her lip, embarrassed by her disregard for his efforts.

As sadness started to cling to her, the sun dipped behind a cloud and the water quickly dulled to a murky grey.

She would call Dom. Just not now.

A voice she was getting used to came from behind. She turned round to see narrow eyes staring at her. It was Cathal Quinn. He was so close she could see his cheeks were threaded with angry red veins and his forehead was flaking. A drinker, her mother would say.

'Are you a resident?'

'Sorry?'

'Are you a resident?'

'I was just having a look at the view.'

'Well, then you can't be in here. It's for residents.'

'Excuse me?' She sounded deliberately irritated. 'And you are?'

'Cathal Quinn.'

Millie shrugged her shoulders.

'The owner.' He was smiling, but only from the teeth out.

'The owner? Right… Suppose you own the Spar too? Oh, and let's not forget the petrol station.'

'That's right. And you need to leave. Now.'

A strange, tense silence lay between them until Millie grabbed her things. Just before leaving she put on her best just-you-wait voice. 'Thank you so much for your kind hospitality. As a journalist I'll be delighted to report on how you treat visitors.'

Without waiting for a reaction, she walked out.

Striding past reception, a sign caught her eye:

Golfing Special… Five nights for the price of three… (Breakfast Included)

Before she knew it, Millie had handed over her credit card. With her cheap plastic room key gripped in her hand, she returned to the resident's lounge.

He was gone.

She wanted to run out the far door that said *Staff Only* to see if she could find him, shove the key in his face. Now alone in the lounge, she became acutely aware of her white knuckled fist and felt foolish. From nowhere, she heard her big sister's voice, '*But you weren't meant to be in there, Millie, were you?*'

As she slumped down onto a sofa, not sure what to do next, she thought about Cathal Quinn. How could someone so awful own so much in the village? She thought about what she'd seen at the harbour and was convinced more than ever that it wasn't just an argument between workmates she had witnessed – but something different altogether.

As she ordered her third cappuccino of the morning, she decided she definitely had a story to tell Tom.

The sun had come back out and Millie thought it might stay. As she fished about in her bag for her sunglasses she headed to the beach. Her head was light from all the caffeine she had consumed and her body felt tight. A brisk walk was what she needed.

Without meaning to, Millie found herself at the bottom of the Lookout. Peering upwards she thought how awful it would be if Finn McFall was on the other side. Then, as if her mind made it happen, he appeared. The same large pad of paper was stuffed under his arm, its edges still flapping frantically in the wind. He was gripping an old tin, maybe a biscuit tin, in his hand and a leather satchel was swung across his body.

He stood like a monument, towering over her. 'Can't keep away, can you?'

Millie wasn't in the mood. 'You know what? How about you keep your thoughts to yourself. And just for your information I was here a long time before you ever were.'

Finn smiled but didn't say anything.

'This is my Lookout,' Millie went on. 'My family has been coming here for years. So don't for a minute think it's yours.'

Only the squawking of seagulls broke the silence.

'Well now. That's me told,' said Finn, sliding down the rock. As he pulled himself clear, his fisherman's sweater rode up his body and Millie turned away sharply. Walking past her, he bowed down like an Elizabethan courtier, throwing his free arm up to let her pass by.

'Now you're just being silly.'

'Yes, that was silly. Very silly indeed.' He was trying not to laugh.

Millie glanced out to sea.

'I wouldn't hang around. It's about to tip down.'

She looked up at the clear sky. 'No, it's not.'

With his free hand, Finn pointed to a large black cloud travelling at speed from the east. 'You'll get soaked.'

Millie watched as he walked away. His curly hair was blowing in the wind and his sweater and jeans were being forced against his lean body. He was wearing battered Chelsea boots, which made her think he didn't always shop in Ballydunn.

A few steps on, he turned quickly and caught her following him.

'I didn't mean to upset you,' he said, pushing curls of hair out of his eyes, swaying slightly in the wind.

'I'm not upset.'

'You seem upset.'

'Well, I'm not.'

'Well, good. I'm glad we've got that sorted.'

He smiled broadly, and once again his perfect smile struck her as unusual.

A gust of wind suddenly pushed Millie towards the sea and Finn tilted his head. Millie felt her stomach tighten with excitement. She didn't want to feel it, but she did.

'Do you fancy giving me a hand?'

'A hand? Where to?'

Finn used his head to nod to the very end of the beach where the sand dunes rose high and then fell to the flat.

'Is that where you store your stuff? The old fisherman's cottage?'

'It's where I live.'

Millie's eyes widened. She remembered the cottage from when she was a child. It barely had a roof back then.

'The old fisherman's cottage?'

'You know it?'

She didn't answer. She'd given away too much information already. Her past here belonged to her. No one else.

'Well, will you help me or not?'

'Oh, alright then,' said Millie, making sure it sounded like it was the very last thing on this earth she wanted to do.

He handed her the rusted Fox's biscuit tin with a thick elastic band around it and dumped a bag on top. Opening her mouth to complain, Millie met his eyes. They weren't dark like she thought, but blue, cornflower blue.

Finn walked ahead of her with big strides and Millie had to double her pace to keep up. They walked in silence to the end of the beach and struggled up the dunes to the flat.

The cottage was the same as she remembered, but different.

It still stood parallel to the sea, perilously close to the rocks, but there had been a lot of restoration to it and the two outhouses that sat at angles to either side of the cottage.

Millie felt excited, returning to yet another place she hadn't been for years. It was here, the older ones had chased her and Kate up and down the dunes and all around the cottage until they were dizzy with exhaustion.

As they walked down the beaten path to the door, the tall grasses prickled her legs just as they had when she was a child.

The cottage had a new front door now. It was made of old wooden planks that Millie could see had been skilfully cut and slotted together. The windows had shutters made in the same way and there was smoke coming from the single chimney.

The outhouses had doors too, but they were different. Boarded up with corrugated iron.

Inside the cottage, Millie blinked in the darkness. The room seemed smaller than she remembered, then she noticed a wall had been erected to allow for a small galley kitchen.

The most striking feature of the new cottage was its walls, which were covered with paintings of every shape and size. When they couldn't be hung, pictures were stacked, sometimes two deep against doors and cupboards. A large paint-splattered easel stood to the side of a long wooden table, which was littered with small pots of paints and brushes. She set the biscuit tin down beside a bunch of letters, mostly unopened, stuffed under a leprechaun paperweight. Small piles of books were everywhere. Fishing nets, buckets and waterproof jackets all hung from hooks in the rafters, and a lantern and torch dangled from a coat rack near the door.

The cottage smelt strongly of burning turf, just like the Fiddler's Inn, and sure enough, there on the left wall was a huge, walk-in fireplace.

This was where she and Kate had played house years before. Using an old kettle pot they had found outside, they'd stand in the fire, pretending to heat water they'd dragged in buckets from the rock pools below.

She lifted a book from a table by the fire. *The Poems & Works of Seamus Heaney.* Remembering the pub reading, she thought about her father and quickly set the book down.

Finn was oblivious to her nosiness. He was relaxed, walking about the cottage, opening windows, stoking the fire. Millie watched him go through the small kitchen to the back bedroom. As he opened more windows, she heard the waves crashing on rocks below. She felt excited and wanted to run to the noise, but she glimpsed his unmade bed and turned away quickly.

'Will you have a bowl of soup? I made it fresh earlier.'

'Soup…?'

Finn cocked his head to the side.

'Oh, alright… But I can't stay long.'

Following him into the kitchen, she noticed a door to the right. A bathroom.

As children, she and the others had been intrigued by the cottage's outside toilet and their young eyes were often driven to peer into the dark, dirty hole they knew, or imagined, a whole family had once shared.

The new kitchen was basic with a sink and wooden worktop, a cooker and fridge. There was an old dresser laden with yet more paints, notepads, and books, including a Jamie Oliver.

Millie smiled at the domesticity.

A rough linen curtain ran the whole way under the worktops and the same fabric had been used to make curtains for the small bathroom window and the three small windows in the back bedroom.

Little was said as Finn busied himself heating the soup. Millie continued to walk around, her mind spluttering with questions she didn't ask. She took off her coat and hung it beside Finn's, all the time gazing at the paintings that were everywhere. She quickly felt she was seeing two different artists.

Some pictures, watercolours mostly, were bright and sea-sidey with seagulls searing over a frothy ocean. Others were darker, oils, created on much bigger canvases. One picture dominated. It was the height of a door and was propped up against the wall to the left of the fireplace. It was bleak and stormy, and as Millie leaned forward, she was sure she recognised the Lookout.

She thought it very good.

'So are you a painter, a poet, or a fisherman?' she asked, leaning around the kitchen door.

'All of the above,' he said, not lifting his eyes from his soup stirring.

They sat at the cluttered table in the main room and ate from black pottery bowls, which reminded Millie of the Nicole Farhi cafe in Notting Hill. She didn't say this as she wasn't sure Finn would know who Nicole Farhi was, or worse, where Notting Hill was.

Finn had cut some wheaten bread, which he brought to the table on a wooden board. The tap water he served from a large, glazed jug was fresh and cold. A world away from anything you would get in a city.

'The devil's food,' said Millie, lifting a piece of bread.

Finn appeared puzzled.

'Slainte,' he said, clinking his tumbler to hers gently.

He talked easily, saying he was a painter most days and sold pictures to tourists at the hotels and shops around the coast. He then hesitated but, helped along by a smile, continued, 'The other stuff, the oils, that's what I really do.'

When they were finished eating, a silence lingered, and Millie played with her spoon.

'So what brings you to Ballydunn?' Finn asked. 'You seem to know the place well.'

Millie was taken aback by his directness. 'Oh, I'm just passing through… you know.'

'Passing through, eh? Going where?'

He was teasing her again.

'Well now – if I told you that, I'd have to kill you, wouldn't I?'

Finn studied her, twiddling his bread knife like a drumstick. Unsure about what was happening.

Millie was playing the game now. 'I've just decided to take some time out, as they say. Line up my ducks.'

It was Finn who eventually made a move. He scraped his chair back from the table and for a moment she froze, thinking he was coming to her. Instead, he leaned over and casually lifted her plate.

Millie poured herself another glass of water.

He came back from the kitchen with an apple as rosy as her hot cheeks. Using a short, stumpy knife with a handle fashioned from blackthorn, he sliced the fruit. Then, stabbing a chunk sharply, he brought it to her lips. She didn't know what to do. So she did what she wanted and leaned in slowly, taking the apple off the knife and into her mouth.

They ate the apple between them, in silence. Millie felt neither embarrassed nor foolish and, as she finished, she purposefully ran her fingers over the corners of her lips. Finn's eyes were on her and she was sure she knew what he was thinking.

The sound of a motorboat passing below the bedroom window broke the moment.

In a flash, Millie had pushed her chair back, pulled her ponytail tight and said she had to go.

'Where are you staying? The hotel?' Finn sounded flustered.

Millie pretended not to hear, instead lifting plates out to the kitchen. Finn followed close behind and as they stood side by side, she was again aware of his bed just feet away. From nowhere, an image of him taking her by the hand, leading her to the bedroom filled her mind. She shook her head, trying to lose the thought.

'Millie.'

She turned, ready to challenge his advances. But instead, he handed her a tea towel.

Forcing her mind to concentrate on drying dishes, her body relaxed. As she hung the tea towel over the draining board, she decided to answer his question. 'I'm staying at the cottage down the beach. Ardmara.'

'The one with the steps?'

'Yup.'

Before he could ask another question, Millie spoke. 'Do you know a man with a black dog? Cathal… Cathal Quinn.'

Finn nodded.

She didn't know why, but she started to tell Finn about what she had seen at the harbour and how he had been with her at the hotel and the Spar. All the time being careful not to sound too dramatic or gossipy.

Finn listened intently, leaning up against the sink, arms crossed. Not interrupting her once.

After she'd finished, she felt a little self-conscious and found herself shuffling from one foot to the other. He could easily judge her, she decided. Tell her she'd got it all wrong.

When Finn was sure she had finished, he spoke with a directness she was getting used to.

'Cathal Quinn and his partners own nearly everything in the village now. The pub, the shop, the new hotel.' Finn paused, uncertain about whether to go on. 'And everyone who works for them. The fishing boats are new, mind.'

As he walked back into the main room, he turned.

'They own this cottage. I just rent from them.'

'And you? Do they own you?' The words came out before she could stop them.

He leaned against the door frame with his arms folded again, 'What do you think?'

His face was so open, with no sign of anger or agitation, and she felt a shot of adrenalin hit her system. 'I need to go,' she said quickly.

'You'll get soaked.'

Grabbing her parka, she could see spits of rain already starting to fall, but she had to get out.

Finn followed her to the door and was now so close she was sure he could hear her heart thumping.

'Thank you. For the soup.'

'My pleasure,' he said, lifting her faux-lined hood gently over her head. 'You'll be needing this,' he added, letting his hands linger.

Millie didn't find his eyes. She didn't dare.

Walking back over the dunes, Millie didn't know what to think. When she thought about what he had done with the apple her stomach tightened, but her excitement quickly turned to agitation.

Who did he think he was?

The hard rain came before she reached Ardmara. It came fast and from everywhere, and as she held the hood of her parka in place, she could feel the trickle of cold water run down her sleeves. It continued throughout the night, pounding the roof of the cottage. The windows rattled like shackles in the wind and as she lay awake, Millie became consumed with thoughts of earlier. One minute irritated someone could be so playful with her; the next, excited at just how playful he was. When she thought about his eyes, the colour of cornflowers, that somehow turned black in the shadow, she pushed her head deep into her pillow.

With the morning came sunshine and resolution. As she mopped up pools of rain that had oozed through the roof during the night, she knew what she must do. She hadn't come to Ballydunn to mess around with a man – she'd had enough of that. She needed to clear her mind, not cloud it. She made a pact with herself to avoid the man at all costs.

She'd be polite and courteous to Finn McFall, but that was it.

No more apple eating.

Chapter 9

Millie spent the next few days avoiding Finn McFall.

She went to the hotel each morning for coffee in the Residents' Lounge and then back again for tea in the afternoon. She thought about staying overnight. The idea of a long bath in a room that didn't smell of damp was tempting, but then she imagined Cathal appearing out of the shadows like a ghost and she quickly changed her mind.

On the third morning of her five-day special, Millie spotted Cathal peering through the back door of the busy reception. When he glanced in her direction, she immediately lifted her jaw. Breathing in, she walked towards the desk, all the time smiling a closed-lipped, tight smile, and before she knew it, she was waving her room key at him. Shocked and delighted at her own defiance, her smile grew into a grin as she strutted past like a pimped-up poodle.

During her early morning visits to the lounge there was a spark in the air as golfers and tourists studied maps and weather forecasts. Then at nine o'clock there was a rush for the door as everyone headed off for the day. Left in a sudden silence, Millie was nervous, half of her always expecting Cathal to come in and confront her, the other half hoping he would.

Standing by the window, she watched the sea swell then splutter disappointingly onto the rocks of the Lookout. As her eyes moved along the strand, she decided she was spending as much time searching for Finn McFall as she was avoiding him.

She took out her phone. A missed call from her mother. She'd have to call back.

Leaning against the window frame, she re-read a text she'd sent Dom earlier.

'*Will call.*'

'*Staying on.*'

She had then added: '*But nothing has changed.*'

Watching the seagulls swoop and dip low over the water, it struck her how easily she appeared to be moving away from Dom and her old life, already thinking about someone else's smile, someone else's eyes. A tinge of guilt spiked her thoughts, but her mind quickly went to the moment in Finn's kitchen when she imagined him taking her hand, leading her into his bedroom, and a rush of desire shot through her. It was then she saw a figure, a man for certain, heading for the Lookout. Focusing her eyes, she saw a leather satchel bouncing against his thigh. It was Finn. Holding her breath, she quickly stepped back from the window, feeling like a guilty schoolgirl.

Moving to a sofa by the fire Millie felt childish, overwhelmed by thoughts of a man she didn't even know. A pinch of panic nipped her. What was she doing? She made herself think. If she didn't get back to London soon, she'd have no job to go back to. She needed to talk to Tom. She knew that. But say what? She had one sighting of a fisherman being harassed; it wasn't much of a story and hardly likely to have Tom asking her to stay on in Ballydunn.

Massaging her temples, she pictured her little basement flat in Battersea next to the railway. She had bought it from the council years before, using a small deposit her mother had given her. Flats were affordable back then and no one wanted it anyway, as it smelt of damp and the old lady who died there. She rented out the box room to a photojournalist, who mostly used it to store his equipment and bicycle. She took on extra freelancing to fund renovations. For as long as she could remember, all her Christmas and birthday money from her mother, and later Jamie, went towards the flat.

As she opened her eyes wide and stared into the fire, which was spitting and hissing with the first turf of the day, her mood dipped. She couldn't afford to lose her job. She had some savings but no more than a few months' mortgage.

She would have to decide what she was doing with the rest of her life. Just not today.

Letterkenny town was back towards the north and although it sat on the border, it was still very much rooted in the south. The one-way system her mother said never worked from the day it was built was at a standstill, snarled up with tractors, buses, and badly parked cars.

Irish music was blaring from speakers outside a small arcade and shopkeepers were standing around on the pavement talking and laughing with each other.

Waiting for a double-parked car to move on she noticed a group of women leaving a nearby cafe. They were dressed up, as if they were off somewhere special. All were wearing heels and their make-up was heavy. Immediately, Karen's voice came into her head, scolding down the phone about a workmate's wedding she had attended in the town a few years before: '*You could tell you were near the south by just looking at the women. Hard-looking tickets they were. Make-up plastered on with a trowel. It's the same with all the border towns and West Belfast – but sure they think they're in the south there anyway.*'

Millie thought about her sister. She still had not replied to her own grovelling text. Leaning her head on the car window she thought how Karen had changed from the girl running through the sand dunes mimicking Mrs Murphy from the Fiddler's Inn.

But then she thought about dad and the divorce and the men from the factories who scared her sister half to death. Maybe if she had walked in Karen's shoes, like her sister had said at dinner, she'd feel the same way too.

Losing patience with the jam, Millie blared her horn until a man finally came out of the cafe, mug in hand, and moved his car on.

She parked in the Dunnes Stores car park. Fifteen minutes later she had bought trainers, tracksuit bottoms, a shower curtain, Paul Costelloe scented candles and a linen dress that felt more expensive than it was. She stopped for a cappuccino in the cafe she had seen the women leave earlier. Sitting by the window, a pink sandwich board advertising *Maura's Beauty Salon* caught her eye. They were offering eyelash extensions for thirty Euro. She was sure she could get her new lashes removed there.

The bubble-gum pink exterior of the salon made Millie feel happy. When Maura herself appeared, with her name sewn into the breast pocket of her pastel housecoat, she was reminded of Frenchy in *Grease*. After some animated discussion, Millie found herself agreeing to have her current extensions removed but replaced with new lashes that were, according to Maura, much more natural-looking.

Minutes later, she was up the stairs in a room with a girl called Olga. Millie could smell Pot Noodle and from the corner of her eye she could see a microwave sitting beside a well-used waxing kit.

Olga had on the same pink housecoat as Maura, but hers was tighter and a lot shorter. Her hair was poker-straight, and she wore hoop earrings the size of bangles. A poster of Kim Kardashian was stuck to the back of the cubicle door.

As she lay on the bed Millie was surprised not to be shown a selection of lashes, but Olga seemed to know what she was doing. When a mirror was produced an hour later Millie froze. The lashes were thick, much more so than the ones removed. She felt like a pantomime horse and immediately started touching them, trying in vain to smooth them down.

Olga was having none of it. 'Now now, stop that. They're gorgeous…' she said, before hollering down the stairs, 'Maura…'

Millie was certain Maura's eyes widened when she came into the room. 'Fabulous,' she said, with a smile as fake as her nails. 'Very glamorous.'

The word glamorous panicked Millie even more and she was now using her own compact mirror to view from every angle possible. She didn't know what to do. Should she ask for them to be removed or just leave?

Oh God, what will Finn think?

'Olga is our best girl for lashes. People come from all over,' said Maura, lifting a Pot Noodle down from a cupboard.

'Give yourself a week or two and you'll be back for infills. Mark my words.'

Millie wanted to tell Maura what she could do with her infills, but she wanted to be away from the salon more.

Driving back to Ballydunn she couldn't stop reaching up to the rear-view mirror. She turned her head left, then right, up, and then down. At some angles she thought they were fine, obvious but fine, then at another angle she thought they were comical – like the ones worn by some of the reality stars she was forced to interview for the paper.

The sun had come out, and in an effort to take her mind off her eyes, she decided to take the Atlantic Drive back to the village. The road that wrapped around the mountain was slow to follow, but the views of the ocean far below were irresistible. She could see the waves were big, rolling to the shore, throwing spray high into the air as they broke. As she turned a corner and glanced down, she saw huge mounds of froth gathering into the corners of craggy rocks. She wondered if the waves would be as big in front of the cottage. She thought about the Lookout and in that moment yearned to be there.

As she turned another sharper corner, the last before the straight into the village, she felt the steering wheel pull violently to the right towards the cliff edge. Millie grabbed the wheel with both hands and braked, bringing the car to a sudden stop. There was nothing behind, but the road was narrow and if anyone came around at speed, there would undoubtedly be a collision.

Driving on for safety, her heart sank. The flapping thud of a shredded tyre was unmistakable. Fear set in. She didn't know how to change a tyre and she wasn't even sure if her mother's car carried a spare. She quickly put on her flashers and lifted the boot. She stood away from the car – something she'd learnt on a driving course she had attended after being caught speeding in Dom's Porsche.

As she was looking down the road towards the village, a red hat appeared in her line of sight. A man in yellow waterproofs was walking on the other side of the road, and as he got closer, Millie felt certain it was the fisherman from the harbour, the one Cathal had been shouting at. When he got parallel to the car, he stopped. Then crossed the road. Millie tried to appear grateful, and the man took off his hat and dropped his head.

'Thanks for stopping.'

No response.

'Can you change a tyre by any chance?' Millie tried to catch his eye.

When he lifted his face, he seemed anxious. She wasn't sure if he understood English. She pointed to the tyre and then back to him. She was nervous and images of him being pushed and pulled at the harbour were filling her mind.

The man signalled to the boot.

'Yes. Yes. You look,' said Millie keenly.

He walked to the back of the car and Millie followed. Seconds later he had lifted the floor of the boot up and there, to Millie's relief, was a tyre.

'Well done. Well done,' she said, maintaining a broad smile.

The man took the tyre and raised it in the air like a trophy. They both laughed, enjoying their shared sense of relief. After digging around in the boot, he took out a red warning sign and gave it to

Millie, who placed it some way back from the car, in the middle of the road.

As he changed the tyre Millie was close enough to see a dirty bandage wrapped over one hand. Lifting the jack, the bandage slipped to reveal crude and irregular stitches across his palm. Millie grimaced. A thick black thread had been used to close the skin. It was just like the fishing wire she had seen in the DIY section of the Spar when she was buying firelighters. She swallowed hard and pulled her parka around her tightly. She wanted to talk to the man, ask him what had happened, but she was sure he wouldn't understand. If she pointed to his hand he might get upset, and as she watched him work, crouching on his knees in his oversized waterproofs, Millie felt profoundly sorry for him. When he was finished, he turned to her.

'Thank. You. For. Helping. Me,' Millie said, trying not to pronounce her words too loudly or slowly.

'No bother,' he said, putting on a thick Irish accent.

Again, they laughed and together they placed the flat tyre back in the boot.

'What. Is. Your. Name?' Millie asked, feeling the air between them soften.

He stopped what he was doing, and after pulling the bandage down over the stitches, he spoke. 'I. Am. Ashmal,' he said, filling his face with another smile. As she studied his features, she saw the mottling of old bruises around his eyes and mouth.

'I. Am. Millie,' she said, mirroring his words.

They stood in a new awkward silence with Ashmal staring down at the ground again. Unsure what to do, she went to the car and grabbed her purse. But this only seemed to alarm him, and he started waving his arms around. 'No, no. Boss man. No.'

Pulling on his red Arsenal hat, he started to walk away from the car. Millie followed, and as she touched his arm, he jumped. Leaning back from him, raising her hands in submission, she saw fear in his eyes. Using one hand, she pointed to herself and then to the car. In desperation she then used both hands to make driving motions.

'I. Take. You…' she said, now speaking very slowly and loudly. 'Home. I. Take. You. Home.'

His eyes darted up and down the road, and only then did he nod briefly.

Millie smiled and sighed at the same time. As she threw her shopping into the back seat, she saw Ashmal spy a box of groceries. Before driving off, she opened a bag of bananas and offered him one. He shook his head hard, but when she took one herself and then offered again, he accepted, devouring it in three bites. She motioned for him to take another and again he hesitated, but Millie prompted, and he relented, this time savouring every mouthful.

As she turned the car in the road, she realised not one other car had passed them by in all the time they were there.

'Are. You. A. Fisherman?'

Still eating his banana, he turned to face her. Millie couldn't work out if he was deciding to trust her or, more likely, didn't understand what she had said. With this in mind she found herself driving with one hand, throwing her other arm away from her like a fishing rod.

'Yes. Me. Fishing.'

'What brings you to Ballydunn?'

Ashmal shook his head hard. Millie knew he didn't understand her question.

She sighed and tried again. 'Born. Where. Were. You. Born?'

'Birth!' Ashmal smiled and this time his whole face glowed. In a slow, low voice, as if he was a student in a language class, he pronounced his words clearly.

'I. Was. Birth. In. Aleppo. I. Am. Aleppo.'

'Aleppo. Syria? You're from Syria?' she said, glancing over to him again. He nodded, smiling as if they were talking about the most beautiful place on earth. Just as Millie was about to ask another question he raised his bandaged hand, pointing to a small track on the right of the road. Millie slowed down and indicated.

'No. No...'

He was flustered.

'You... No...' He was almost pleading.

Millie brought the car to the side of the lane, and after saying thank you many times, Ashmal got out, all the time watching the road. As he hurried up the track, she saw smoke bellowing from a distant chimney, assuming it belonged to a cottage or house which was out of sight. She wanted to follow him, find out what was up there – but she knew she couldn't. He had made that very clear.

Driving back down to the village, Millie didn't know what to think. Instead of turning down Sea Lane, she drove on, slowly pulling up by the old fisherman's cottage. The chimney was smoking and a window was ajar. Millie inhaled deeply. Finn was home.

Moving over the grass towards the cottage she stopped. *What if he isn't alone? What would I say?* Turning on her heels, she crouched down below window height and started to make her way back to the car, but just before she reached the road, feet appeared in front of her eyes. She threw her head up and there, right in front of her, was Finn.

He was carrying a pint of milk and a copy of the *Irish Times*. 'You alright there?' he asked, his now-familiar smile creeping over his lips.

Millie touched her new eyelashes.

'I thought you maybe didn't like my cooking.'

All Millie could think about was apples.

'I wasn't sure if you had company. I... I didn't want to disturb you.'

'Disturb me. Sounds serious, that,' he said, frowning. 'Come on in and take the weight off your feet.'

Once inside, Millie took a seat by the fire. With her coat still on she perched nervously on the edge of the chair. Finn made real coffee with a pot that bubbled on the stove and produced a plate of tray bakes that made Millie think of her sister. She sat hugging her parka, staring deep into the grate.

'Are you okay?' he asked, sitting opposite her.

'I had a flat tyre up on the Atlantic Drive earlier. The fisherman I told you about stopped to help.'

'Did something happen?' Finn leaned forward in his chair, trying to get her to face him.

'No. No.' Millie shook her head. 'Why does everybody always think the worst of them?'

'Them? Was there more than one boy up there?'

'NO…! No. Just one. Ashmal. His name's Ashmal.'

Millie finally met Finn's eyes. She tried to raise a smile, but the corners of her lips turned down, not up.

Finn lifted his coffee, the plate of tray bakes untouched on the floor between them.

'Tell me what happened.' His voice was, once again, calm and measured.

Millie went over everything. The flat tyre, the cut on Ashmal's hand, the stitching that she was sure was self-applied with something awful like cat gut or fishing line from the Spar.

She said she'd heard about this type of thing before and was worried Ashmal was being abused. Pausing for breath, taking her mug of coffee between her hands, she went on to say she was sure Cathal Quinn was the boss man Ashmal had talked about.

Like before, Finn let her speak. Never interrupting, just listening, observing.

Leaning back in his chair, stretching out his legs, he finally spoke. 'Look, I'm not saying it's a great situation. God knows, I know Cathal Quinn and he's got a temper on him. I've seen that for sure. But this? I'm not sure…' Finn sipped his coffee. 'Those boys have only just come to the village, Millie. There's about a dozen of them. All from the Middle East somewhere. Migrant workers.'

'Aleppo,' Millie cut in. 'He's from Aleppo. I'd call him a refugee myself. Not a migrant. And I'm telling you, he was frightened. Even just talking to me.'

'Jesus, Millie. Are you surprised he's frightened? He's probably traumatised.' Finn leaned forward again. 'Sometimes what you see isn't all the story.' As soon as he said this, he looked into the fire and seemed to drift away from her. The sound of a tractor outside made him start, and he was back as quickly as he had left. 'You need to watch yourself. This is a small place.'

'Watch myself?' Millie felt warned off. She turned to the fire again, trying to hold her temper. 'I think I might go to someone you know. The police.' She spoke with a finality to her words, not wanting a response.

'Jesus, Millie, hold your horses there. You're running away with yourself.'

She could feel a ball of anger gathering in her chest. 'Running away with myself?'

'I didn't mean it like that.'

'Listen, you weren't there.'

Finn exhaled. 'You're right. I wasn't. But I'm just saying that going to the Garda is coming on a bit strong.'

'Really? Is that because Cathal Quinn is your landlord? Maybe even your friend?' Millie knew she was sounding angry, too angry. She bit her lip to make herself stop talking, then stood up quickly, digging her fists into her pockets.

'Don't be like that now. Sit down. Please.' He smiled, his head slightly tilted, trying, Millie suspected, to ease the tension that had slipped between them. 'Don't get me wrong, I'm no friend of Cathal Quinn,' he said, standing up to face her. 'But you've no real proof, Millie. A cut hand. Grazes. He's a fisherman, for God's sake.'

Millie pushed her head back. 'I shouldn't have come here. It was a mistake. I'm sorry. I don't even know you. I just thought…'

'Thought what?'

Dropping her arms to her side, she exhaled. 'I suppose I thought I could talk to you.'

'You can.'

Millie knew she was about to cry. Her chest was rising and she could feel her eyes filling with tears. Trying not to blink, she glanced past Finn towards the kitchen, trying to find something to focus on.

'Are you sure you're telling me everything? You seem very upset.'

Millie couldn't bear him being nice to her. Not now, when she had been so short with him.

She did want to tell him everything. About the clinic, the drugs, coming home. She wanted to tell him about the pub and the poem and her father. Tell him she felt scared and sad most of the time and didn't know what to do. But she couldn't. She couldn't tell him any of this. He'd judge her before he even knew her. She felt desperate to be away from him now. Back at her own cottage, the door locked against the world.

Finn came towards her, and she immediately diverted her eyes. He was so close she could hear his breathing. She felt his hands lift her face gently up to his.

No longer smiling, he appeared serious. She'd seen it before, after their lunch together. Now, leaning in, he kissed her softly on the forehead, just the way her father used to do when her brothers had been rough with her. Or the way her mother had done at bedtime, before Dad, when she had time for such things. Millie immediately closed her eyes and two tears that had been clinging to her new lashes fell silently down her cheeks.

'I have to go.' Her voice barely audible.

'No, you don't,' said Finn, his forehead resting on hers.

Without replying she turned to leave, wiping her face with the back of her hand. Finn followed behind, and as they reached the door, he leaned over in front of her to open the latch. As he did so, he said he would ask a few questions about the fishermen. His tone was gentle, encouraging. Millie knew she didn't have to ask him to be careful. To be mindful of Ashmal.

She turned to say goodbye, not wanting Finn to think of her as sad, or worse, mad.

She knew what she had to do.

Looking up into his face and using all the strength she had left, she smiled. The smile she knew men liked. He tilted his head to the side again.

'Have you done something to your eyes?' he asked. 'They seem, I don't know, different somehow.'

Millie touched her new lashes. 'Well now, that's another story altogether.'

With that, he leaned in towards her. But this time the kiss was different from before.

Chapter 10

Millie woke and for the first time in months her mind didn't go to the clinic.

She grabbed her duvet and brought it to the chair by the living-room window. Cocooned in the remnants of sleep, she lay with her head back; her hair was messy and strands caught the ends of her new lashes. She felt different. As if the blood in her body had started to pump again. Aware of her skin, she stroked her arm under her sweatshirt.

Outside, the ocean was still. She knew if she opened the window she would only hear the lapping of the water as it broke on the shore. It was early and she wondered if Finn was awake, padding about his cottage, not half a mile away, making coffee, reading the paper, or maybe painting.

She hoped he was thinking about her.

To stave off the cold she pulled the duvet up to cover her mouth and tugged the edges of her sleeves over her fingers. The sky was full of cloud and there was a haze hanging over the grey water. Even without the sun, it was strangely beautiful.

Closing her eyes, Millie now allowed herself to relive what had happened.

She knew Finn hadn't planned the kiss by the door; her smile had made him do it. A silent primal act – it never let her down. Millie needed the kiss. She couldn't bear to walk away, leaving him to think she was angry, unhinged. Like her sister.

Wearing her duvet as a cape, she went to the kitchen and made a cafetiere of coffee. Too distracted to light a fire, she brought a blow heater she found in the bedroom cupboard and placed it close to her armchair.

She recognised the PSNI logo on the mug she drank from. The words '*Keeping People Safe*' were printed underneath. Kate maybe came to the cottage more than the others realised. Millie smiled, deciding the empty beaches of Donegal would be well suited to her little sister and long-term flatmate. Trying to decide if the rain was coming or going, Millie let Finn once more fill her mind.

She couldn't believe one kiss could be so remarkable.

When he took her face in his hands, there was a moment, she was sure of it, when he almost stopped. But her smile brought him back.

Millie lifted her legs up into the chair and, playing with the ends of her hair, decided he had really kissed her twice. The first one was eager and strong; the second, although his mouth never left her lips, was gentle, playful. As she hugged herself tight, she thought he might even have nudged her nose with his. With this thought she spluttered, pulling the duvet over her head.

Jesus. What was going on?

After the kiss – the one that was really two – she remembered feeling a rush, as if a drug had invaded her being. The charge of anger in her chest had evaporated, leaving only lightness.

Finn had pulled back from her, shocked by his action. He had laughed briefly in disbelief, amazed at his own recklessness. Pacing in front of her he clasped his hands above his head, making his T-shirt rise, and again Millie had been aware of his physical being. When she finally said she had to go, he had smiled, tilting his head ever so slightly.

A silent request for her to stay.

She didn't dare smile back.

The dry air from the heater was making her nostrils itch and her lips felt chapped, but she didn't want to move, worried the slightest shift might take her out of the moment. She allowed herself to go over it all again and was excited in a way she hadn't been since her school days, when she would sometimes duck inside a darkened doorway with a boy she had been to the cinema with.

Lifting her phone from the floor, Millie read Sasha's text from the night before. Her friend was going to be in Ballydunn for the weekend and had asked her over for tea that night. At six o'clock.

Who eats at that time anyway?

Then she remembered her mother saying most of the country did and to get off her high horse, as Millie herself had done it all her life, before moving away.

She laughed again. She'd lived in London too long.

As the haze drifted off the water, a fine drizzle of rain started to fall, creating tiny dimples on the flat sea. She wanted to be in the ocean, feeling the salty drops burst on her skin. She imagined being there with Finn, her legs wrapped around him, her head back. A sudden warmth crept up her body and she closed her eyes.

Her phone vibrated. It was Dom.

The interruption hit her like a slap. Jumping off the chair, standing in the middle of the living room, she felt foolish. It was only a kiss, for God's sake, not a marriage proposal. Pulling her hair away from her face she could feel her neck sticky with sweat. Embarrassed by her fantasies, she headed to the bathroom for a shower.

Millie stayed away from the beach that day.

She went to the hotel in the afternoon and did some research on migrant fishermen in Ireland. She was surprised how many there were: mostly from Somalia, and now Syria. Some had refugee status; most did not.

She thought about Ashmal and the other men, and then about what Finn had said. Maybe they weren't being held against their will, but maybe they had no option either.

What did he know anyway?

Throughout the day Millie managed to convince herself, once again, that any sort of cavorting with Finn McFall was out of the question. She didn't need the complication of a man in her life. Especially one that lived in a fisherman's cottage in the middle of nowhere. She needed to be on her own. All the self-help books said it.

She forced herself to put on some make-up for dinner, or was it tea, at Sasha's. Taking time to study her lashes from all angles, she was still undecided about them. After more deliberation she pulled on a low-cut white T-shirt she had bought in Paris and her leather jeans. Looking in the bathroom mirror, she again felt some of the old Millie had resurfaced.

As soon as she started walking over the dunes, she regretted her shoe choice. Heels and sand – particularly damp sand, do not mix. When she reached Main Street, her calves ached. She stopped to catch her breath and drifts of music from the Fiddler's Inn found her ears. She wanted to run to the window, peek inside, but she kept walking. She didn't need Finn McFall in her life. It was all wrong.

But even saying his name silently made her tingle.

Millie wanted to tell Sasha what had been going on. Her oldest friend had been kind to her since arriving home, but as well as being big-hearted and loyal, Sasha was a gossip. No. She couldn't trust her. Anyway, Finn was a Catholic, and Millie was sure Sasha, even now, would have something to say about that.

Her early morning euphoria had faded, and she decided to walk down to the pier. Fifteen minutes wouldn't matter. Sitting on a bench by the harbour, the day not quite gone, the night not yet arrived, Millie thought about the past she and Sasha shared.

Even after Dad, Millie knew not all Catholics were bad; just as she knew not all Protestants were good. Sasha was different. She grew up in a family of staunch Unionists, who thought Catholics were '*out to get them*' or, at least, wanted to '*get them out*'. Michael's murder had sealed their family's sectarian fervour.

Millie looked out at the horizon. Leaving home had softened her own edges, she knew that. She wasn't party to the everyday prejudices life at home so often held. Her friend had never left the town; it would be hard for her not to still be angry. No, she couldn't tell Sasha about Finn. She then thought about her sister and took out her phone. Still no reply to her text.

She now didn't want to go to Sea View for her tea. It would be loud and bright and full of happy children. She wanted to go home. Be alone with her thoughts.

Passing the gift shop by the cafe she spotted a watercolour in the window. She was certain it was Finn's. A village scene – the type of picture a wealthy golfer would buy to be reminded of their time in Ballydunn. Absorbing the image, Finn's smiling face came into her head. She knew he was Catholic from the moment she saw him. She didn't need to ask his surname or try to find out what school he'd gone to. His dark features and easy manner answered her question. As a young child, she remembered once asking her mother why people had to be one or the other – Catholic or Protestant. Could they not just be the same? Her mother had been shocked.

'*Don't be silly, child. Catholics and Protestants are far too different to be the same. They're like night and day.*'

Back then, she wasn't sure what her mother meant exactly, but as Millie grew older she began to notice the differences for herself. For one thing, Catholics laughed more. It was a fact. She saw this in the golf club when her parents took her and the others there for tea. They seemed to enjoy themselves more than Protestants and were always buying drinks for everyone. They had a God who forgave them anything, which Millie soon decided was very useful. They were also better-looking. No doubt about it. Most of the boys she fancied as a teenager were from St Malachys, not the Protestant Royal – a fact that caused much eye-rolling from some of the family, mostly Karen.

Sea View dazzled in front of her like a giant doll's house. As she approached the front door, having been buzzed in the electric gates anonymously, she saw the fountains were spouting out water in unison. Ringing the bell, she noticed the Union Jack door mat. No. She wouldn't tell her friend about Finn.

Anyway, there was nothing to tell.

When no one came to the door, high-pitched squeals brought Millie to the back of the house, where she was confronted by a steaming hot tub full of children. Stringy arms and legs were thrashing about in the bubbling water and Millie was reminded of her Ibizan holidays. Shivering in the cold night air, she waved over to the giggling mass, but no one said anything as she passed by.

There were so many cars parked up, Millie wondered if Sasha had invited other people. Then she saw the number plates: the Range Rover, Porsche and pick-up were all part of the *CH1K* family fleet. She glimpsed a jet ski and speed boat in the triple garage and a trace of a smile passed her lips. Stepping through big glass doors, she found Sasha, in gym gear, working out enthusiastically to a Davina McCall DVD – her tan, hair and neon nails all glowing under an army of spotlights nestled in the high ceiling.

'You're here,' she said, throwing her arms every which way.

Millie blinked, surprised to see the whole kitchen in total order, not a removal box in sight. There were even family pictures on the wall. All shot on the main beach of the village. There was one with Sasha and the children and then one just with David, then all alone draped over some rocks that might have been the Lookout. Millie suspected they were professionally taken and hung.

Curating a life not yet lived.

'You wasted no time.' The words stuck in her throat.

Sasha beamed. 'I know. Dave got men from work to help unpack this week. They worked like… hard. They worked really hard,' she corrected herself quickly.

Millie took off her coat and sat on a white leather bar stool by the island. Two crystal flutes with coloured stems sat on a tray.

'God, I didn't bring a bottle, Sasha. I wasn't sure if you'd be drinking at this time… I should have stopped at the Spar or somewhere…'

Sasha's face darkened. 'God, don't go into that hole. The new owner's a real Shinner apparently. I'll be buying all my groceries from Tesco at home and bringing them up.'

Millie flinched. The '*Shinner*' was Finn's landlord.

Sasha took a bottle of Prosecco down from a well-stocked wine rack. 'Watch this,' she said excitedly, placing the bottle into a suction pack. 'Sixty seconds and we're in business.'

Sure enough, one minute later, a buzzer went off and the bottle came out ice cold. Sasha dried it off with a Union Jack tea towel.

'Slainte, as they say in these parts,' she said, clinking her glass.

Millie was now glad she had come. Sasha, for whatever reason, always lifted her spirits.

Standing by the island, her friend wagged a mahogany finger towards her. 'Great eyes.'

'Oh, thanks, I'm still not sure they're me—'

'Are you mad? They're fab. Very Kim K.'

Just then, a booming voice came from behind. 'Well, look what the cat dragged in.'

David, Sasha's husband, was standing in the doorway. She saw his cheeky smile hadn't changed, but he was different. There was less hair and more gut.

'David!'

'Well, well… Home from the big smoke,' he said, leaning in to kiss her on the cheek, letting his hand linger low on her back. 'Sasha says your mother's not well. Sorry to hear that. She's a good woman.'

Millie watched as he lumbered over to a white leather sofa, a large glass of red wine in his hand. 'I see her sometimes at the council meetings. Does she say? She's got balls. I like that.'

'Language!' snapped Sasha.

Millie was reminded of what her mother had said about David at the council meetings over the years and flushed. 'She likes you too, David, it's just all your workers, you know – Foreign Nationals as she likes to call them.' She forced out a laugh. 'She thinks there's too many in the town.'

Silence.

She fumbled on. 'Sure she's old and doesn't like change.' Instantly, Millie was annoyed for betraying her mother.

'I'm just getting a top,' shouted Sasha.

'So, home from the big smoke, eh?' he said again, looking at her in a way Millie was certain Sasha wouldn't like. 'Believe you're a big journalist now. Writing about all those celebrities my wife is obsessed about.'

Millie smiled but said nothing.

'Suppose you think we're all big culchies now. Anyway, how's the love life?'

'David!' Sasha bounced back into the kitchen wearing a pink velour tracksuit top with diamante hearts all over it. 'Sorry, Millie. He's as nosy as sin, that one. And you know full well, Millie's got a man. Isn't that right? Works for a big bank... Isn't that right?'

Millie briefly thought about spewing out that it was all over between her and Dom and that she'd met a lovely fisherman. A Catholic from God knows where.

'Very rich... that's what my wife really means,' said David. 'Is he with one of those banks that caused all the trouble?'

Millie stopped smiling.

'Give over, will you?' said Sasha, taking a swig out of her newly filled glass. 'He was out to lunch. Celebrating a deal round here. He's half cut.'

Millie decided it was time to speak. 'Do you know London, David?'

'Can't say I do, Millie.'

'Shame.'

'Sure it's very grand. But wild horses wouldn't drag me to a city. I'm the country type and, sure, I've not done too bad for myself – even if I am a hick from the sticks,' he said, waving his wine glass around precariously.

Millie seemed to remember David's butcher father making a lot of money from illegal smuggling of livestock over the border at night. He was caught a few times, maybe even went to prison for a short time. Just as she was about to ask him how his father was, she heard the familiar voice of Betty McKillen, Sasha's mother.

'Millie Malone. Is that you?'

Glad for the interruption, she went to Mrs McKillen, hugging her tightly. As she pulled back Millie saw a shrunken version of the woman she remembered. Her hair, which had been as shiny and black as a stallion's, was speckled grey and she stooped.

She was old now, just like her own mother.

'How's your mum?' Mrs McKillen asked. 'I haven't seen her in a lifetime.' Her voice was hoarse with age.

'Oh, you know Mum, she's a fighter.'

'You're right there. They broke the mould when they made Maggie,' she said, as she tried to lower herself down beside David on the sofa. 'Why don't you have a normal couch like other people?' Mrs McKillen scolded. Sasha pretended not to hear. Giving up, she slowly moved to the island and heaved herself up onto a bar stool, next to Millie. 'Well now, it's just lovely to see you,' she said, as she reached over and cupped Millie's hands softly.

Millie knew what was coming but felt powerless to stop it.

'So your mum's on the mend. That's good to hear. It hasn't been easy for her over the years. Lord knows, it hasn't been for any of us.' Looking down at their hands, she went on. 'You know, I still remember the day your father was killed. There was a wind that would have cut corn. It was as if the very gods themselves were angry.'

Mrs McKillen turned her head, smiling limply at some of the children who were now playing with huge water guns outside the window.

Millie couldn't bear the silence. 'Auntie Lizzie said she heard the banshees.'

Jesus. What am I saying?

Mrs McKillen didn't respond. She appeared to be in a world of her own, a world of ghosts and memories.

'Then it was George Sharpe a week after your dad. A week to the day. Then Kenny Shaw at Christmas, then… and then…' She stumbled.

'Give over, Mummy.'

'They wiped out half of G Battalion in a few months. Did you know Rhonda Sharpe said George was hanging out his car window like a burning candle after the bomb exploded? Right there in front of her own eyes. Imagine that?'

'Well, that's just lovely, Mummy.' Sasha's voice was shrill. 'Why are you bringing all that up now? Millie came out for her tea, not to hear all this… crap.'

Millie felt her hands hot under Mrs McKillen's.

'No one cares, Mummy. Our Michael died for nothing. Sure, we're the baddies now. Isn't that right, Millie?'

'No one cares? Well, let me tell you, my girl, if it wasn't for the likes of our Michael and Walter Malone and all the others in the UDR, there would have been a lot more killing in the town.'

Mrs McKillen tried to catch Sasha's eye, but her daughter was having none of it. She was too busy wiping down the already spotless worktops.

Millie was reminded of her sister.

Mrs McKillen was now shaking her head and Millie felt sorry for her.

'I see there's been a few more shootings,' she said, trying to show solidarity.

'That'll be drugs or women,' David shouted from the sofa, not taking his eyes off the football.

'The paper said something about the New IRA.'

'There's talk. But I can't see it myself. Sure all the old brigade are dead and buried – in hell hopefully, or up here in cosy wee holiday houses. Paid for by yours truly.' Then, as if he had something important to say, he muted the TV and looked over. 'If this place is to work, we'll have to bed down with the Shinners and probably Dublin. Whether we fuckin' like it or not.'

'Language!'

'Well, all I can say is thank the Lord I'll not be here to see it. Sharing power with murderers. It's not right.' Mrs McKillen's head was so low, it was nearly touching the island.

'Oh God, let's all slit our wrists now,' said Sasha, marching to the glass door and hitting it hard with her ring finger. 'Ben… Jamie… Tea… Tell the others.'

To Millie's relief, Mrs McKillen finally removed her hands from hers.

After much more shouting, all the children were inside, queueing for lasagna and garlic bread, made by Mrs McKillen. Under instruction from their mother, the siblings said hello to Millie before running off into another room to watch a different TV.

Millie, Sasha, and her mother ate at the island. David stayed in front of the football, shouting and swearing at the screen every time a goal was scored or missed.

With effort, Millie answered lots of questions about London, sometimes even making up stories about celebrities she had interviewed to keep the mood breezy. When asked about Dom, she again pretended they were together, and she could see her friend's face light up.

'Would you like a cappuccino, Millie?' asked Sasha, waving a finger at a coffee machine of industrial proportions built into the sleek kitchen. 'Santa brought it. Isn't it fab?'

After a latte topped with mini marshmallows, Millie said she had to be going.

'But what do you do all day?' asked Sasha. 'You don't even have Sky!'

Millie heard herself say she was working on a story and her friend made a face, as if she had said something unpleasant.

Mrs McKillen disappeared into the utility room and came out with a pavlova. It was topped with fresh cream and fruit, and Millie immediately thought about the nuns across the road from the house in Dungrillen and made a point of thanking her profusely.

Sasha hugged her tight and whispered that they'd have to get out for a drink over the weekend.

Without being asked, David got up and walked Millie out of the house.

Leaning against the electric gates, his wine glass re-filled, Millie knew he wanted to talk.

'You know I'm the devil himself around home.'

'I'm sure that's not true,' said Millie flatly.

'But I'm keeping the bloody town afloat. No locals want the work. They're lazy bastards.'

Millie knew David wanted her to agree.

She didn't speak.

'At least the houses I keep are decent. Not stuffed to the rafters like some.' Then, as if thinking out loud, he went on. 'The men keep themselves to themselves, send money home to their families. What's wrong with that, for Christ's sake?'

Even in the dark, Millie could sense David's anger. She wanted to leave, but he had his arm over the gate's exit button. Leaning close to her, he went on. 'Your mother needs to look closer to home. See those car washes, that's real slave labour, and the houses they stay in. Well…'

Millie tried to think of words to silence him.

'Anyway, enough of that. It was good to see you, girl,' he said. Then, letting the wine talk, he went on. 'That banker's a lucky man.'

His mouth was so close to hers she could smell the sweetness of red wine. 'You know, Millie, everybody wanted you, because no one could have you. You were different from them all. Did you know that?'

'Catch yourself on,' said Millie, trying to shift the melancholy that had settled on them. 'You've done well for yourself: Sasha… the kids… the hot tub.'

Suddenly both of them were laughing.

'Don't be a stranger now… Keep her lit…' said David in a pronounced Belfast accent, finally letting her through the gates.

On her way home, passing the pub, the music had stopped; the serious drinking would be starting. A blustery wind had picked up and was pushing her along Main Street. As she cut through the dunes, she thought she could see a light flickering at the very far end of the beach. Certain it was from the fisherman's cottage, her breath quickened.

Chapter 11

In the dunes, it was only the wash of moonlight on the water that kept her from being in utter darkness.

She felt unnerved, and couldn't stop her mind churning through images and words from earlier. Mrs McKillen's memories were so painful to listen to and David's insinuations about Jamie had caught her by surprise.

Millie thought about her brother. The son who bought his mother a new kitchen; the husband who did everything his wife told him. Could he be involved in something so awful? Millie shivered. He didn't say anything about learning Irish. He was very quiet about the houses. Jamie did have secrets.

Her eyes, now accustomed to the dark, moved past the Lookout towards the light she saw earlier, the one she thought was coming from Finn's cottage. But it was no longer there. Maybe she'd been mistaken: maybe it had come from a fishing boat making its way slowly round the headland.

She wondered if he was home.

He hadn't said anything when she left the night before. He hadn't even asked for her number. When she thought about it, she couldn't remember ever seeing Finn with a phone. Maybe he didn't have one. God. That would be odd.

But it all didn't matter, because even if he did come to her door and ask her to walk with him on the beach or sit on the Lookout watching the day turn into night, she wouldn't go. She'd say she was busy.

A sudden gust knocked into her and the pavlova she had been carrying so carefully toppled to the ground. Swearing, Millie tried to gather it up, but she could feel the base had broken and felt sand everywhere. Straining her eyes in the darkness, she could just see the outline of a beach bin and threw the cream-splattered bag inside, letting the lid bang shut in the wind.

Turning towards the cottage, holding her hood down to shield her ears from the wind, she could still hear the waves beginning to thunder on the beach below. So different from the still harbour earlier.

As a child, a big sea at night had terrified her. Her father would tease Kate and herself – who almost always had to go to bed before everyone else, to keep their swimmers close just in case the sea crept up during the night and stole them away.

Stopping to look back over the dark ocean, Millie remembered the fear she felt then. It had no end. It would smother her, making her so scared, she would have to get out of bed and run to find her father.

Millie smiled, remembering how he would scoop her up in his arms like a baby and kiss the top of her head, promising to never let the sea take her or her sister away. She lifted her face into the cold air and closed her eyes. As the wind blustered around her, she allowed herself to imagine the touch of her father's hand on her hair once more.

Back in the cottage, she welcomed its loneliness. She tried to stoke the fire back to life, turning the coals for heat, but she couldn't stop Mrs McKillen's voice seeping into her mind. She glanced at her watch. She could go to the bar in the hotel, drink away the talk of car bombs and car washes, but then she thought Cathal Quinn might be there. Maybe she could watch a DVD from the pile she'd found in the old sideboard or even run a bath; but the heat of a long soak would only agitate her already fizzing mind.

No, she wouldn't do any of that.

She needed space, to be free from her thoughts.

When she felt like this in London, she would pull on a coat and walk through the streets of Battersea to the embankment. There, she would stand under the lights of Albert Bridge, watching river life pass under her, until she felt still again. But tonight the wind had been joined by heavy rain and she couldn't face fighting such weather in the dark.

She'd go for a drive instead.

It was nearing ten by the time she left the cottage. The roads around the village were poorly lit, and as the car climbed up the mountain, Millie ascended into a pitch black. She clutched the steering wheel hard, but every so often, a gust would pull the car to the right and she could feel her knuckles repeatedly whiten in response. The forecast had predicted unsettled weather, but not this. The rain was heavy, arriving on the windscreen so fast the wipers couldn't keep up and the wind was billowing under the car, making deep horn-like noises.

Slowing down, trying to find the entrance to Ashmal's lane, Millie was about to give up when she passed a track that was more worn than others. The thickets on either side were bent where cars, or maybe something bigger, had pushed by. Even with the wind and the rain battering the car she knew she had found it. Without thinking, she indicated. Only then did she bring the car to a slow stop and turn off the lights.

The old trees around her were stooping down to meet in the middle – some branches were even being dragged across the roof of the car in the wind. It was beyond dark.

As she started to inch up the track, she could feel her legs twitching. The heat in the car was making her sweat, but she didn't turn it off, fearful the windows would steam over completely.

Then, from nowhere, something large moved quickly in front of her, into the bushes.

Millie inhaled sharply and slammed on the brakes.

Without thinking, she leaned over and locked the passenger door and then her own. She screeched the car into reverse and looked over her shoulder, trying to see the road behind her.

A sudden tap on the passenger side window made her swing round, and there staring in through the window was Ashmal, lit by a small torch held to his face. The badge on his red Arsenal hat was glowing in the light.

Millie froze.

Even though she knew it was Ashmal, she was afraid. Not of him but who might be with him. In the light of his torch she could see rain dripping off his nose and chin – but there was something else. Something red, smearing. Blood.

Her instinct was to push on the accelerator and just drive backwards, praying she wouldn't end up in a sheugh. But then she saw Ashmal try to smile.

Millie's eyes darted around and when she was sure he was alone, she leaned over and opened the window to the wind and the rain.

There was blood smeared all over his face. One eye was swollen, nearly shut, and there were dark red crustings around his nostrils. When he tried to smile, more blood smudged on his teeth and his bottom lip was thick with a deep opening that was still oozing.

'Jesus, Ashmal, what happened?'

He didn't reply, dropping the torch down from his face and hanging his head.

'Get in the car,' she said, struggling to push the passenger door against the wind and the weight of his body.

'No. No.' He was now shining his torch through the open window onto her face. Millie turned her face away, then without thinking, was out of the car, fighting against the wind to get round to him. As soon as she touched his arm, he winced.

'Oh God, Ashmal. Who did this to you?'

He didn't answer.

'You need help.'

Still not speaking, Ashmal dropped his arms so they were hanging limply by his body, his torch dancing light on the ground.

'Get in the car. Ashmal. Please.'

He lifted his head, putting the torch to his face.

'Excuse.' He was quiet, defeated.

Standing there, rain now running down both their faces, she was sure there were tears in his eyes.

Millie helped him into the passenger seat. She had to use both her hands to bring the door shut against the wind. At one point she caught her nail, but she felt no pain; the adrenaline made sure of it. The gusts were so strong, she had to hold on to the car as she walked her way back to the driver's seat. When she got in, she leaned over and closed his window.

Now only silence filled the car.

Ashmal sat with his head down, clutching his torch.

'You need help. A doctor… you need a doctor. The police… we need to get the police.'

Shining his torch towards her: 'Po… lice. No. No.' His voice was loud. Urgent. 'Doctor? No doctor… Po… lice? No po… lice.'

Squinting again in the light, Millie saw Ashmal try to find the door handle, but he cried out when lifting his left arm.

'Okay… Okay, Ashmal. House. We go to your house,' she said, pointing frantically up the lane.

Breathing heavily, he eventually spoke. 'Okay, house,' he said. 'Okay.'

Millie gripped the steering wheel hard and again started to move up the track. All the time trying not to think what Karen had said about foreign workers and how they lived.

The stone building was in total darkness.

'Thank. You,' said Ashmal, pronouncing his words slowly and quietly, as he had the day before. He went on. 'Thank. You. Millie,' using the light of his torch to illuminate a sad smile.

Seeing his bloodied teeth and lip in the dim light, a rush of tenderness hit Millie. 'I can help you, Ashmal,' she said, touching his good arm gently.

'Go. You. Go,' said Ashmal, throwing light towards her.

Millie ignored him and got out of the car. The rain was starting to ease and the property appeared to be protecting them from the worst of the wind.

Ashmal finally handed her a single key attached to a large, knotted piece of fishing tackle. She was surprised how easily the door opened; the lock was loose, almost broken.

As she shunted the door, the stench that met her nostrils made her wretch. Twisting her head to the side, she was grateful for the darkness.

Trying to work out what the smell was, she recognised gas. Then fish. Fresh fish. And then old sweat. Keeping the door open and holding her breath, she instinctively felt around for a light switch on the wall. She found one but it didn't work.

Ashmal came from behind and bent down with his torch, his wellington boots squelching against a hard floor. Immediately there was light. Harsh, intense light that made Millie's eyes hurt.

There were five or more lines of cord tied to an old central light fitting. Each cord had at least one halogen lantern hooked to it and an array of plug extension leads dangled from the cords.

The leads fed into one over-loaded double socket hanging from the skirting board. Alongside the lanterns, there were three, maybe four, makeshift washing lines made of rope, all looped between hooks in the ceiling. Millie could see yellow and black waterproofs, tracksuits, towels, socks, and underwear almost double-layered on the drooping lines. Underneath were two old-fashioned gas heaters.

Ashmal touched Millie's shoulder and she jumped.

'Excuse. Excuse,' and he covered his eyes with his good hand to show embarrassment.

'It's okay, Ashmal. It's okay.'

The floor was stone and covered in an array of tatty, stained mats. The walls were whitewashed but yellowed with age. Amongst all of this busyness were six metal fold-up beds, the type you would get in a camping shop. Millie was immediately struck by how neatly they were positioned. Lined up, just like her dorm in boarding school where she went before Dad.

Two rows of three beds. Each one a small, tidy island of life. A zipped navy sleeping bag lay on top of a bare mattress and a pillow, plumped and straight, lay on top. At the bottom of each bed, identical plastic flip-flops sat on the floor beside a pile of neatly folded clothes: fleeces, vests, T-shirts. On top was a clear plastic bag. The type you would get at the airport. Inside, Millie could see a comb and a toothbrush and toothpaste. Again, all identical.

There were large plastic boxes under all the beds, each one stuffed to the brim. She thought she could see a photo frame pushed up against the side of one but couldn't make out who was in the picture.

Ashmal slowly made his way to the large open fireplace, where another mobile gas fire was placed. Using his good hand he pumped the handle, and the clicking noise reminded Millie of a heater they had in Dungrillen when she was little. Even then, in their big kitchen with its high ceilings, the smell was pungent. Here in this small space, it was choking.

On the right-hand wall there was an old kitchen unit with a sink and draining board. Tea towels were laid out and mugs were washed and turned over to dry. Plates and cutlery were on a table left of the unit, as was a two-ring hob. A small gas cylinder stood on the ground beside a neatly folded plastic shower hose.

Pots and pans were stacked up on the gas rings and there were two shelves above it, rammed with cans and bottles, and packets of spices. Razors and shaving foam were in an old Bewley's tin sitting on top of a small fridge that was wedged between the table and the wall.

A card with a flag and writing she didn't recognise, possibly Arabic, was stuck to the fridge door.

Ashmal shuffled through to the back room and Millie followed, more intrigued than afraid now. Again, he turned on a switch near the floor and the room lit up as before. Six more beds lined the walls. The only difference between the two rooms was the smell. It was thicker here. Millie felt nauseous. She needed air. She didn't want to offend Ashmal, but she didn't want to vomit either. She went to a window which had been painted over, but no matter how hard she pushed she couldn't open it.

Tasting some lasagna in her mouth, Millie watched as Ashmal moved to the far-left corner of the room. He sat down on a bed and exhaled slowly, lowering his head to the pillow, his feet still on the ground. Millie could see his waterproofs were dripping water onto the sleeping bag, but he appeared to neither notice nor care.

She searched for a door or a curtain, something that would lead to a bathroom. But there wasn't one.

'Ashmal. Bathroom?'

He didn't understand.

'Toilet? Shower?' she asked, lifting her arms up, pretending to wash.

'*Salle de bains?*' asked Ashmal, still lying on his side. '*Aucune salle de bains*,' he said, pointing to the window Millie had tried to open.

'*A l'extérieur.*'

'*Salle de bains.*' French. He was speaking French.

'*Parlez vous Français?*'

Ashmal was more alert now, sitting up, his bad arm resting in his lap.

'*Oui, et vous?*'

'Ah, *un peu*. Very little,' she said, desperately trying to remember her O level oral.

Ashmal lay down on the bed again.

Millie could feel her wet hair sticking to her hot cheeks. Her T-shirt was damp with sweat under her parka and her throat was parched.

She'd read about this. Whatever this was. But she was confused. Ashmal had a key to the door. He wasn't a prisoner. But the cottage, or was it an outhouse, was uninhabitable and twelve men or more lived here. Millie decided Cathal Quinn was behind it all and in that moment felt total rage towards him.

Again, she tried to remember her French, but she could only find a handful of words and phrases.

Then she recalled the translation app she had used when interviewing a Polish actress for the paper. She quickly took out her phone and prayed she could pick up a signal from the cluster of masts she had seen on the mountain the day before. Ashmal immediately sat up on the bed again, waving his good hand furiously. 'No…! No telephone.'

'No. Wait,' said Millie, waving her phone back at him as she walked to his bed.

Sitting beside him, her hands trembling, she typed in '*French to English translation*', willing the phone to pick up a connection. Just when she thought nothing would come through, various sites popped up. Smiling wildly with relief, she shared the phone with Ashmal, who was now leaning towards her. Within a minute, Millie was holding the phone and Ashmal was typing slowly with one finger. She was breathing through her mouth to avoid the smell of the cottage and all the time trying to ignore the stitched gash on his palm.

After he typed, she would hit the translate button and the English version would appear. They looked at each other and laughed as if they were the oldest of friends.

Millie could see from the phone it was now after eleven. Surely the others would be coming back soon. Maybe driven back. Millie thought of Cathal Quinn's pick-up filled with men and her stomach lurched with fear.

Over the next five minutes Ashmal typed in that he'd had a fight with another worker. He wanted no doctor or police. When Millie gritted her teeth in frustration, he wrote that he had no papers and would be sent back. They all would.

Millie nodded, trying to process his words.

She took the phone and reversed the translation. 'Are you being kept against your will?'

'No.'

'Are you being paid?'

'Yes.' But he turned away quickly.

Ashmal then wrote that their wages were kept for the cottage, clothes, and food. They were told they would start to get money in their hand after four weeks. They'd been there three.

'Do you have a passport?'

'No. Boss Man has.'

'Boss Man…? Cathal Quinn?'

Ashmal nodded quickly.

Still typing.

'What time will the others come back?'

'Cleaning boats. An hour.'

'Is there a First Aid kit?'

'Under the sink.'

Millie helped Ashmal take off his waterproof jacket. The fleece underneath was wet and, as she helped him wriggle out of it, he shouted in pain. Once off, Millie made him slowly move his arm and fingers to check nothing was broken. She then helped him put on a T-shirt and fleece from the pile at the end of his bed.

Lifting the First Aid kit from under the sink, a thick needle and some black wire was sitting on top of a tea towel. An open bottle of methylated spirits sat beside it. Breathing deeply, she tried to focus on the task in hand. She took out a bandage and between them they made a sling for his arm. Millie boiled some water in a pan. She added salt and then, with a clean tea towel she found folded by the sink, cleaned Ashmal's face and lip, putting a plaster over the cut on his eye.

She took his right hand and cleaned it slowly. They didn't speak, but she found Ashmal's eyes, wanting him to know she saw the stitched wound.

Rainwater had run off his waterproof trousers and pooled on a mat. Millie pointed to his waterproof trousers and then helped him take those and his wellington boots off. His tracksuit bottoms underneath were damp but his socks were sodden. She dried his feet gently with a towel she found hanging over one of the washing lines and pulled new socks up over his toes.

Ashmal pointed to his tracksuit bottoms and for a moment Millie thought he wanted her to change them. He registered her panic and shooed her away.

Relieved, she left the room.

Needing air, she walked outside and, using the torch on her phone, felt her way around the side of the cottage. The wind had all but died and now only sudden spats of rain were falling. She found the bathroom Ashmal had talked about – it was an outhouse with a large piece of heavy plastic nailed over the entrance. Pushing it aside, Millie saw a toilet. The cistern was open and there was no seat, and using a torch, she peered inside. The bowl was dark, but not from filth, just age.

It was so cold that Millie could see her breath smoking into the air. Her mind went to Dom's luxurious en suite in London and flashes of her privileged life rained over her.

There was a small sink hanging dangerously loose from the wall. She turned on the tap and freezing water spluttered into an ancient basin again heavily stained from age. A plastic box under the sink housed toilet paper, soap, and shampoo. Some cleaning products and a new toilet brush were also stacked neatly to one side.

Millie was struck by the order of everything. She sensed these men, whoever they were, had once lived normal lives. Aleppo was a city. They would have had houses with heat, warm water. They could have been doctors or lawyers.

She wondered about their families. Did they have wives and children they left behind? Or worse. She closed her eyes. *They must think they are in hell.*

Then, as she closed the box, she thought about what Finn had said. Maybe they were just glad to be alive.

Carefully following the torch, she made her way back to the cottage.

As she walked, she felt lightheaded. Her T-shirt was starting to dry and she was shivering. She couldn't believe anyone would stay in a place like this of their own free will. She didn't care what anyone said. This was abuse.

Inside the cottage, the smell quickly hit Millie's nostrils and she tasted lasagna again.

Ashmal had changed his trousers and was wearing what Millie could only think of as long johns. Even with his battered face and sling, he appeared more relaxed. He was sitting on the edge of his bed looking into a small wooden box. As Millie got closer, she saw the box had intricate carvings all over it. She was struck by how something so beautiful could end up in a place like this.

He motioned Millie to sit by him. As she got closer, she saw the inside of the box was lined with a rich fuchsia silk. A tatty plastic bag lay on the bed and Millie could see small parcels, the size of pebbles, wrapped up inside.

Ashmal carefully shook the plastic bag and several of the parcels, all wrapped in different coloured silks, fell onto the bed. Millie watched him handle the little bundles as if they were precious jewels. Unwrapping a piece of silk with a bird of paradise pattern on it, he lifted his hands towards Millie. She peered in but wasn't sure what she was looking at. Ashmal raised his hands further towards her nose and smiled proudly. Then, an intense smell of lemons filled her nostrils and lingered in the air around her. It was so unexpected, she pulled back and Ashmal let out a small laugh.

'Aleppo. My. Aleppo,' he said slowly, closing his eyes, inhaling deeply.

The aroma continued to press through the air.

'Soap?'

'*Savon*,' he said, smiling and pushing it towards her again.

Millie took the soft pebble in her hands, cupping it gently. It was the colour of sunshine and soft to touch, like plasticine in her hands.

He pointed to her phone on the bed and started typing again.

'His wife had made soaps and oils in Aleppo.

'Beautiful scents… lemon, rose, orange.

'Beautiful woman.'

When Millie saw the translation, she touched his arm gently with her hand.

Using one hand, Ashmal wrapped the soap up and handed it to her. She tried to refuse it, but he shook his head. '*Amie*,' he said, and firmly pushed it back towards her.

He started typing again.

'He was trying to get to Europe. To his brother. The boats were the best way to get there.'

Millie pointed to her phone. 'Telephone?'

Ashmal shook his head.

'You have no phone?' asked Millie.

Typing… 'Not allowed,' and suddenly the lightness that had briefly landed between them evaporated.

As they sat on the bed, he unwrapped another flat piece of silk. Inside was a photograph. From where she sat, Millie was certain the man in the picture was Ashmal. He seemed happy, leaning up against a convertible car with a beach in the background. Standing beside him was a woman with long black hair loosely tied back, leaning her head on his shoulder. She was wearing a pretty printed summer dress and she had her hands on the shoulders of two small girls in matching swimsuits with mermaids on the front. Twins.

As Ashmal traced the faces of the woman and children with a finger crusted in dirt and blood, Millie felt her chest tighten. A noise she didn't want to make was threatening to leave her throat. She bit the inside of her lip hard, trying not to think about the people in the picture and what had maybe happened to them.

'*Famille. Mon famille*,' Ashmal said proudly, holding up the photo.

Millie reached for the photograph. Studying it, she spoke quietly. 'Beautiful, Ashmal. They are beautiful.'

He glanced at her and then kissed the picture before carefully wrapping it up again and placing it inside the box.

His shining eyes were now spilling tears. Millie laid her hands over his. She had no words.

He pointed to the time on the phone. 'Go... Go. I okay,' he said, wiping his face with the back of his fleece.

'I will come back. Tomorrow.'

Ashmal didn't understand.

'*Demain*,' said Millie pointing to herself. '*Demain*.'

'*Non*... No.' He took the phone and typed faster this time. 'Too dangerous.'

Millie wanted him to know she cared. She pointed around the room and then typed, 'Wrong.'

Ashmal took the phone. 'Better than before.' Then, after thinking, he wrote again. 'We are alive.'

Millie stared at the translation. No one spoke and then it was Ashmal's turn to gently touch her arm, the way she had his.

She saw his eyes were shining again. It was true. He was glad to be alive.

Millie quickly typed that she would bring him a phone over in the next few days. She would leave it in the bathroom. In the box.

Ashmal looked worried.

'No one will know. I promise.'

As she stood up, she took the small bar of soap wrapped in silk from the bed and put it deep in her pocket. 'Thank. You. Ashmal,' she said, putting one hand on his shoulder.

'Thank. You. Millie,' he replied, using his practised tone, his thick lip now making his smile lopsided.

Millie drove quickly. The road was empty and dark until a set of bright foglights came hurtling towards her. Blinded by their intensity, it was only when it passed that she saw the pick-up truck with men in the back. She picked up speed, all the time going over in her head everything she had seen and heard that night.

Chapter 12

Finn's cottage was in total darkness.

She had driven home and then walked, stumbling in her heels, over the beach, allowing the moonlight to guide her. She couldn't decide if it was raining or not, and the sand on the beach was damp and heavy to tread. As she stood on top of the dunes that ran down to the flat, she knew the wind from before was heading around the headland, towards Mullaghmore.

Pushing her hands into her pockets for warmth, she felt the silk-wrapped soap under her palm and took it out. It smelt so exotic, so far away from where she had just come. She tried to imagine Ashmal's life before. The elegance, the beauty; all gone now. Blown to smithereens.

Millie thought of the bombs and killings she had known. She wanted to tell Ashmal she understood. But she knew his hell had been worse than hers.

Before knocking on Finn's door, she paused, again worried he might not be alone. A woman, a friend, anyone could be there. What would they think of her, this person, soaked to the skin, calling at this time of night? Her courage deserted her, and she pivoted round. But then Ashmal's battered face appeared in her head. She didn't care if Finn had company; she had to tell him what she had seen.

Millie knocked the door twice. A light went on and she cleared her throat. 'Finn? It's me, Millie.'

The door opened and Millie could only see his outline against the lamp light behind him. He was wearing sweatpants with no top and she was struck by the paleness of his torso, which stood out against the darkness.

'Jesus. Millie, are you okay?'

Millie tried to repeat the words she had prepared on her walk over. But as soon as she started to speak her voice broke. Her head was down and her hood had slipped low, swaddling her neck. She had no tissues and was using both her hands to wipe away tears.

'Come here,' said Finn, pulling her towards him just inside the door.

He held her so close Millie could feel his heart beating against her. Then she was sobbing. Her face was leaning on his bare shoulder and she could feel his skin, warm and soft. She wanted to put her arms around him, but they felt too heavy to lift. He smelt of sleep and as he held her tight, she thought she heard him whisper her name. After a time, when she was still, she pulled back from him.

'I'm not mad,' she said, sniffing tears back up her nose.

'We're all a bit mad.'

Finn closed the door and helped her take off her coat, then her boots, which were thick with mud and sand. She let him take her hand and lead her to a seat by the fire, the one he normally sat in. She watched as he expertly stoked the fire into life.

'Where have you been? You're soaked through.'

'God, I don't know where to start.'

Millie could still feel some wet sweat patches on her T-shirt, and even though she was exhausted, she panicked, worried she smelt of Ashmal's cottage.

Without speaking Finn left the room and came back with a large towel and a sweatshirt. As she took them, her mind raced.

He read her thoughts.

'Dry off and change your top. I'll put the kettle on.'

Millie hugged the towel close to her face. It smelt fresh.

As soon as he was in the kitchen, she pulled the pale blue sweatshirt over her head. It had never been worn and had a large Vancouver logo on the back.

Hugging herself, she stared into the fire, watching small flames start to dance around logs. 'I didn't know where else to go,' she said quietly, watching Finn bring in two mugs of tea.

'Tell me,' he said, moving to the seat on the other side of the fire.

In the low light, Millie noticed how lovely the chairs were. They had high curved backs with fine armrests. Her mother would have called them elegant. She cupped her mug of tea and told Finn everything from when she drove up the lane to Ashmal's cottage.

Like the night before, he sat silently across from her, nodding and sipping his tea as she spoke. He had pulled on a white T-shirt and his elbows were resting on his knees. When he leaned forward, Millie could see his muscles making his arms lean and strong.

Only when he was sure Millie had finished did he speak.

'They're not what you think, Millie. I've asked around. They can go anytime.' Again, Finn spoke with no insinuation or told-you-so malice.

'Can they? And go where exactly? He… that man has their passports, Finn! They're not allowed phones.'

Finn's eyes narrowed but he said nothing.

'It's not right.'

'It doesn't sound right. But it's probably a whole lot better from what they came from.'

Millie's eyes swept the room and saw things she hadn't before. A lamp was throwing light on a framed picture propped up on a bookshelf. For the second time that night she was confronted with a picture of a man, woman and two children.

She thought about the photograph in Ashmal's box.

'Who's that?' she said, nodding towards the picture as she sipped her tea.

'Oh, that's Daniel. My brother,' said Finn, smiling. 'Lives in America. The boys are wee rips.'

Millie regretted asking the question. She didn't want to think about fathers and happy families.

She was once again aware of her exhaustion and even though her cheeks were flushed from the fire, she was cold and shivery.

'I should go,' she said, but felt too heavy to move. 'I need to sleep. Think about what to do.'

'Do? Millie, you can't do anything,' said Finn quietly. 'This man. What's his name? Ashmal? He doesn't want you to do anything.' Finn was running his hand through his hair.

The rage again.

'I'm not like that. I can't do nothing,' When he didn't speak, she went on. 'Maybe you can, but I can't.'

Finn set his mug down on the floor and came towards her. Kneeling down, he placed a hand on the side of her face. He pushed some stray hairs that had caught her lashes away from her cheek.

'You know what I think?'

Millie didn't answer. Her heart was racing.

'You need to sleep on it.'

'Yes, yes. I need to go,' said Millie quickly, raising a hand to remove his. But instead, she kept her hand on top of his.

Finn then leaned in and kissed her forehead, the way he had the day before: gently with no agenda. He kept his forehead against hers and they stayed there silently. Their eyes shut.

It was Millie who pulled back first. Waiting, wanting Finn to do something.

'I'm not letting you go. Not tonight.'

Taking her hand, he walked her through the kitchen into the bedroom. Millie was sure of what was to come and was embarrassed by how hungry she was for it.

Chapter 13

The sea woke her.

When she opened her eyes, she wondered how the windows had moved. Then she remembered, and quickly turned her head to see if Finn was beside her. He wasn't.

Sitting up quickly, Millie looked under the duvet. She was still wearing her underwear and the sweatshirt Finn had given her. Her jeans were neatly folded over a radiator. Everything from the night before came at her. Supper at Sasha's. Ashmal's face. Finn's kindness. She rolled onto her side and hugged her legs close to her chest. Facing the other side of the bed she thought she could see a faint outline of where Finn had slept. She gently stretched her hand over it. Cold. No, he hadn't slept there. She was sure of it.

The shutters were pulled back and the three small windows were all slightly open. Sunlight was bouncing off the whitewashed walls and the light was sharp and intense.

Like the other rooms, paintings of every shape and form were pushed up against the walls, two, sometimes three deep. The only picture hung was a huge oil at the far end of the room, facing the bed. Similar in size and composition to the one in the living room, it dominated the space. Dark and haunting, Millie was certain the two pieces were connected. There was a rocking chair with a rug on top and some of Finn's clothes were thrown over it. An old Art Deco-style wardrobe was up against the left-hand wall, just beyond the closed door.

On the other side of the bed, there was no table, just a simple reading light, a glass of water and a couple of books sprawled on the floor. Millie couldn't resist stretching over and lifting one. *Irish Myths and Legends*. She smiled.

Lying on her back, her mind came back to Ashmal. She still couldn't accept the way he was living. She had to help him. Getting him the phone was just going to be the start. She then thought about Finn and the way he had controlled the situation, their situation last night. The way he had taken her by the hand into the bedroom, somehow managing to neither make advances nor avoid them.

Millie blushed when she considered her desire. She had wanted him to take her in his arms, kiss her the way he had the day before. Instead, he had stroked her hair, helped her gently take off her jeans and lifted her into the bed. After that, nothing.

Opening the door as quietly as she could, and without looking further into the cottage, she dived into the bathroom. The small room was the warmest in the house. There was a bath with a shower and a basin with a mirrored unit above it. The radiator was tall and modern and had two white towels hanging off it. Everything was clean and neat. She smelt the towels and imagined Finn loading a washing machine and smiled.

After throwing water on her face, she couldn't resist peeking in the cabinet above the sink. Almost scared at what might be there, she was relieved to only see mouthwash, a skin and lip balm, shaving foam and a razor.

Using her finger as a toothbrush she washed her teeth and gargled some mouthwash. She studied her face in the mirror and was shocked at how tired she looked. One finger had crusted blood on it and as she ran it under the tap, her mind flashed briefly to helping Ashmal into her car. Millie squeezed her eyes tight to dislodge the image and, after a few deep breaths, opened the door.

Finn was asleep on the sofa. A patchwork quilt covered most of his body and head, except for one foot which was dangling off the edge of the sofa. The room felt cold and his tracksuit bottoms and T-shirt lay in a pile on the floor.

Millie tiptoed towards him and, after pausing, gently inched the quilt away from his face. She studied his eyelashes, which were long and thick. His stubbled face was even more weather-beaten than she had thought and his lips were slightly open. He was breathing heavily, but not snoring. He was so peaceful and she wondered if he was dreaming.

Millie knelt on the floor, her legs to the side of her body. She wondered, what was it that so attracted her? They were so different and yet she felt they were somehow alike.

Just as she thought about who he was, he opened his eyes and slowly smiled. Her stomach tightened. He didn't move and she knew she must decide what happened next.

Silently, she got off the floor and pulled the quilt back. She lay down beside him, carefully spooning into the contour of his body.

Hot from sleep, his arms enveloped her. As he pulled her hair back and kissed her neck, she heard him whisper her name.

She closed her eyes, allowing her mind to empty of all thoughts.

'One lump or two?' Millie woke to Finn's bright smile.

He was dressed only in sweatpants and Millie could see tiny splatters of paint across his chest.

'What time is it?' she asked, sitting up quickly, pulling her hair off her face.

'Past noon.'

Painfully aware of her nakedness, Millie used her legs to fish around under the quilt for her underwear and top. Finn returned from the kitchen just as she pulled the sweatshirt over her head, but he appeared not to notice, too busy focusing on the small wooden tray in his hands. It reminded Millie of the way a child would walk in an egg and spoon race.

On the tray there was a black teapot with two small matching mugs with swirly handles, all made from glazed pottery. A simple tea strainer and teaspoon were on a matching saucer. Using his left leg, he dragged a small table made up of different woods in front of the sofa.

'Real tea?'

Finn raised his eyebrows. 'We're not all peasants up here, you know.'

She smiled but couldn't meet his gaze, too conscious of everything they had done earlier. Then, as he leaned down with her mug, he kissed her tenderly on her cheek.

'Drink up.'

Millie finally found courage and met his eyes. Her cheeks flushed with a mixture of embarrassment and desire.

'I was just thinking. Do you have a second name?' Finn was scratching his chin, moving to his chair by the fire.

'Malone. I'm Millie Malone. My mother calls me Matilda.'

'McFall. Finn McFall. My mother called me many things.'

They laughed and Millie blew on her tea.

'Well, there you go, we're old friends now,' said Finn, letting his legs stretch out in front of him.

Millie was surprised how easy he was with her. When she talked about Ashmal, he wasn't gruff or impatient. He just let her be. And when they talked about other things, there were no awkward silences, no painful stumbling over words. It was as if they were indeed old friends, not new lovers.

Finding a hair bobble on her wrist, she pulled her hair up into a ponytail. With Finn watching her she decided to smile that smile. The one she knew men liked.

'Now, you're going to get into all sorts of trouble if you keep looking at me like that.'

Millie laughed, letting her whole face soften this time.

'Do you always play with people, Finn McFall?' she asked, pronouncing his surname slowly.

'Only with the ones I like.'

Millie knew what they were doing, and she was enjoying it.

'Now, I was thinking about making us a fry? Would you like that, Millie Malone?' Finn asked, mirroring her slow pronunciation. 'I think you could do with a big feed.'

Millie nodded eagerly, realising she hadn't eaten since the lasagna at Sasha's.

When Finn was busy in the kitchen, Millie went to the bathroom. She quickly washed her teeth again – this time using Finn's toothbrush, before crawling back under the quilt on the sofa.

Familiar smells and sounds wafted into the room: bacon being fried, eggs being crackled, bread being toasted.

Leaning against the arm of the sofa, she thought about earlier. How Finn had touched her and how ready she had been for him. Her cheeks coloured, and she quickly pulled the quilt up to her eyes.

Then, with no warning, a niggle of worry poked her.

Since the clinic, she had worried if she was somehow different. Inside. Now, she wondered if Finn could somehow know she had allowed a life to be sucked out of her? Millie shifted around on the sofa. She was hot and as she kicked off the quilt, she felt a familiar sensation start to spread over her.

Finn then appeared from the kitchen. He was carrying a different tray, bigger than before, and was walking like a butler. 'Madam, your food awaits.'

As soon as Millie saw him, and all the effort he was making, her body relaxed and her panic vanished as quickly as it arrived.

Plates on their laps, they ate greedily. Again, they talked easily with no point-scoring. Finn told her about his life in Ballydunn. How he fished for a man called Rafferty around the headland in Mullaghmore, because his sons had all left the village and Finn felt sorry for the man.

Millie listened, enjoying his relaxed manner and funny stories about the village and the characters in it. He told her he came from Belfast, west of the city, but had gone to Canada after getting sponsored in his twenties.

'So that's where your weird accent comes from,' she said smiling. 'That drawl must stick out like a sore thumb when you're back home.'

'You're one to talk! But in truth, I haven't been back to Belfast in a lifetime.'

Millie felt Finn momentarily pull away from the conversation.

When asked, he said he had only returned to Ireland five years ago and found himself in Ballydunn. He'd visited often as a child, stayed with his aunt who ran the Fiddler's Inn. When Millie heard this, she had beamed with delight, and they decided they'd probably seen each other years before.

Millie wanted to stop quizzing him, but the journalist in her kept throwing up questions.

'Where did you learn to paint?'

'Everywhere.'

'Why did you stay in Ballydunn? Why not move back to Belfast or Dublin?'

'Why not? It's one of the two most beautiful places in the world.'

'The other?'

'Vancouver Island.'

Millie thought about the sweatshirt logo, imagining a life Finn had away from Ireland.

'I like your art.'

'Not all of it, surely?'

'Most.'

Finn smiled broadly.

'I love to paint,' he said, turning his palms over. Sounding more unsure than she had heard before, he went on. 'It's as if my hands come away from my body.' Finn looked into the fire. 'I've never said that to anyone. Not in my whole life.'

Millie felt warmth flood her body and without thinking she went to him. Kneeling in front of the fire, she lifted his head and placed her hands on either side of his face, kissing him gently on the lips. Then without saying anything, she took his hand and led him to the bedroom.

As darkness fell, the fire caused shadows to dance across the cottage. Finn and Millie lay together on the sofa.

'I can't stop thinking about Ashmal.'

Lifting her hair in his fingers, Finn spoke softly. 'It's difficult to imagine, alright. But I honestly believe they don't want help… or to be saved. They want to be here, Millie. It's just part of their journey to get to where they're going.'

Wind rattled the window, breaking the intimacy.

'Listen, I have to go to the pub. I'm on tonight,' he said, nuzzling into her neck. 'Will you be alright?'

Millie allowed her thoughts of Ashmal to slip away and, in a low, theatrical voice, spoke. '*"Mid-Term Break" by Seamus Heaney…*'

'Aw, now there's a poem,' said Finn, pulling Millie to him and holding her, like Rhett Butler held Scarlett O'Hara. 'I suppose you think I'm daft doing what I do up in the pub. But you know, I enjoy it. Most of the lads in the band are from the boat. They're great craic.'

Kissing her head, Finn jumped off the sofa and pulled on his sweatpants. He appeared not to be self-conscious in any way about his body, and in turn, Millie responded, not embarrassed to look. In the shadowy darkness of the cottage, his torso appeared milky white. His body was lean, but his shoulders were broad. The type of body you would see on a building site.

Millie stayed on the sofa as Finn pottered about the cottage, lifting the tray from earlier into the kitchen, going to the bathroom, running a shower with the bathroom door open, the smell of eucalyptus wafting through the rooms.

All this time Millie thought about Finn. She had stayed with him since last night and not once had he been harsh or careless with her. Even when she had asked him so many questions, he appeared happy to answer them openly and honestly, amused, even, by her curiosity.

When she had talked, he had listened.

She had been cautious. Only telling him she was from Tyrone but not saying where exactly and he hadn't pushed. She said her father had died a long time ago and she was one of seven.

When she told him about moving to London for college and about her work, he appeared very interested, raising his eyebrows and nodding in all the right places.

He thought she was a Catholic. She was sure of it. Her surname wasn't obviously from one side or the other: like a Paisley or a Rafferty. Her family had a cottage in Donegal, not the north-west, like other Protestants, and she had told him she was one of seven. Anyone could have made that assumption.

At one point, when he had taken her hand and was tracing the lines of her palm, she thought she should somehow drop into the conversation a funny story about her high school or tell him casually about the Presbyterian church she had attended. But she hadn't, choosing instead to talk about her many holidays in the village.

When Finn was dressed in his faded jeans and fisherman's sweater, Millie thought how handsome he was.

'You can stay, you know,' he said, walking over to the sofa, bending down to kiss her on the cheek. 'I'd like that.'

In the shaded light of the cottage, his blue eyes appeared dark again.

In that moment Millie wanted nothing more than to stay under the quilt and sleep by the fire in his sweatshirt, waiting for his return. But she said no, she'd go back to Ardmara.

'I could come by later,' said Finn, picking up a copy of *The Dubliners* and a Seamus Heaney book of poetry from a shelf by the side of the fire. 'Tuck you in,' he said, raising his eyebrows.

'I actually need to get some sleep, not get tucked in,' said Millie, laughing. Before he could come to her, she jumped off the sofa and darted into the bedroom to get dressed.

She let him hold her hand as they walked over the beach and up the steps to Ardmara. The light had all but gone and they were mere shadows in the dark.

Finn cleared his throat. 'I don't do this, you know… I'm not one for this,' he said, turning to face her.

'What? Walking a girl home at night?' asked Millie, the darkness encouraging her flirtation.

'No. You know what I mean. I'm—'

'A good Catholic boy,' said Millie before she could stop herself.

Finn laughed. 'Well, that's up for debate,' he said, taking her face in his hands.

'For your information. I'm not one for this either,' said Millie, trying not to sound prim.

Then, pulling back from her dramatically, Finn spoke in his theatrical voice. 'How lucky I am to have something that makes saying goodbye so hard…'

'Let me guess. Seamus Heaney.'

'Nope.'

'Joyce?'

'No way.'

'Yeats?' asked Millie, trying to think of other Irish poets.

'Winnie the Pooh,' said Finn, laughing, his white teeth shining through the darkness.

After kissing goodbye several times, Finn walked towards the burning lights of the village. After a few steps and without turning around, he called back, '*Oiche mhaith mo alainn.*'

Millie smiled after him, clueless to what he had said. Searching her pockets for the cottage key, she felt something soft in her fingers. The soap.

'Finn. Wait… What about Ashmal? I need to get him a phone,'

Millie shouted into the dark. 'I could drive into Letterkenny in the morning, maybe,' she said, mostly to herself.

'No. I've a better idea,' he shouted back. 'I'm not on the boat tomorrow – I'll pick you up in the afternoon.' And with that Finn all but disappeared into the night.

Millie's heart leapt. She'd see him again soon. And they'd help Ashmal.

Together.

Chapter 14

'Well, child. I thought you'd died up there in the cottage.'

'Of hypothermia?'

Her mother didn't laugh.

'I meant to call sooner. I've just been, well… busy.'

'Doing what?'

Millie blushed. 'I can't believe none of us come up here anymore.'

'Well, that's why Jamie's of a mind to sell.'

Millie thought about Jamie's car washes.

'Mrs McKillen was at Sasha's. She was asking after you.'

'Aw, that's nice,' said her mother. 'Betty never got over young Michael. Even with all the money in the world. Just shows you.'

Millie imagined her mother in her new kitchen, in the chair by the Aga, her eyes closed.

'How's Karen? I texted her, you know.'

'Well, you're the bigger girl for that, Matilda. And so you should be. She's not had it easy.'

Millie grinded her teeth.

'Your sister will come round. Give her time.'

Millie wanted to remind her mother how everybody had their problems. Like they had discussed the morning before she left.

Her mother's tone turned cheery. 'I've news.' Then, without waiting for Millie to enquire, she went on. 'Jamie's given up the Irish. Told Eimear after our dinner. Said it was ridiculous. Ridiculous, he said.'

Millie couldn't help but smile at her mother's glee.

In truth, she was glad for her mother, but in turn she was now thinking about the Gaelic Finn had left her with the night before. It had sounded so natural coming from him and she was surprised, and now, speaking to her mother, even embarrassed, at how much she had liked hearing it.

'When are you coming back?' her mother asked, then added quietly, 'Do you have a date for London?'

'Actually, I'm following up on a story for the paper.'

'Story? There can't be many celebrities in Donegal, unless it's Daniel O'Donnell you're after.'

Her mother laughed and Millie sucked her teeth in annoyance. She now wished she hadn't called home. 'It's something more serious.'

'Serious, is it?'

Just then Millie heard a different voice in the background.

'In here,' called her mother. 'It's Lizzie. I have to go. She's brought stew.'

Glad for her aunt's interruption, Millie promised to call her mother again in a few days.

'Will you not be back by then?'

Millie ignored the question, sending love to her aunt before hanging up.

Passing the hotel, Millie wanted to go into the Residents' Lounge. She could sit by the window and let her eyes drift towards the Lookout and beyond. But her Weekday Special was over and although Cathal Quinn was nowhere to be seen, she didn't dare risk a showdown.

Instead, she went to the cafe and settled into her favourite window seat. She ordered a cappuccino and set about drafting an email to Tom, laying out the basis for a feature on migrant workers on the fishing boats of Ireland. All the time being careful to use the words '*abused*' and '*inhumane*', rather than '*trafficked*' and '*prisoners*'.

As an afterthought, she added she could substantiate the story with an interview. She had no idea if Ashmal would talk to her, but she'd have to try.

Finn had told her more men had arrived over the last week – apparently now working on boats further around the coast. She'd have to find a way to talk to them at some point.

Happy with her proposal, Millie pressed send.

She then re-read an email Dom had sent her in the early hours of the morning. It was very business-like, and the tone had irritated her. He had said he was going to Singapore for work and as she wasn't taking his calls, could they set a date to meet as soon as he was back?

Without warning, an image of what she had done with Finn slipped into her head. She closed one eye tight but was unable to stop a wave of guilt wash over her.

Sasha had also made contact. Texting the day before, wanting her to go to the Fiddler's Inn for a drink. She felt bad she hadn't replied. She wondered if her friend had gone anyway, maybe with David. If so, they might have heard Finn read. She imagined him standing tall by the smoking fire, reciting Heaney and Joyce to another eager audience.

She tapped her phone, thinking about what to do. If she spoke to Sasha, she'd surely have to tell her about Finn. How could she not? Then she thought about how Sasha was the other night at supper. She texted instead. Explaining she was on a deadline for a feature, suggesting they meet the next weekend, if Sasha was planning to be up again?

Waiting for a second coffee to arrive, Millie felt pleased with her plans. She leaned back in her chair

Now, she had all morning to think about Finn.

Millie heard him, before she saw him. The throaty growl of a motorbike on the lane to the cottage made her run to the window. She was just in time to see him drive around the back, like her father used to do, pulling up fast at the front door. He was wearing a white T-shirt and an old-fashioned helmet. The type you'd see in vintage war movies.

'Well, hello there, George Clooney, or is Steve McQueen more your vintage?' she asked, leaning against the front door frame.

'Isn't she a beauty?' asked Finn, grinning widely, stroking the bike like a horse.

Millie walked round the old Triumph, and just as she went to put her hand on the fuel tank covered in old stickers, Finn revved the engine and Millie jumped in fright.

He laughed and handed her a helmet. 'Jump on.'

'Won't you be cold?'

'Listen, love,' said Finn in his best Belfast accent. 'I'm from the Falls. Hard as nails.'

'Where did you get her?'

'Fergal Rafferty. For helping his father out on the boat. She's been all round Europe. I'm only minding her really.'

Millie jumped on behind Finn, as excited as she was frightened.

The sun had kept its morning promise and was out for the afternoon – there was hardly a cloud in the pale blue sky. As Finn drove through the village, he shouted back they should take the long way into town and turned up onto Atlantic Drive.

The bike scrambled high, and Finn leaned into the twists and turns of the narrow road. Millie gripped his torso tightly. After a while, when she knew she wouldn't fall off, she relaxed and began to enjoy the journey.

The sheer cliffs and craggy coves that lay beneath her felt perilously close. It was exhilarating to be so near danger. She could almost reach out and touch the seagulls and guillemots that swooped and dived around her. Speeding down a steep hill onto a flat by

Mullins beach, the salty scent of the ocean filled her nostrils. Then they were climbing up and over and round and down.

When they hit another flat near the top of the mountain, Finn slowed down and pulled into a lay-by where the tourist coaches stopped to take pictures. Climbing off the bike, Millie could feel her feet still tingling from the journey.

Finn stood behind her, his arms wrapped around her waist. 'It's the second biggest ocean on earth, you know,' he said, nuzzling his face into her hair. 'Separates the old world from the new.'

'Is that right?' Millie asked, watching a fishing boat with yellow dots of life on board chug parallel to the shore, wondering if Ashmal was on board.

'What's Canada like?'

Finn waved his hand over the sea. 'Well, it's way out there somewhere.'

Millie was nervous, unsure about what might come, but she wanted to know everything about him.

'The people are nice,' Finn paused, then went on, 'Not angry like us.'

'Us?'

'The Irish. Sure, we'd fight with our shadow.'

Millie didn't know what to say. She wasn't really Irish. She never could be. Not after Dad. She was about to try and explain this when he went on.

'Vancouver Island is beautiful. A bit like here, but the weather is better and the water is warmer.' He nuzzled into her hair again. 'People have boats, ordinary people. And there are whales to watch. People keep bees.'

'Just like here then,' Millie said, laughing, happy for the subject change.

'The food is class. All fresh and not full of crap. There is this one place on the island, Sooke Harbour. There's a wee hotel there with an amazing restaurant. Everything is grown in the gardens and the food…' Finn stopped talking.

Millie felt a pang of jealousy. She now wished she'd not asked him about this place she'd never been to. A place he so obviously missed.

'What, no big Ulster frys?' she asked, trying to hold back a mood that was settling on them.

Finn didn't answer. His mind had already left.

'Will you go back?' She squeezed her eyes shut, regretting her question.

Finn tightened his grip around her waist. She could feel him breathing deeply. 'I would like to. Someday. I've built a house there. On the beach. Glass windows from ground to ceiling.'

Millie was about to turn around to see if he was being serious. But he went on. 'A good client gave me the land. He's like a father to me. His daughter and I built the house.' Then he added hastily, 'She's an architect.'

'An architect?' Millie's mind was racing. 'Sounds expensive.'

'It was that alright. But I've a good few clients over there who like my work. The oils. I'm lucky.'

Millie couldn't bear it any longer and wriggled around, searching his face for some clue as to who he was. But she just met his bright, open smile and she immediately felt foolish. Why couldn't he have had this life? She thought his work was wonderful; why wouldn't others? But she now thought of Finn in a different way. A successful painter living in a beach house with floor-to-ceiling windows. In Canada. She breathed deeply, trying to calm her mind. She didn't like to think of Finn like this. She certainly didn't like to think of the architect. Who was she? An ex? A wife, maybe? God, there might even be children. Millie's mind was racing. She didn't want this Finn; she wanted the one who lived in the fisherman's cottage with no phone and no car and who picked up his letters from the post office, when he remembered.

She turned around and leaned her head back on his chest, trying to rid her mind of questions. Then, as if he knew what she was thinking, he bent down and kissed her cheek tenderly.

'I'll tell you a secret,' he whispered into her ear. 'I never had this in Canada.'

Millie's heart soared.

Back on the bike, they turned inland, roaring through country lanes. The engine sounded much louder now as they were hemmed in by high brambles and thickets laden with unripe berries.

When they reached Black Lane, where the trees bowed so low over the road they met in the middle, the temperature dropped and Millie shivered. Then, back with the sun on her face, she inhaled the smells of cut grass and early summer. A plane flew overhead, leaving a white stream in its wake. Noises blurred into one: tractors in the fields, cars on the road, seagulls cawing.

Best of all, every so often Finn would reach back and gently touch her leg.

They drove through the village of Glenary with its old chapel and ancient Gaelic gravestones. They passed the posh hotel, which had an indoor swimming pool all those years ago. Millie remembered how she and her siblings yearned to swim there but couldn't, because you had to be a resident.

She squeezed Finn tightly and he turned round briefly. At that moment she never wanted the journey to end.

At the phone shop they decided on a pay-as-you-go for Ashmal.

Finn took charge and paid cash for the phone and £100 worth of credit. Millie gave him a look and Finn returned it, opening his eyes wide in a what's-wrong-with-that sort of way. He then leaned in towards her ear, whispering, 'Don't tell anyone, but I rob banks when I'm not painting.'

'For all I know you do.'

Finn suggested they also buy Ashmal a radio. They went to a small electrical shop near the shopping centre where Finn knew the man serving. Millie insisted she pay for it and a pair of good earphones.

They went to the cafe she had been to before for tea. The sandwich board sign for '*Maura's Beauty*' was still on the pavement opposite and Millie touched her eyelashes, having all but forgotten about them.

Just then Maura appeared from the alleyway leading to the salon. She moved like an old-school Hollywood starlet, her pink hips swaying from side to side. A passing van honked its horn, which made Maura smile and her hips swing even more. Millie wanted to nudge Finn and tell him about her visit to the salon, but he was staring intently at the instructions for the phone, and she decided he might not think it was quite as funny as she now did.

After setting up the mobile, Finn put batteries in the radio, and they shared the earphones like lovestruck teenagers. Millie brought up the frequencies for Arabic stations on her phone and Finn tuned them in. They jotted these and Millie's mobile number down in a small notebook they bought in the newsagent.

Millie insisted on buying some large bars of chocolate to leave with the phone and radio, even though Finn thought the boys now had plenty to eat.

'Do you have a phone yourself?'

'I do,' said Finn with mock pride.

'I never see it.'

'It's in a drawer.'

'Useful.'

'You're just jealous,' he said, teasing. 'I'm free from all that nonsense.'

'How do you expect people to get in touch with you? Friends?'

'I don't. If it's urgent they know to call the pub or the post office. If I want to see someone, I find a way.'

Millie liked what she was hearing. No regular contact surely meant there was no one special in Finn's life.

'I do check it the odd time,' he added, 'but there's never anything much on it. A few calls from Canada, maybe.'

Canada again.

'I have a radio, mind. I listen when I'm painting in the cottage. It can be lonely enough there.'

Millie suddenly felt full of desire and leaned over, kissing him on the mouth.

'We'll be told to get a room,' he said, grinning, as he went to pay.

Pleased with their purchases and research, they headed for the bike.

'Do you fancy a bite before dropping the phone off?' asked Finn, taking out a leather jacket from a side saddle. 'We could head round the coast. I could show you the boats. My other life.'

Back on the bike, she closed her eyes and again wrapped her arms tightly around Finn's middle. It was only when Millie saw the signpost for Mullaghmore her mood dipped. It was her father's favourite place to fish, according to her mother, but it had other, terrible associations. The killings were before she was born, but a recent anniversary was all over the news. The senior royals out on their fishing boat, blown to bits. A local boy dead, too.

She felt an eerie sense of anticipation as they drove into the village and parked by the harbour. The sun had all but disappeared behind grey-edged clouds and Millie was cold.

'Shall we eat first and then I'll give you the grand tour?'

Millie tried to smile.

'You okay? You look frozen.'

'I just need to warm up.'

The Harbour Hotel was everything you'd expect from a small Irish inn. Burning fires, swirly carpets, and busy bars.

They got a table by the fire and Millie allowed Finn to persuade her to have half a Guinness. He suggested they both have the chowder. Said it was the best in Donegal. Then he added quickly, 'Because I caught it.'

His knees were pressed up against hers and he was stroking her hand as they talked.

'What really brought you to Ballydunn?' he asked.

'Oh, I don't know. I needed to get away. Think about things.' Millie stared out the window. 'I think Mummy's in a mind to sell the cottage – I'm glad I came up.'

'Do the others not come?'

'Well, three are away and the others, well, they're busy. It's pretty run-down and it reeks of damp. It'll be the site that sells.'

Millie felt uncomfortable. She didn't want to talk to Finn about her family and everything that meant.

'What about your family? Do they ever come?'

'I've only got the two brothers. Both in Florida,' said Finn, draining his Guinness. 'My dad had an accident just after I was born. Blinded. Couldn't work. Died not long after.'

'Blinded? God, that's awful,' said Millie, 'Your poor mother.'

'She found it hard, alright. We all did,' said Finn. 'She died when I was away.' Finn was now drumming his fingers on the table, staring out the window.

'God, Finn, I'm sorry. It's my job. It makes me nosy.'

'Two chowders?' asked the waitress, who Millie decided straight away was wearing a too-low top. 'I gave you extra wheaten, Finn. It's just out of the oven.'

Watching the girl grin at Finn, Millie couldn't decide if she was blushing or just wearing too much make-up.

'Thanks, Eilish,' said Finn.

'Do you think Ashmal will be okay?' Millie asked quickly, wanting Finn's attention.

'You know what? Those lads are survivors, Millie. They'll get to where they want. Eventually. Like most of us.'

'That man… Quinn. There's something about him.'

Finn didn't speak.

'I just don't like him. He's a creep.'

Finn took a sip of his second half Guinness.

'He shouldn't be allowed to treat people like that.'

Finn finally squeezed Millie's hand. 'Forget him. He's just an old man.'

'Why do you rent his cottage?'

Finn lifted his head, as if he had seen something important outside. 'I wasn't sure how long I'd be staying.' Then, talking directly to her, he smiled. 'But that was over five years ago.'

After lunch, when Finn was paying the bill, Millie watched Eilish openly flirt with him again. Leaving the hotel, she laughed. 'She'll know you again.'

'Away with you now,' said Finn, pulling her close and kissing the top of her head. 'Her father owns the hotel. He's a big client of old Rafferty. I need to keep them sweet.'

The weather had turned, and it was cold. As they walked hand in hand around the half-moon harbour, Finn had his arm wrapped tightly around her. He showed her *Iola na Mara*, the boat he worked on, two, sometimes three days a week. It was bigger than Millie thought it would be, and she tried to imagine Finn hauling in nets or steering the boat in rough seas.

After Millie asked, Finn pointed out other boats in the harbour – the ones he said migrant workers were starting to appear on.

They walked along the pier wall to the end and stood gazing out over the ocean. There was a dullness in the light that made Millie think it was later than it was.

'My father loved it here. It was his favourite place to fish.'

Finn squeezed her waist but didn't speak.

'He was here the day Lord Mountbatten was killed.'

'That was a terrible thing,' said Finn, staying perfectly still.

When he didn't say anything else, she went on. 'It was a long time ago.'

'The royals were here last summer, you know,' he said, sounding chattier. 'They're back fishing. The wee blond boy was in the boat. It was good to see.'

'You could sell that story.'

Finn pulled her into him, this time wrapping both his arms around her, again kissing the top of her head.

'I love to paint here,' he said, throwing his arm out over the ocean, 'The water and the sky change all the time. Angry, calm, warm, dark. Just like a woman I know.'

'Hey!'

Just then, Millie felt a presence behind them.

They turned round together.

'Not out today?'

'Cathal.' Finn's voice was dry and cold. Millie hadn't heard him use this tone before.

Another man hung back. The type of man you'd see on a street corner is how her mother would have described him.

'Rafferty not out today?' Cathal repeated the query. This time with a threatening tone.

Millie was aware of his thick grey hair dancing wildly in the wind, his puce face an angry splodge of colour set against the greyness of the afternoon.

'Not today.'

'Introduce us then, lad,' said Cathal. 'I think we've met – a few times now.'

Millie turned away sharply.

Finn responded to Millie's defiance and ignored Cathal's request. 'We have to be going.' He grabbed Millie's arm and started to pull her back along the pier.

Cathal gripped Finn's elbow as he passed. 'We have to have that chat.'

Finn shook Cathal off and walked on silently. His hold on her arm was so tight, she was sure she was bruising.

Neither spoke until they got back to the bike.

'Jesus. What was that about?'

Finn ignored her. His face was set hard, and he was breathing through his nose, his nostrils slightly flared. In the fading light, his eyes appeared darker than ever, almost black.

It was the first time she had seen him angry, and it frightened her.

As they drove out of the village, Millie turned back, just in time to see several fishing boats pulling into the harbour. On one of the boats, Millie was sure she could see Ashmal's Arsenal hat darting around between an army of yellow waterproofs. She thought of his battered face and sore arm and closed her eyes, allowing a fine mist of sadness to fall over her.

The clouds had joined together and the sky had darkened for the day. Rain was threatening. They drove up the Atlantic Drive, and just before they got to Ashmal's lane, Finn shouted back to her. 'That's where Cathal lives,' nodding to a lane on the other side of the road.

Millie had to squint, but in the poor light she could just make out a run-down farmhouse behind some trees. The gate to the front yard was hanging off its hinges and she would have said the house was derelict, if asked.

A few minutes later Finn stopped the bike halfway up Ashmal's lane.

'Best you wait here.' His face was grey, like the sky.

Finn walked up the rest of the lane carrying the plastic Dunnes bag under his arm. Millie took off her helmet and in the half-light kept her eyes on the entrance to the lane, all the time wondering what she'd do if a black pick-up truck appeared, growling its way towards her.

Less than five minutes later, Finn was back.

'Job done,' he said, his bright smile back in place. Brushing strands of her hair away from her face, he went on. 'He'll be okay, Millie, they all will. I promise.'

'I hope so.'

Millie could feel spits of rain through the overhanging trees and she was chilled to the bone but didn't say. Finn turned the bike lights on even though it wasn't yet five.

As they descended into the village, Millie clung to him, her head bent down. The wind was cutting through her, and she found the pull on her body at every twist and turn of the road exhausting. She was glad when they turned down Sea Lane towards Ardmara.

Finn didn't get off the bike and Millie was glad for that. She sensed an uneasiness lying between them and when Finn said for her to come over later, she declined, saying she'd walk over in the morning. Give them both a chance to sleep.

Turning the bike to leave, Finn saluted like a soldier. Just as he roared off down the lane, heavy drops of rain started to bounce off his jacket.

The cottage smelt of damp more than ever. Millie lit some scented candles and thought about lighting a fire but didn't have the patience. She turned on the immersion for a bath and poured herself a large glass of wine.

Waiting for hot water, huddled over the blow heater, she thought about what Finn had said earlier, about the Irish being angry. She knew her mother would eagerly agree.

Once in the bath, Millie went over the day in her head. She still hadn't managed to tell Finn she was a Protestant. It wasn't important, not these days, but she felt he should know. With her eyes shut, she thought again about what she could say to him: '*Well, Finn, I know it doesn't matter, but just so you know, I'm a Protestant from Dungrillen.*'

Millie moved around in the bath for heat.

Maybe she needed to be more casual.

'*Finn, it was so interesting what you were saying about the Irish being angry. My mother thinks that too and we're Protestants from Dungrillen.*'

No. No. She'd just slip it in as a by-the-way comment, the way you might tell someone you're a vegan.

This thought, along with the wine, made Millie giggle.

In London, she made a point of calling herself Northern Irish. A cultural mongrel, she'd say, grinning. But no matter how many times she said it, she was still considered full-on 'top-of-the-morning-to-ya' Irish. People seemed unable or unwilling to distinguish between the north and the south, Catholic and Protestant.

You were just Irish, bog standard.

When she explained she had never learnt the language or even the dancing they were bewildered, or worse, annoyed. They wanted her to be Irish. They liked the Irish. Even though the Irish didn't like them.

To add to her problem, and Millie now cringed thinking about it, she sometimes play-acted Irish. She supported Ireland in the rugby, but so did every Protestant she knew. Well, not every one. Not her sister.

St Patrick's Day was the worst. Each year, Millie would somehow find herself celebrating with the hordes of Irish, and everyone else who thought they were Irish, in London.

She now wondered if she was the only Northern Irish Protestant who behaved like this.

Lying on the bed, enjoying the coolness of the room, she wondered what Cathal wanted to '*chat*' to Finn about. Whatever it was, it made Finn angry. He wasn't telling her everything, she knew that. But quickly, her mind went to everything she had not yet told him, and her face flushed. Then, as if her mother had brushed by her, she heard her voice. '*People with secrets don't say much. It's their way.*' Millie sat up quickly, glancing round the room.

She decided she didn't care. Even if there were half-truths and hesitations between them, she still felt close to Finn. She didn't know why, but something connected them.

Brushing her hair by candlelight in front of her mother's old dressing table, she imagined him there, leaning up against the door frame, watching her, his head tilted to the side. She knew she would tell him all about herself in the morning.

He would understand.

Chapter 15

'Do you ride?'

'Excuse me?' asked Millie.

'Horses. Do you ride?'

Millie tried not to laugh. 'I did as a child. Did you?'

'I didn't have lessons if that's what you mean? Not much call for it up the Falls,' said Finn, laughing. 'I learnt in Canada,' he went on, flicking through a mail-order catalogue he'd been sent in the post with horses on the front cover.

Millie was lying on his sofa, her bare feet up on the armrest. She was combing through a book of Irish folklore Finn said he liked to read in the pub on winter nights. But no matter how she tried, she found it impossible to concentrate. When Finn was in the same room as her, she was excited, restless, and wanted to talk to him all the time.

'The Raffertys have stables. We could take some horses to the beach.'

'That could be fun.'

Millie hadn't ridden since childhood. Back then, she had gone to the Argory stables every Saturday morning. Just as she had gone to badminton, ballet and piano lessons every week. But that was all before Dad. 'I'll need an old nag, mind. It's been ages.'

Finn's brow crinkled as he rifled through the rest of his letters which he had picked up from the post office earlier. Catalogues from art suppliers and Irish book publishers were randomly tossed into the fire. A few unopened envelopes were saved, and placed on a shelf by the fire, which Millie now realised he used as a desk.

When he came to a postcard, Finn studied the front and then the back of the card at length. He paused, pursing his lips, unsure whether to speak or not.

'Anything interesting?' Millie tried to sound casual.

'Actually, yes,' said Finn. 'Look at this,' as he threw the postcard like a frisbee across the room towards her.

Catching the card in her hand, Millie sat up. It was the type of postcard you ordered online, using one of your own images.

On the front was a picture of a man and a woman, probably in their late sixties or seventies. They were good looking – '*well put together*', her mother would say. Their hair was greying but attended to, and their clothes were casually expensive. They were standing in front of a walk-in fireplace, above which hung a huge oil painting. Millie knew immediately it was Finn's work.

Her eyes were then drawn to a younger woman, sitting on an Ottoman in front of the couple. She had long blonde beachy hair and had the type of body only regular Pilates achieved. Her teeth were straight and white. Just like Finn's. As Millie studied the image, she was immediately reminded of a Ralph Lauren image.

She had seen the family before. Well, this type of family. They holidayed in the same smart hotels Dom liked to take Millie to. They travelled in groups – two, maybe three generations, all glowing with health and laughing over dinner about the day's golf or skiing antics. She and Dom would watch them silently, like uninvited ghosts.

The grandfather would hold court, lifting the bill quickly with a smile, the younger ones, rolling their eyes, half-heartedly trying to pay. The men with their logos and gin and tonics; the women with their diamond tennis bracelets and glasses of champagne they rarely finished.

Millie used to imagine their lives – full of noisy family dinners, expensive schools, and fundraisers. Certain no one in these clans had been murdered or blown up, or adopted and lonely, like Dom had been.

It was the type of family that made Millie burn with envy.

She turned the card over and saw the Canadian postmark, and her skin itched with resentment. The message was typed but was made to read like a scribbled note. It simply said, '*The Best Yet*'. It was signed '*KKK*'.

Millie knew they were referring to the painting. She turned the card over again. The oil must have been six feet high. Even in the homespun photo Millie could see it had intensity and depth. It was so dark, it was almost black. She recognised the location straight away.

'Is that the Lookout?'

Finn nodded shyly.

'It's wonderful, Finn. Actually, it's more than that.'

'Hold your whist now!' he said, laughing. 'You'll give me a big head.'

He walked back to the fire, casually throwing the last of the unwanted post into it.

'They must be nice people to send you that,' said Millie, digging deep to find kindness.

'They're good friends. Like I said, family really.'

'The girl in front. The one with the good hair. She's pretty.'

'That's Kelly.'

'Kelly?'

'Their daughter.'

Millie studied Finn's face, searching for clues. But there wasn't a flicker of emotion. Millie pressed on, trying to control her nerves. 'Is she the architect?'

'Yes, that's her,' he said quietly.

Millie's heart was beating so hard against her chest, she worried Finn could hear it.

'Were you an item?'

'We were,' said Finn finally, staring at the card Millie had now put down on the small table.

'Did you love her?' Millie couldn't believe the words coming out of her mouth. 'Oh, God. Sorry. Don't answer that. I'm sorry.'

'I did. Well… I thought I did,' said Finn, sitting down on the sofa beside her.

Millie said nothing and closed her eyes.

'I met her father when he came to the village here. I'd somehow ended up here after Belfast. Painting for the tourists.'

She opened her eyes to see Finn now holding the postcard, staring at it as he talked.

'Kevin Murphy was… is… a great man,' he said, smiling broadly. Then, mimicking a Hollywood voiceover, he went on. '*A giant of a man.*'

He touched the postcard with his fingers. 'He traced his family back to Ballydunn. They left during the famine.'

Millie thought about the old stone cottages on the far side of Black Mountain.

'He loved my oils. Saw something in them.'

'Well, he's right.'

'Self-made, you know,' said Finn, nodding. 'Pharmaceuticals. He sponsored me to go to Canada.'

'When was that?'

'Fifteen or so years back. A lifetime ago.'

Millie tried to remember what was going on in her life back then.

'What happened?'

'A lot. Everything,' said Finn, throwing the card on the table, running his hands through his hair. 'I was in my mid-twenties,' he said, coming back to the sofa. 'Kelly was just out of college.'

'Young.'

'Kevin and Karen, the Murphys, couldn't have children. She's adopted.'

Finn leaned towards her, pushing her hair back over her shoulder.

'She was spoilt.' A trace of nostalgia crossed his face. 'She always had to get what she wanted.'

'Did that include you?'

'We were friends for a long time before…' Finn lay back on the sofa, his legs outstretched.

'What happened?'

'She was wild.'

'What do you mean, wild?'

'She would drink, pick fights. Then it was drugs, parties. You name it. She did it.' He turned around to face her. 'It was as if the devil himself came into her. I often said she must be part Irish.'

Millie's mind wondered, and for a moment she thought about Dom and his demons.

'"*She had money and bought everything it shouldn't buy.*"' Finn suddenly spoke in his Hollywood voice again. 'Who said that?' he said, frowning, trying to remember.

'And you?' asked Millie, ignoring his question. Trying to imagine Finn caught up in this world.

'Oscar Wilde, I think. "*They tasted everything and still had no taste.*" I'm pretty sure that's Oscar Wilde, too. Don't you think?'

Millie knew what he was doing. She leaned over and touched his mouth with her finger.

'Is that where your lovely teeth came from?'

'Aw, these,' he said, mirroring her smile and taking her hand in his, kissing it gently. 'Well, I sure wasn't born this way.'

Then, without warning, he grabbed Millie, pulling her down the sofa, tickling her manically. Afterwards, they lay still. The silence of thought only broken by their own short breaths.

It was Finn who spoke first.

'In the beginning, it was fun. Even though I knew she was troubled.'

Millie didn't speak; she just closed her eyes.

'But by the end it wasn't. We had broken up and got back together too many times. I think I did it for Kevin really. He thought I could save her.'

'Save her?'

'From herself.'

'And did you?'

'I tried. God, I tried,' said Finn, sitting up. 'But some people just can't be saved.'

He got up abruptly and walked to the fire, stoking it roughly, pushing some half-burnt logs over red ambers.

His mind had left her.

Millie felt lightheaded. She knew Finn wanted to stop talking, but she couldn't bear to leave it there.

'When did it end?' She winced at her own persistence.

Another silence. Millie worried she had gone too far.

'Finally? About six years ago. I couldn't do it anymore.' Finn looked back at her. 'I felt terrible leaving them all.'

'That must have been difficult.'

'She checks into rehab regularly. She's a survivor.'

Millie thought about Dom again.

'And you?' she asked, deciding this had to be the last question.

'Me? I came back to Ireland.' Then, talking mostly to himself, he went on. 'I knew it couldn't work. She didn't know who I was. Where I came from.'

'But you stayed friends, right?' asked Millie, reaching over and lifting the postcard again.

'God knows how,' he replied, raising his eyebrows. 'She's with someone now. From rehab.' Finn stretched his arms out as he stood up. 'Hopefully it will work for her.'

Millie stared at the perfect family portrait.

Picking up the poker Finn began playing with the fire again. 'Kevin's still my biggest client. Has houses all over. So do his friends. I paint for them all,' said Finn, turning the coals slowly. 'I'm bloody lucky. I think he understood I just wanted a normal life. After everything...' He stopped himself going on.

He then turned to her, poker in hand. 'It's silly, I know, but that's all I've ever wanted, really. To be normal. You know... What everybody else has. A home. A family.'

Millie, breathing quickly, held his gaze, letting him know she understood.

She tried to stay calm, but she couldn't stop her mind from racing. All the time thinking about a future, a family with Finn.

Suddenly, without warning, she felt hot. Her body was jittery, and as she squirmed around on the sofa, she felt the familiar metallic taste come into her mouth.

It was happening.

She could feel her blood starting to pump through her veins and her heart was banging against her chest wall. She tugged at the neck of her T-shirt which was irritating her. Closing her eyes, she tried to clear her mind, like the therapist said. Breathe. But another familiar sensation started to crawl over her. She tensed, gripping the edge of the sofa. Her mouth was so dry she could hardly swallow.

Finn was watching her.

She felt trapped, suffocated. Everything seemed too close to her. She thought she might vomit. Then it came. The shame.

It rained down on her, filling every part of her, until she thought she might drown.

Millie pushed the small table away from the sofa with her feet and it scraped back hard across the tiled floor. She stumbled to the door – she had to get outside – to fill her lungs with fresh air. She yanked hard on the door handle, but it wouldn't open.

Then, Finn was behind her. She turned sharply, careering away from him. Her arms were hitting out and she could hear a noise. Someone was crying.

She felt a heaviness around her, smothering her. It was Finn. Hugging her, squeezing her so tight she thought she might burst.

'Millie, Jesus. Millie. It's okay. I'm here… I'm here. Don't be afraid.'

Crumpling into Finn's arms, listening to his words, Millie was afraid. Not of one thing but everything. Who she was. What had happened to her. What she had done.

Letting Finn guide her, she stumbled back to the sofa, lying down with her head on the armrest. Her throat was tight, but the wailing noise, which she now knew belonged to her, still came. She shielded her eyes. She couldn't bear him seeing her like this. He took the quilt from the back of the sofa and gently wrapped it around her. Then, lifting her like a sick child, he carried her in his arms to the bedroom, laying her down on top of the duvet.

Without speaking, he closed the shutters and the door. He lay down beside her, all the time stroking her fringe away from her forehead, just like her mother used to do.

When the adrenaline left her veins, Millie's body felt empty, but her mind was full of disgust. She wanted to close it down, forget the images and thoughts that were appearing like flash cards before her eyes: the clinic, the bloodstained glove, her own pathetic weakness and, always, the shame.

Then nothing.

It was night when she woke. Shards of firelight danced across the open door to the bedroom. A side lamp was on. Finn was talking to her gently, the smell of jasmine tea wafting under her nostrils. Her head ached and her throat still hurt. She could feel her puffy eyes straining in the semi-darkness and her skin prickled with dryness.

'Well, hello there,' said Finn, smiling down on her gently.

Millie didn't speak. Peering down at her crinkled clothes, she closed her eyes. Finn wrapped her hands around a mug of tea. The mug with the swirly handle, the one she always had at Finn's.

'I can't get it out of my head.'

'What, Millie, what can't you get out of it?'

'Something I did,' she said, gulping air, her eyes filled with fresh tears.

Finn's eyes narrowed. Millie could see he was thinking, imagining maybe, what she might have done.

'Millie,' he said, taking the mug from her hands, before holding her again. 'Nothing you could have done is that bad. Nothing.' He pulled her away from him and looked into her face. 'Whatever it is, whatever you did, you must have had good reason.' When Millie didn't speak, he went on. 'Sometimes in life we don't have a choice.'

'No, Finn, stop,' said Millie angrily. 'I did have a choice. But I was weak. You know what I did?' she asked, grabbing Finn's face hard with her hands, her own face now close to his. 'I aborted my baby, a perfect baby. A baby I wanted, because my boyfriend asked me to. That's what I did.'

Millie kept hold of Finn's face, staring at him defiantly, daring him to hate her. Then, almost spitting the words, she went on. 'There you go. I killed one to keep the other. What do you think about me now?'

Millie waited for Finn to pull back in disgust. For his eyes to grow dark and cold, the way they had at the harbour.

Her heart was pounding and she felt terrified. Another panic was trying to come up through her, but she was numb to it.

Finn gently took her hands away from his face. 'I'm so sorry, Millie,' he said, pulling her into him again.

With a voice so small, it was hardly audible, Millie spoke. 'How can you not hate me? I killed a beautiful baby. My baby. What does that make me?'

The last words were rasping, choked through more tears.

'Hate you, Millie? Jesus, woman, don't you know it yet? I love you.'

Finn squeezed her into him even tighter, as if he was trying to absorb her pain. Repeatedly kissing the top of her head, he rocked her slightly in his arms.

'People do things they don't want to do all the time, Millie. They feel trapped.'

And in that moment, Millie stopped crying. She pulled back from him, gazing up into his face. He wasn't angry or disgusted with her. He didn't question or pity her. All he did was love her. With this certainty, Millie sighed so heavily, her body once again crumpled into his. Finn stroked her hair in long, slow movements from behind and she felt her lids close. A light swaying motion came over her. Finn was rocking her to sleep again.

When Millie woke in the morning she felt better. The heaviness, which so often followed her around ready to descend on her with any sad thought or cross word, had dispersed. She wasn't afraid anymore. Not about her past or her future.

Finn didn't mention Canada again. The postcard disappeared and that suited Millie. Finn knew about the clinic, about Dom. That was enough for now. In this new world she inhabited with Finn, nothing mattered. Not really. She would have to tell him about her father. Of course she would. But there was no rush. She'd do it when the time was right.

Later that day, when Finn was out fishing, Millie thought about calling home. She wondered what her mother would say if she told her about Finn, about how happy she was. Just as she reached for her phone a text came through. It was from Ashmal. Writing in English she half understood, he thanked her for the phone and radio and wanted to give her money, as he was now being paid. Millie hugged her phone to her chest, then wrote back, saying she was so glad for him, adding the phone and radio were gifts. She then asked if they could meet up. She wanted to talk to him.

Scrolling through her emails, Millie re-read Tom's reply to her feature idea. She felt elated every time she read it. He'd agreed to her proposed story about the fishermen – as long as she could secure an interview.

Finally, she was maybe getting the chance to write about real people with real issues.

Chapter 16

The weather was the talk of the village. Summer, it seemed, had come early to Ballydunn.

She had agreed to meet Finn on the beach, just by the steps of Ardmara. Enjoying the sounds of the ocean, she heard a different noise and, blinking into the sun, saw Finn cantering along the hard sand towards her. His horse was dark and glossy with legs that worked hard against the sand. A second horse was running beside him, the reins of which were in Finn's hands.

Millie covered her mouth with her hand.

It was like a scene from a period drama.

Soon, the mirage was in front of her. Finn's cheeks were shiny and his hair was waving in the wind. The horses were pulling on their bits, eager to continue their journey.

'Meet Donald and Trump.'

'Are you serious?'

'Totally. I've got Donald. He's a feisty wee article,' said Finn, trying to keep the horse still. 'Trump's a bit more timid. But she'll go like stink if you push her.'

Millie was scared to even touch the animal.

'She won't bite.'

Millie ignored him, finally patting the side of Trump's white dappled head and pulling on her ears gently. The horse's nostrils flared, and she shook her mane manically in appreciation. After hopping around in circles, Millie managed to climb into the saddle, insisting Finn kept hold of Trump's reins with one hand. After a few minutes of gentle persuasion, she agreed he could let go.

Nervously, she followed Finn towards the sea. Very quickly, she discovered he was not stopping at the water's edge but leading his horse into the waves, allowing him to splash in the surf. Millie tried to divert Trump away from the water, but no matter how hard she pulled right on her reins, the horse wouldn't turn.

'Finn. Stop.'

Looking over his shoulder, Finn rolled his eyes. He turned Donald with ease and came up beside her. Leaning over, kissing her on the cheek.

The waves were now splashing against their knees, soaking their jeans.

'Finn. Please…' Millie pleaded, looking down at the waves.

'Aw, don't panic now. They love it.'

With that, he geed Donald up, and before she knew it, Finn was cantering through the splash towards the main beach of the village.

'Come on.'

The command was enough for Trump to follow.

Millie's anxiety had grown into full-blown terror. She gripped her reins hard and dug her knees into her saddle. She kept telling herself she knew how to ride; she just had to remember. Her leg muscles ached and when she couldn't hold her grip any longer Trump broke into a gallop, desperate to catch up with her stable-mate.

Millie's heart was racing, but she felt excitement too. She remembered how to sit in the saddle and hold the reins. She began to relax and soon she had caught up with Finn, who turned sideways just in time to see her pass him on the outside.

Screaming and whooping with joy, they teased each other with the horses. When they came to a stop near the rocks that curled around to meet the main beach, Millie was almost crying with laughter.

Finn came up beside her and took Trump's reins, pulling her towards him. Leaning over the horse's head he kissed her on the mouth and then, letting go of the reins, took her face in his hands. Exhausted, the horses were happy to be still.

'I could not love you more,' he said, smiling wildly at her.

Millie responded, leaning her head into his left hand. 'I love you too, Finn,' she said, now holding his hands on her face.

'But I love winnin' more,' and with that he threw Trump's reins back at her.

'Come on,' he shouted, geeing the horse up into another canter.

Without a thought, Millie brought Trump alongside him, and they raced down the beach, back towards the Lookout.

Later, back at his cottage, they lay in bed.

Finn was propped up against some pillows, one hand behind his head, the other delicately tracing her vertebrae. She was leaning over his torso, trying to concentrate on James Joyce.

'Is it just Irish writers you like?'

'Are there any others?' asked Finn, feigning disbelief.

'Well… a few.'

'Aw, but not like the Irish. We're the best at everything. Don't you think?' he asked, raising his eyebrows.

Millie seized the opportunity. 'Well, you know, I'm not strictly—'

Finn talked over her. 'There's no getting away from it: I'm going to have to paint you,' he said, leaning down and kissing her back.

Relieved at the interruption, Millie put on her best Irish accent. 'Away with ya', you big eejit.'

'No, seriously, I can't have something as beautiful as this in my presence and not paint it.'

'Who said that?'

'I did!'

With that he was up, naked, rummaging around inside a box by the big picture at the far end of the room. He came back to the bed with a scrap of art paper and a thick dark pencil. Then he was quiet, sketching frantically, using his spit and thumb to rub and shade his work.

Millie was protesting lamely but enjoying the attention. She rolled over and arched her back, asking him provocatively if he liked that. But he didn't respond.

Then she was on her front, her legs kicking up behind her, pulling her hair to one side of her face, laughing into her pillow. Minutes later, he studied the paper, moving his head from side to side, as if he was judging someone else's work.

'Not bad. Not bad. Even though I say so myself,' he said, throwing the sketch to Millie. When she saw what Finn had done, she was shocked. The work was so rough, so quick, but also full of mood and movement. She loved it. She dropped the paper on the floor and crawled down the bed as seductively as she could, pulling Finn towards her.

Listening to the waves land on the rocks below, Millie spoke.

'Where did you learn to paint?' she asked, twirling Finn's curls rhythmically in and out of her fingers.

'Belfast.'

'Really?'

'I had a great teacher.'

'At the art college there?'

Finn put on a dramatic voice. 'Her name was Purdy Perrili. Can you believe that? God, she got some stick for that,' he said, laughing. 'We all thought she was a goddess. She had this lovely long hair that shone in the light of the studio, and she always wore these wrap dresses that somehow—'

'Okay, okay, I get the picture,' said Millie, sitting up. 'I think you're a brilliant artist, Finn. I think you could be very successful.'

'What do you mean, "*could be*"? Let me tell you, my girl,' he went on, leaning forward to whisper, 'I just sold a piece in Canada for… well… let's just say, enough.'

'How much is enough?'

'Now that would be telling.'

'Where do you keep these big pieces you talk about?'

'I've a wee studio in Dublin. I keep the ones that go abroad there.'

'Dublin?'

Over the next few days, Finn painted relentlessly. If it was dry, he was on the Lookout early in the morning and again, before dusk, taking full advantage of the long stretch in the evenings. Some days he was picked up by two men to go out on Rafferty's boat. It was a puzzle to Millie how Finn communicated regarding these lifts, as she never saw him use his phone – but she never enquired, instead enjoying the sense of mystery that so often surrounded him.

Chapter 17

Millie had now been in Ballydunn for sixteen days.

'What do you mean, migrant workers?'

Millie left a silence just long enough for her mother to pick up. 'They're being treated badly on the boats here.'

'Well, they should maybe have thought about that before they came over on those other boats.'

Her mother was using a familiar tone. She didn't try to argue back.

As she doodled a heart on an unopened envelope on Finn's table, her mother went on. 'It's bad enough here with the factories, but at least they're legal.'

Millie turned her head to the side, proud of her design, she added an '*F*' and '*M*', and smiled.

'Don't you be encouraging any more to come in now.'

When she was sure her mother had stopped talking, she changed the subject. 'How's Karen?'

'Well, there's been a development.'

'What sort of development?'

'Colin and the other one.' Her mother paused for effect. 'They're as good as over. He wants back.'

Millie stopped doodling, imagining her sister's face when she told their mother her news. It would have been victorious. Like a jubilant gladiator holding down his opponent.

'Will she take him?'

'She will.'

Millie thought of Karen at that awful dinner. Her vitriol and bitterness spilling over everything. She felt a knot of irritation gather in her gut.

As if reading her mind, her mother went on. 'She can't cope without him, Matilda.' Her mother's voice softened. 'She doesn't eat. She's not sleeping.' Her tone was almost conspiratorial. 'The children need him.'

'He'll have a dog's life. They all will.'

Her mother cleared her throat. 'Jamie came to see me.'

Millie started doodling again.

'We've decided to sell the cottage. He's spoken to that big agency in Belfast.'

'We?'

'Yes, Matilda. We. Jamie knows about these things.'

'Does he now?'

'He's been a great help to me over the years…' Her mother paused briefly, then carried on. '…When others weren't around.'

Millie sat back in her chair, raising her eye to the ceiling.

'Anyway, I don't know why you're bothered. This is the first time you've been near the place in years. Some big developer will buy it. It'll be money from America. Think about that.'

But Millie could only think about why she hadn't come to Ballydunn earlier.

Over the next few days, Millie spent her mornings driving around the surrounding coastal villages. Finn had marked them out on a map for her, writing out the names of the biggest fishing families in the area. She soon discovered migrants were now working for most of them, bar old Rafferty and the Dolans of Malin Head, the two oldest fleets on the coast.

Millie thought about Finn's warning. If the workers were illegal, and she was sure they all were, they would not want her asking questions. Nor would their employers. The way Finn had talked to her about the situation made Millie sigh with pleasure. He had asked her to sit at the table. His voice had been serious, his face concerned. She saw him as half protector, half collaborator. They were a team.

With Finn's words in mind, she was careful with her research. She only took pictures of the boats when she was sure no one else was around. Like Ashmal, the men wore yellow or sometimes red waterproofs and the colours jumped out of her screen against the blue sky. She liked the images and felt certain Tom would too. Her afternoons were spent in the cafe or at Finn's cottage, editing her photographs and researching the boat owners.

She wrote a list of questions she planned to ask Ashmal and made a list of the pictures she wanted to take at his cottage – if he agreed.

One morning on her way round the coast, the early sunshine persuaded her to stop off in Mullaghmore for a coffee. She went to the Harbour Hotel where Finn had taken her for lunch, where she sat at a table outside, enjoying the powerful smell of fresh fish and seaweed.

Peering through the harbour mouth, she imagined what it must have been like the day Lord Mountbatten was killed. The noise of the explosion in such a quiet place. The realisation of what had happened. The sheer panic.

Her thoughts were interrupted by Eilish, the waitress who had flirted with Finn the week before. Millie smiled but only got a pinched show of teeth in return.

She looked at her phone. Sasha had been messaging her. The night before she had received pictures of her friend posing in a kaftan, standing in a lush tropical garden, a fish mouth fountain in the background.

For one moment, Millie thought Sasha had created a botanical fantasy in the grounds of her house in Dungrillen. But the attached message simply read '*Dreamy Dubai…*'.

On asking for details, another message had appeared that morning revealing the family had just gone away for the week. A last-minute deal in a six-star hotel. Worth taking the children out of school for.

Millie had laughed. She and Sasha were so different, yet their shared pasts secured a friendship she believed would last a lifetime. She hoped her friend felt the same way. Sasha had suggested Millie move into Sea View while she was away – if she was still in the village. She had given her the code for the gates, '*1066*', and told her there was a key under the front mat. The Union Jack mat, Millie remembered.

Sasha reminded her about Sky.

As she drove away from Mullaghmore, Millie celebrated Sasha's spontaneity. It saved her, for now, from having to explain about Finn.

Fiddling for her sunglasses, she considered how secretive she was. Cagey, her mother called it. It had started after Dad. Ever since then she had felt different, when all she ever wanted was to be the same. She became skilled at giving people just enough information, but never all of it. She learned to navigate life that way; it made her feel safe, protected.

Millie pondered the one big secret she was still keeping from Finn. She had to tell him about her father; it was such a big part of who she was. She just needed to find the right moment.

Leaning across the passenger seat, she opened the window to let air into the car, and the smell of the first hay cutting filled her nostrils. As she passed a rickety tractor lurching over the road with a hedge cutter on the back, small blades of grass hit the windscreen and flitted in through the widows, speckling the seats and her new linen dress. The smell was potent and Millie inhaled deeply, allowing herself to relax back into her seat.

On the winding coastal roads, surrounded by hedges now heavy with buds and early berries, she imagined living here. With Finn.

They could build a house by the sea with windows from floor to ceiling. Just like Canada. She could be a freelance feature writer, working for the papers in London and Dublin. Even Belfast. Finn could paint. They could be a family. She smiled broadly, enjoying her fantasy.

With her right elbow leaning on the open window frame and her sunglasses on, Millie enjoyed a strange, sweet sensation spreading through her body. She turned the radio up and picked up speed.

Chapter 18

On Friday, Finn asked Millie to go to the pub with him.

It was the first bank holiday of summer. The weather was good, 'The craic will be '90,' he said.

Millie wanted to go. She hadn't been to the Fiddler's Inn since the day she had called in with Sasha and loved the idea of now being there with Finn, listening to him enthrall the audience with his poems and tales of Gaelic legends.

It was just after six when they headed out. Finn pointed to a lobster pot near the front door, saying there was always a key there, in case Millie wanted to come home early. She smiled brightly and leaned her head on his chest. His cottage did feel like home.

The day was ending, but the sun was still out and there was a light haze settling over the sea. The beaches were more busy than usual with happy families, and speedboats with water skiers motored back and forth parallel to shore – and every time someone fell over a wake, distant laughter rippled over the water. The village was different now summer was coming. It was alive, full of purpose and expectation.

As they reached Main Street, traffic was at a standstill. She could see drivers and passengers turning their heads every way, searching for a parking space. An ice-cream van selling whipped 99s and candyfloss had positioned itself on the pavement and a snaking queue of eager children was waiting patiently.

O'Neils was still open, buckets and spades hanging from their doors and windows as usual. A giant inflatable swan had been added to the collection. It made them both giggle. Even the hotel was ready for the season with two new picnic tables outside the entrance. As they walked past the abandoned digger still by the front door, Millie nudged Finn and they laughed even more.

Passing the first caravan site, Millie saw men hammering windbreakers into the ground, to protect their barbeques from the beach breeze. Children were running around with crabbing nets and water pistols, and nearly every caravan had two cars outside, many with northern number plates, which made Millie happy.

Finn had one arm around her shoulder, his chunky fisherman's sweater was tied around his waist, and he was carrying his favourite book of Irish poetry under his arm. He pulled Millie close and kissed her cheek. She was conscious of people ogling from their cars, but she didn't care. She liked it. When she turned her face up to his, he quickly found her mouth. The next kiss was lingering, and she liked that even more.

In the pub, she sat at the big table by the smoky fire, her cheeks slowly roasting with the heat. She was surrounded by the band who had trudged past her the night she had been there with Sasha. Tonight, she was part of it all. Some of the players were sitting quietly, studiously tuning or cleaning their instruments; others were standing around, laughing about something or other that had happened on the boat that day. Everyone, it seemed, was buying her drinks.

One lad, Connor, she heard Finn call him, the youngest by far of the band, kept smiling over at her. He had bad skin and a front tooth missing. His face was the colour of smashed raspberries, and each time he reached his hand up to take a drink of his beer, his alabaster hand glinted like sugar against his scorched face. Watching his fellow band members, it struck Millie that the good spell of weather had taken them all by surprise.

Trying not to stare, Millie observed how people wanted to be in Finn's company. At that moment, he was deep in conversation with two men, golfers. He had his arms draped amicably around both of them and his head was down, close to their mouths, so he could hear what they were saying over the din of the pub. They were laughing, then listening intently to whoever was speaking. One was trying to show Finn a golf swing, but in the packed pub, it was proving impossible. She saw how he had an ability to put people at ease, feel good about themselves. Like they counted.

Every couple of minutes, he looked over to her, raising his eyebrows, his way, she now knew, of asking if she was okay. She grinned back, raising her glass, happy to sit and watch the shenanigans around her. As the pub buzzed, the boy with the scorched face started to hand out the grubby, laminated sheets of music to the delight of the tourists. Dermot brought a round of drinks over to the table. He had to carry the tray high above his head to avoid the crush and a squall of delight went up all around her.

Millie now understood why Finn did this thing in the pub. He loved the banter with the boys from the band and the mutual backslapping with the ancient locals. He enjoyed the chat with the over-familiar tourists, who, because their ancestors came from the area, felt they belonged here too. He even had time to listen to the golfers about their swing.

The young Goths Millie had seen before were back, huddled around the jukebox, still drinking cheap cider. She knew they'd be hitching lifts to some club or other in Letterkenny later. One tall, skinny boy was wearing a full-length leather coat and Millie winced thinking how hot he must be.

With no one in particular to talk to, she went to the bathroom. She held her wrists under the cold water tap to cool down and remembered the last time she had been in there. In the mirror, she saw a new Millie gazing back at her. She lifted her cold hands to her hot cheeks, hardly daring to believe how happy she was.

The door opened and the noise of the pub fell in on her – pulling her ponytail high, she headed back into the sweltering heat of the bar.

As she pushed her way to the table she heard the familiar first bars of 'Teenage Kicks' from the jukebox and stopped, remembering the last time she'd heard the song. Finding Finn in the crowd, she looked up into his face and he squeezed his arm tight around her. He was singing along with the crowd, not embarrassed to be just like them. She studied his curly hair, then his long dark lashes and believed she was obsessed with every detail of him. The way he tilted his head to the side when teasing her, his constant hair stroking when anxious or worried – she loved every part of him. With Finn by her side, she decided, nothing in her past could hurt her anymore.

After the song finished, Finn waved his arms above his head for quiet. Behind the bar, Dermot played along, hitting a glass hard with a knife. 'Enough, lads, enough now. Time for another wee bit of culture.'

Millie twisted and turned her way back to the table. The boy with the burnt face squeezed up to let her sit down and then pushed a new glass of white wine up the table. Even though her head was spinning, she was thirsty and took a large gulp.

Finn lifted his book of poetry and, as always, Dermot finally clinked a glass for attention. The silence that quickly fell around the pub was full of anticipation. It was theatre.

Finn pushed his hair back and cleared his throat, a small smile, maybe only one she would see, traced his lips.

Her eyes went around the pub. The tourists, unsure of what was to come; the band members holding their fingers to their lips; the bar staff, smiling as they cleared glasses – were all playing their part in this play.

'"The Song of Wandering Angus" by William Butler Yeats.'

A small cheer and a ripple of claps rumbled through the crowd and Finn began…

'Though I am old with wandering through hollow lands and hilly lands. I will find out where she has gone and kiss her lips and take her hands …'

With this, Finn turned purposefully to Millie and smiled, his eyes shining brighter than she had ever seen.

Just before closing time, Millie was aware of two men ploughing through the crowds towards the bar. They weren't smiling or apologising for their brusque manner. They were drunk and one of them was Cathal Quinn. Millie tried to find Finn's eyes, but he was chatting to the band, getting ready for their final set. Watching Cathal push through the crowd, she recognised the other man from their encounter on the pier wall in Mullaghmore.

When the men reached the bar, they stood stony-faced and silent. Cathal had lifted a Guinness bar mat and was turning it on its edges repeatedly. She saw him mouth Dermot's name and the barman quickly dropped who he was serving and went to him. Two pints of Guinness and whiskey chasers were set down; no money was paid.

The men lifted their glasses and smiled blurrily. She sensed they were maybe celebrating something; but it was furtive, not for everyone's eyes. The chasers brought back memories of her father. She remembered him sitting at the very same bar, watching the rugby, a pint in front of him, a Bushmills to the side.

The shouts and hollers that followed Finn's recital brought her mind back to the bar. She watched how the men drained their whiskey then lifted their pints and moved unsteadily round the counter towards the back of the pub.

When Cathal passed Finn, he was in the middle of a group of

tourists, having his photograph taken. Millie could sense he was distracted, maybe aware of the shadow that had just stole by. Straining her neck to follow the men, she watched as they propped themselves up against the wall of a dark corner, next to the toilets.

Without warning, Cathal leaned forward and darted her a look. He raised his pint high and gave her one of his ugly, sly smiles; she ignored him and glanced away.

Leaving his friend where he was, he then came out of the darkness towards her. Millie tried to stay calm, but she could feel her heart thumping against her chest.

Does he know about Ashmal's phone?

She wanted to call out Finn's name or make for the door, but before she did any of this Cathal stopped a few feet away, next to the band. Leering, he banged his pint hard on the table, making wine spill out of her glass. As soon as the musicians saw him, a tension settled about them. She couldn't work out what it was. There was a tightness in the air suddenly: a stressed cough, a shift in their centre.

A new mood was lingering and she tried to catch Finn's eye. She wanted to go home. When Finn's eyes finally found her, she saw an anger in them, just like that day on the harbour wall.

Cathal was then beside Finn, pulling him from the tourists, whispering in his ear. He was unsteady on his feet and Finn was tugging away from his grip. Finn's face was set hard, and in the shadows of the pub, his eyes were once again dark. He was shaking his head, but Cathal was insistent they spoke.

After slapping Finn hard on the back, Cathal produced another empty smile as he moved round the table to young Connor. Leaning down, he cupped the lad's hot ear. The boy listened as if his life depended on it.

In turn, Connor then pushed himself up to the bar and waved Dermot over. A few words were spoken and Millie could see the barman curse to himself, before bending down under the bar, reappearing with a handful of old papers. Song sheets, Millie decided, but not laminated like Finn's.

The boy began handing the sheets to the tourists and the golfers, who, again, took them eagerly. The locals watched on, chatting and laughing as they had before, and when all the sheets had been handed out, Dermot clinked a glass for silence. When the noise didn't quell, he clinked again, harder this time. 'Well, folks, it's time for a song,' he said roughly, and everyone cheered. With little warmth, he went on. 'But it's from the second sheet you have there now.'

Millie tried to catch Finn's attention again, but his eyes were fixed on Cathal. She wanted to go to him, tell him she was leaving. Maybe ask him to come with her, but the band had already started scraping their stools together, their drums and fiddles on their laps, and she didn't want to have to cut through their preparations.

As the music started, Millie didn't recognise the tune, but then the words struck her like a bullet:

'... the bravest men, the bravest ten, they died in H-Block holes...
They shut their mouths and gave their lives ... to free our Irish souls...
... Thatcher was the devil, she never won the fight...
but don't despair, the war goes on... to make one ireland right...'

Millie swallowed hard. The heat from the fire was unbearable.

The scene reminded her of being in church as a child, when a hymn few knew played and the minister and choir tried to carry the congregation along. Here, it was Cathal and his friend, singing, almost shouting the words to each other and those around them.

Her eyes scanned the room for collaborators. The locals appeared to be in two camps. The older ones were sitting upright on their bar stools, singing along proudly, banging the wooden counter with their fists. They didn't need song sheets. The younger ones and the Goths were not singing, choosing instead to laugh at the drunken performance.

The tourists and golfers, eager to be part of the show, studied the word sheet eagerly and tried to sing along, looking to Cathal for encouragement. Millie turned to the band, who were now concentrating hard on the music, not one single smile between them.

Behind the bar, Dermot was leaning against the counter, shaking his head. His eyes were roaming the pub, trying, Millie thought, to see the effect the song was having on his customers.

She looked back at Finn – whose eyes were still glaring at Cathal. His arms were folded tightly around his body and his mouth was clamped so hard, his nostrils flared like bellows when he breathed.

Making fists of irritation as each new verse started, Millie wondered what she could do to make this man stop. She tried to get out from behind the table, but on one side, the band was blocking her way and on the other, so many people were huddled around the table, she didn't feel strong enough to push through them.

She was trapped.

The whites of her knuckles were now showing and she felt her hands somehow didn't belong to her body anymore. She opened her palms wide and then sat on them to keep them from doing something terrible.

Millie couldn't believe what was happening. Here she was, in a pub in Donegal, listening to a Republican anthem. The shame came without warning. She put her head down but, at the same time, tried to lift her eyes to survey the faces around her. Darting between people and over the heads of the band, she suddenly saw everything differently from before.

She watched the old men singing along at the bar and hated them. The tourists, mostly Americans, she now thought stupid. Here they were, singing away, nostalgic for a time and place they never knew. She watched Dermot behind the bar. His huge stomach and sweaty skin repellent to her now.

Then there was Finn.

She studied his face, searching for answers.

Why wasn't he doing anything?

She wanted him to march up to Cathal Quinn and tell him to stop. She wanted him to grab the sheets from the tourists, to tell the band to stop playing and everyone to go home. But he did none of this. Instead, he stood there letting this man sing about martyrdom and murder.

As the verses went on, Finn finally looked over at Millie and gave her a weak, 'how-awful-is-this' smile.

She lifted her head but didn't smile back and for a moment she thought she saw a flicker of concern cross his features. It was only for a moment, something about his eyes or the way his mouth opened then shut quickly that made Millie think he knew there was something more than embarrassment etched on her face.

Just before the song ended, Finn stood in front of Cathal, waving his arms in the air, using his dramatic voice to gather attention.

'Well now, folks, how about something a bit more fun to end the night?' And he turned to the band, who were nodding in unison.

'Let's go with "The Irish Rover", shall we? It's on the other song sheet you have there.' And with that the music kicked in. The atmosphere around her immediately softened and all she could see were happy smiles.

The first bank holiday of summer.

Millie felt her skin sizzle. She began to rehearse in her head the words she would say to Finn, but she had to get out of the pub first.

As she looked towards the front door, calculating how to get there, a shock of blonde hair caught her eye.

It was Sasha. Back from Dubai.

The warm, cheap wine Millie had been drinking all night suddenly hit her stomach. Had Sasha just arrived? Or had she heard Cathal sing? Millie felt rising panic. She couldn't let her friend see her like this: sitting with the band, drink in hand. She'd never be forgiven.

For a brief moment, Millie considered hurling herself to the ground or maybe even crawling to the toilets on all fours. She fumbled around for her bag and pashmina, and with her head still down, heaved through the crowd to the ladies – her feet barely touching the ground in the crush. Just as she reached Finn, she saw Cathal reach out and grab his arm. Millie couldn't hear what was being said, but they were shouting into each other's faces, and she was confused, frightened about what she was seeing.

Just then two of the band dropped their instruments and stepped in between the men. Finn shrugged himself clear and Millie saw Cathal's friend pull him towards the back of the pub. She was about to speak when she heard Finn shout after Cathal, '... *There's been too much dying for Ireland... not enough living.*'

The words made Millie stop and for a moment the noise of the pub disappeared. She could see mouths opening, but all she could hear was her own fast breathing. Seconds later, she was back in the fray. She felt unsteady on her feet and had to put her hand on the shoulder of one of the band members to steady herself. She had to get out of the pub. Keeping her head bowed, she pushed past Finn and kept pushing until she was through the swing door of the pub's kitchen.

A young woman was peeling potatoes.

'Sorry... I need to get out,' said Millie, her eyes flickering around, searching for the exit.

Without waiting for the girl to speak, she walked towards a door at the side of the room. When she opened it, all she could see were sacks of potatoes and shelves stacked high with tins.

'Where's the door...? Please...'

'You okay?' the girl asked with a strong accent. She was rubbing her hands on a tea towel tucked into one pocket of her jeans, staring at Millie suspiciously.

'I just need to get out.'

The girl came towards her, wearing a perfume of fried food. 'Man?' she said, nodding, pulling her plump red lips into an upside-down smile.

Millie sighed deeply, 'Let me out... Please.'

The girl pointed to a heavy plastic curtain, the type Richardson's butcher's shop had when she was a child. Millie tried to smile at the girl, who simply crossed her fingers on both hands.

Once outside, she gulped air manically and let the coolness settle her cheeks. She pulled out her ponytail and shook her hair free. The moon was full and it added an inky greyness to the sky above.

As she ran down the hill from the pub, she passed the Spar, and a fresh spike of rage came into her. She stopped in front of the large window and had a sudden urge to break it; that would show Cathal Quinn.

She searched for a stone, but then saw the red hair of a woman serving and suddenly felt spiteful and childish. She walked on, all the time pulling her pashmina around herself for heat.

As she crossed the road towards the dunes, she didn't know where to go. She couldn't go back to Finn's cottage; that man owned it. She swore in frustration, deciding her only safe space was back at Ardmara.

Over the last two weeks, she had all but moved in with Finn, only going back to her cottage for clothes and to check on the leaky roof. Without the fire lit or the candles burning, it was cold and damp. Jamie was right to sell it.

Walking as fast as she could, she went over again in her head what had just happened in the pub.

The wind had picked up and it was now helping carry her from behind. As she reached the edge of the beach, she heard a noise. She turned back, sure her name was being shouted. In the darkness she could just make out a figure. The big frame was unmistakable. It was Finn.

For a second she thought about running to him, throwing her arms around his neck, asking him why he had said those words to Cathal. But her anger kept her moving – the stamp of her feet throwing up sand behind her. Her fists were tight and she could feel her nails digging hard into her palms. Another shout made her turn again. Finn was close.

Waiting by the steps of Ardmara, Millie could just make out the white surf of the waves crashing hard on the sand. The wind now seemed to be coming off the water and was whipping her hair all around her face. She dropped her head as Finn approached.

'Hey, why did you leave?' asked Finn, pulling his jumper off and wrapping it around her shoulders. 'You're foundered.'

'What?'

'Why didn't you say you were leaving?'

Smudges of cloud had darkened the moon and Millie could now only see the outline of Finn's features. But she knew his eyes were on her, waiting, wanting an answer.

'Why would I want to stay and listen…' she tried to control her voice, 'to that crap?'

'What? Cathal?' A small, forced laugh escaped from Finn's mouth. 'He's just an old man living in the past. It's nothing.'

'Nothing? You were almost fighting, Finn. For God's sake. Anyway…' said Millie, pulling strands of hair away from the corners of her mouth. 'What the hell were you talking about… *too much dying for Ireland*? I mean, why would you say that?'

The noise from the waves was now loud in her ears and the wind was trying to push her across the sand. She stood firm, determined to stay until she got answers.

'Jesus, Millie. What is this?' Finn looked away from her. Then turning back, he went on. 'Why are you so obsessed with him? Just leave it, will you?' He was angry with her. It was the first time.

'Finn. Listen. I'm just going to say this, okay?'

'What?' Finn was straining to hear her. 'What? Say what?'

'Well… my father was… I mean…' Millie stumbled over the enormity of what she had to reveal. 'Well… it's just that… we're Protestants, Finn. I'm a Protestant. From Dungrillen.' Millie's shoulders shrunk as her courage deserted her.

'What?' said Finn, now also shouting to be heard, 'You're a Protestant? From Dungrillen?'

'Yes. Yes. That's right.'

'Why did you lie?'

'I didn't. You just assumed. Assumed I was like you. Catholic.'

'What? I can't hear you.'

'It just never came up. I did try—'

'I don't understand,' said Finn, running his fingers through his hair.

The clouds had moved on again and it was a little brighter. Bewildered, he brought her face close to his. 'Look… it doesn't matter what the hell you are… or where you are from. Who cares, for God's sake? That's all over now…'

In the darkness Millie could feel his yeasty breath heavy on her skin.

'Not according to everyone apparently.' She shrugged his hands away and turned towards Ardmara. She was not going to spend the night with Finn. Not in that cottage.

He came up beside her and took her by the shoulders, turning her around. 'Millie. I'm sorry. I didn't know. That's all.' He tried to hold her face in his hands, but she kept pulling it away. The wind was so strong now, there was a rushing noise inside her ears.

'Millie, please.'

This time, Millie let him pull her into him. His body felt warm and his arms were strong.

'Jesus, Millie. It's nothing. Nothing, do you hear?' Finn was trying to laugh.

Millie pulled back from him. 'I don't know what it is about that man. I really don't. But he's horrible. Disgusting. I don't want anything to do with him.' Then she added, 'And I don't want you to either.'

'What do you mean?'

'Well …' Millie's mind was racing. 'Well… I think you should move out. Not rent from him.' She stopped, unsure if she should go on. 'Listen, he's a real Republican. Jesus, Finn. I can't believe we're having this conversation.' She closed her eyes again and lifted her face up into the wind, moving her feet further apart to keep herself balanced. She scraped her hair back from her face and pulled Finn's sweater tight about her neck.

Finn took hold of her, more gently this time. 'Let's get back,' he whispered close to her ear, letting his head rest on hers.

'I'm not going back there,' she said, defiantly. 'I'm staying here.'

'No, you're not. You said yourself, it's cold and damp. You're coming back with me.'

They didn't speak until they were inside his cottage.

'I'm going to bed.'

'It was only a song,' said Finn, kissing her forehead gently.

Millie's body sagged and she closed her eyes, thinking it was so much more than that.

She woke up to a noise, probably a tanker far out to sea. The room was dark, with only a crack of light seeping under the door. Finn's side of the bed was empty and when she found her phone she saw it was just after four.

Her mouth was dry and sour, and her head ached. She'd drunk so much wine she needed water. As she got up, she started to remember what had happened in the pub and her face creased with irritation.

When she opened the bedroom door, she could see Finn sitting in his chair by the fire. The only light in the room was from the small flames he was stoking rhythmically with a poker. A half-empty bottle of whiskey sat on the shelf he used as a desk.

She was about to turn away, tiptoe to the bathroom, when he spoke.

'Stay,' he said, without looking at her.

Millie silently went to him and, like a small child, clambered up into his lap, resting her head gently on his shoulder, pulling her legs up to rest on his thigh. He wrapped one arm around her tightly and with the other he gently smoothed out her hair.

Millie now wanted to tell Finn why she was so upset. She wanted to talk to him about her father, share everything that had happened.

But something was stopping her. She could smell the whiskey on his breath and heeded her mother's advice about never talking to a man with drink taken.

'I love you,' he said, breathing deeply into her hair.

'I love you too,' said Millie, emptying her mind of everything.

Chapter 19

Millie's stomach ached and her neck hurt when she moved. She hadn't nursed a hangover like this in years.

Leaving Finn to sleep, she tiptoed into the bathroom. She needed time to think about the night before. She had no choice now. She had to talk to Finn, tell him how her father died. He had said it didn't matter she was a Protestant. But he was surprised. No doubt about it. Sinking deep into her morning bath, careful not to let the water spill out over the edge, she decided that was completely normal. She would have felt the same – if it had been the other way around.

As she washed her face, shards from the night before kept crashing through her head. The music, the boy with the scorched face, Cathal's song, and then Finn's outburst.

A barking dog made her sit up. She recognised the angry, urgent sound. It was his dog. Cathal was here. She jumped out of the bath, forcing water to slop over the edge, spilling onto the tiles. She quietly checked the door was locked, even though she knew it was. Naked and shivering, the tiles cold under her feet, she could hear herself breathing. Drips of bathwater puddled around her. She wanted to dress, go out and confront Cathal – but about what? A song? She'd come over deranged. Grabbing a towel from the rail, she sat on the toilet, imagining herself shouting into Cathal's ruddy face, telling him her father was murdered by the type of men he sang about. As she pulled a second small towel around her neck for warmth, she thought about Cathal's leering smile. No. She wouldn't go out.

Back at the door, she was sure voices were being raised, but between the birds cawing past the open window and the sea crashing on the rocks below, she still couldn't make out what was being said. Then a door slammed. More barking. But this soon trailed off, fading into the distance. She sat back down, now shivering from the damp towels. Staring at the floor, she watched small pools of bathwater join up on the tiles, making soft, cloud-like shapes.

She didn't want to confront Finn, but she was sure there was a connection between him and Cathal, and she had to know what it was.

'Why did he come?' asked Millie, making tea in the kitchen.

'He was drunk.'

'Still?'

She was wearing one of Finn's thick fisherman's sweaters she had found behind the door in the bathroom and the heat of the fire was making her cheeks glow.

'But want did he want?' She handed him a mug of tea.

'He was talking about Ashmal and the lads. Said they were getting paid now and have their passports. Wants me to stop asking questions.'

'I thought I heard raised voices?'

'Don't think so.' Finn's voice was calm, practised.

He was lying. She knew it.

She studied his eyes and the deep, dark circles which had appeared underneath. There was a faint smell of stale whiskey all around him. He seemed tense.

'Has he been involved?' Millie surprised herself with her words.

'Involved? What do you mean?' Finn busied himself with his post.

'You know... involved... Is that why you said to him about too many people dying for Ireland?'

Finn stared at a particular letter. It had been lying on the table and then the shelf by the fire for a week now. It was stiff and white with loopy, scrolled handwriting on it. Like a wedding invitation.

Finn studied the envelope hard. 'I'm not sure. I think he might have been years ago.'

Millie wanted more than anything for Finn to turn round, look her in the eye. But he didn't.

Still avoiding her gaze, he shuffled the post to make one neat square, throwing some opened envelopes and flyers to the side. Then turning to her, he flashed a smile. 'Now that's a bit more Protestant-looking.'

Millie laughed, happy for the light he had let into the room.

He moved towards her, his head tilted. 'That sweater suits you,' he said, pulling her forward.

On Sunday, Millie arrived at Ashmal's cottage just after six as he suggested. He would be alone, cooking. They wouldn't be disturbed. The wind which had blown through the village for the last two days had moved on round the headland and it again felt warm in the early evening sun.

A washing line made out of orange fishing rope had been tied from the corner of the roof guttering to a big branch on an old oak tree at the front of the cottage. The array of underwear, sweaters and socks hanging on the line reminded Millie of the cover of a book her father had given her as a child.

The front door was open and Arabic music was filling the space. The radio she and Finn had bought was on the counter. As she stepped inside, she saw all the lights were on and the smell she anticipated had gone, replaced with a rich aroma, reminding her immediately of a souk she had visited with Dom.

She knocked the door. 'Hello, anyone home?'

Ashmal came out of the back room, sharing his big, eager smile. A tea towel was tucked into the waist of his sweatpants, chef-style, and he was still wearing his Arsenal hat.

'My turn cook,' he said, throwing his arm out towards the camping hob. The cut on his lip had all but disappeared and the dark bruising around his eyes had faded into his dark skin. 'English good, no?'

Millie wanted to go to him. Put her arms around him.

'Very good. Yes.'

'I make friend Spar. She helping me English good.'

Millie flinched at the mention of Cathal's shop but managed to stretch her lips into a smile. 'Smells good.'

'From me country. Smelling coriander, yes?'

As Ashmal dished out two bowls of lamb and white bean stew, Millie found she had little appetite. She had left it in the pub on Friday night.

With the confidence of a waiter, Ashmal ushered Millie outside. They sat in a sunny spot by the door, on two white plastic chairs he produced from around the corner of the house.

'I buy chair. With me money. We sit.'

He was wearing sweatpants and thick walking socks, and his feet were stuffed into plastic sliders that were too small for him. The arm sling had gone, as had the bandage on his cut hand.

Millie forced herself to eat and, as she did so, discovered the taste was delicate and fresh. Afterwards, Ashmal brought out tea. The fresh mint leaves got stuck in the spout as he poured, and they laughed as he attempted to pull the stalks out through the hole. Without asking, he sweetened each cup with two sugar lumps.

They spoke little, Ashmal appearing to enjoy the company without the effort of translation.

Millie finally broke the mood. 'Ashmal. There's something I want to talk to you about.'

By the time Millie left the cottage, the sun had all but gone. As she drove down the winding lanes into the village, she couldn't tell where the grey sky ended and the sea began. A dull mist was spreading onto the empty beaches. The bank holiday weekend was nearly over and many had packed up and gone home.

Millie felt as empty as the roads around her.

The cottage was in darkness and she thought no one was in, but when she opened the door, she saw Finn kneeling in the light of the fire. She turned on a side lamp and saw he had spread out paintings, many of which she'd never seen before, over the floor.

'Where are these from?'

'Everywhere. I keep a lot in the outhouse across the way,' he said, not looking up. 'Most of them will sell over the summer,' he went on, waving his hand casually over the floor. He pointed to a few larger canvases propped up against the table. 'I'll not sell these, mind.'

Millie went to the pile and her eyes settled on one picture in particular. It was full of colour and light. Different from the others.

'Where is that?'

Finn followed her gaze. 'Mullaghmore. From a boat in the harbour.'

Millie leaned over and gently touched the canvas. 'Ashmal told me his story.'

'God. Sorry. I should have asked,' said Finn, standing up, giving her his full attention.

'Was it what you thought?'

'Pretty much.'

He went to her, but she moved away; she didn't want to be comforted.

'His wife and twins died in a hospital in Aleppo. It was bombed when she was giving birth. They were all there. He only survived because he went to try and find a doctor.'

'Jesus. Did he tell you all this?'

Millie nodded. 'We used the phone a bit, but his English is much better. There's a woman in the village helping him.'

Millie started pulling off bits of imaginary fluff from her sweater, all the time biting her lip. But it was no good. The tears she didn't want Ashmal to see began to fall down her face. Again, Finn outstretched his arms, but she pushed him away. 'Don't,' she said, walking towards the kitchen. 'I just don't know how this can happen. Not in this day and age. We all knew what was going on – why didn't we do something about it?' Blowing her nose on a piece of kitchen roll, she went on. 'It's just not fair.'

'You're right, it's not fair, Millie. But life isn't. Is it?' Finn walked away from her, dragging his seat close to the fire. 'Ashmal lived. His family didn't. He has no choice but to go on.' Finn's words were flat. He didn't expect a reply.

Millie thought about the choice she made, the one in the clinic – and her shoulders dropped. Watching Finn stoke the fire, in a world of his own, she knew he was right. Sometimes people, living different lives, do what they do because they have no option.

With new flames in the grate, Finn reached over and lifted a picture. A small pastel that had been leaning against the wall. 'I can't believe I actually painted this,' he said, breaking the canvas in two with his knee, throwing it roughly into the fire.

As the canvas burned, flames threw shadows over Finn's face. A darker mood had appeared in the cottage and this time it had settled over both of them.

'Listen, I've spoken to Cathal,' he said, turning. 'Told him I'm finding somewhere else. You were right. I should have done it a long time ago.'

'How was the old bastard anyway?' said Millie, sniffing, trying to make things better.

'He's been drunk for a week. He'll go to the nuns soon. Come back sober.'

Millie managed a smile, even though she was full of sadness. 'Finn, listen, there's something I want to talk to you about.'

He walked towards her, his shadow dancing all over the cottage walls.

'It's about my family. My father.'

Rubbing smudges of mascara away from under Millie's eyes with his thumb, he put on his pub voice. 'Don't tell me. He was pure orange and hated all Taigs.' He was teasing her. He could do that now. So sure he knew who she was, where she came from.

'Don't be silly,' she said. 'Dad hated all that. He really did.' Then speaking more quietly, she added, 'He was a good man. Everybody loved him.'

'God, sorry.' Finn pulled her close. 'Jesus, I'm a complete eejit tonight. Go on, tell me.'

'Well… it's… it's… something that happened when I was young.'

'When you were young? Did someone hurt you, Millie?'

'Yes. But not in that sort of way…'

'What then?' Finn was staring at her, his jaw hard. Millie suddenly felt a little frightened.

'Listen, I'm… I'm… sorry. I'm just being silly. I'm tired. It's Ashmal. I just need to sleep.'

'If I thought anyone had hurt you. Jesus, I don't know what I'd do.'

Millie heaved herself straight. 'Aw… My prince has come… and yes, by the way, you are a big eejit – the biggest in all Ireland,' she said, straining to laugh.

'Well, if you won't talk. I will,' he said. 'I've news.'

He went to the shelf by the fire and lifted the stiff white envelope from the shelf.

'Someone in Dublin wants to exhibit my work. They've a gallery in London, too.'

'That's fantastic.' Millie felt a flush of relief run through her body at the shift in the conversation.

'They want to see me in Dublin,' he said, then, pausing, went on. 'I wasn't bothered at first. Then, I don't know, I thought, why not?'

'Not bothered? Are you mad?' She reached out for his hands. 'When will you go?'

'I called them. I'm meant to be seeing them tomorrow. But I could always change it.'

'Called them, did you? You must be keen.'

'Will you come? We could stay at the hotel on the green. You know. The big one with the bar.'

'No. No. You go. I want to start writing up Ashmal's story – it's all I can think about.'

'A wee break might help you.' Finn tilted his head.

'No, it's better I stay.'

Finn went to her, pulling her close. 'Ashmal will be alright, Millie. I promise you that. He and the lads will get to Europe, like they want. The boats will get them there.'

Millie didn't say anything. Too consumed with Ashmal's past to even think about his future.

Chapter 20

They had ended up sleeping on the sofa in front of the fire.

Millie had dreamt about being a child. She was on the beach in front of Ardmara with her father. They were throwing a ball to Patch, just in front of the Lookout. But the dog had disappeared and then her mother had called them in for tea and they'd left without finding him.

She had tried to tell Finn about her dream and how uneasy it made her feel, but he was busy getting annoyed with his mobile, trying to work out what his own number was.

'Give it here,' said Millie, shaking her head, taking hold of the old Nokia. 'This will be an antique soon, if you're lucky.'

After finding his number, she wrote it and her own on a scrap of paper she tore from an art pad lying on the sofa.

'That's the one,' he said, tucking the scrap inside his wallet.

She then put her number into his empty contacts and, after pausing, added her flat details: '*Flat 1, 131 Albert Bridge Road, London SW11*'. Reading her old address, she felt unnerved. The thought of living somewhere else, away from Finn, was now unimaginable.

Watching him study his phone, Millie knew this was her future. She was sure of it.

She leaned forward and placed her hand on his cheek and, tilting his head, Finn lifted her fingers and kissed them gently. Patting his pockets, he then muttered something about keys.

Finn was anxious, she could tell. He rarely left the village and maybe, like her, he had become accustomed to their isolation. She didn't ask him where he was staying in the city, and he hadn't said. He had a studio; maybe he'd sleep there. He'd have friends in Dublin, she was sure of that. As she watched him pat his pockets again, her brow crinkled with thoughts of him going out in the city without her.

Millie arrived at Ardmara just after eight. The smell of damp made her feel queasy and after opening all the windows, the place was Baltic. She briefly toyed with the idea of going back to the comfort of Finn's, but then thought about Cathal and instead went about her ritual of lighting candles and turning on the immersion heater for a bath.

Wanting company, she went to the record player. Crouching on her hunkers, she flicked through the various albums, stopping at any familiar cover. She came across the *Best of Van Morrison* and immediately had a strong sense of her father bounding through the door, smiling broadly, the LP tucked under his arm.

Millie's eyes moved to the door, half expecting to see him. When he wasn't there, she stared back at the record and fragments of a warm weekend came to her. She read the date on the back of the album: *1993*. One year before he was killed.

It must have been summer, because Uncle Joe was there, and they only ever had guests in summer. A jeweller by day and a frustrated magician by night, he was Millie's favourite. She touched her ear – remembering how he had pulled a shiny coin from behind it when they were on the beach one day.

Walking to the window, she looked over the empty strand. For a moment, she could almost see him dancing there, a big straw hat on his head and a paisley handkerchief around his neck. Her father had always called him a '*natty dresser*'.

Uncle Joe died the year after Dad. A drunk driver knocked him over as he crossed St Stephen's Green in Dublin. She wondered if it was true what her mother had said, that he had been buried with his magic set inside his coffin.

She went into the kitchen and opened the cupboard under the sink. She was hunting for a big pot, the type dinner ladies use. Her mother had one she used for stews when the house was full, and Millie clearly remembered it being out that weekend.

Poking around in the darkness of the cupboard, her fingers sticky with grease, she found it. It was grimy and full of dust, so Millie boiled a kettle and washed it out. She wanted her mother to have it, before the cottage was sold.

Millie lay in the bath, the thin curtains pulled against the harsh grey light of the morning. Candles flickered all around her and as she listened to 'Brown Eyed Girl', she again imagined her mother and father dancing in the living room, sofas pushed back.

Just as Millie felt herself drifting into sleep, the record stuck. When it didn't move on, she got up, running through the cottage naked, dripping water everywhere. She felt cold and a little lonely and now regretted not going to Dublin.

Back in the heat of the water, she got annoyed with herself for yet again not telling Finn about her father. She should just have forced it out, and in turn he would have sympathised, saying how awful it must have been for her. Then, he'd have gone on to Dublin and when he came back it would all have been okay.

She dropped her shoulders beneath the waterline.

She promised herself she'd tell him the next day, on his return.

As the record started to play again, Millie wondered if her father was already a marked man when he bought the Van Morrison album. Had '*those boys*', as her mother called his murderers, already decided they were going to kill him?

Millie's mind was full of questions she hadn't asked herself for years. What was the exact date, the day of the week her father's killers decided his fate? Where did they meet to talk about it? Someone's kitchen? A car park in town? Why did they decide to shoot him rather than hide a bomb under his car, like they had with George Sharpe and so many of his friends?

From nowhere, Mrs McKillen's description of her father's friend hanging out of his car window like a burning candle once again slipped into her mind and she closed her eyes.

Millie knew it was time to talk to her mother about Finn.

Convinced she would like his big, easy presence, she imagined him standing by the Aga in Dungrillen, telling one of his stories, rubbing his hands together as he finished, just the way her father used to do. Her mother would like that. She'd say he was an artist, a successful one, with a big house in Canada. Her mother would like that even more.

She wouldn't need to say he was a Catholic. His name and looks would do that for her.

As she wrapped her toes around the taps of the bath, careful to avoid any boiling drips, she thought about Eimear, her sister-in-law. She was a Catholic and the family all liked her. Well, everyone except Karen.

Hours after the shooting, Eimear had arrived at the house. She'd stayed for those first terrible days, making endless pots of tea and sandwiches for half the country, who trooped through the door, telling her mother how sorry they were. '*A saint*,' was how her mother described her back then.

Laying a hot face cloth over her cheeks, she thought about the Irish-language class Eimear had signed up too. Was it just to be part of this '*New Belfast*' her sister had ranted about? Or was it something more tribal? Millie wondered how it was for Eimear. Living in a family from the *other* side, never quite belonging. No doubt suffering years of innuendo and little jibes the others might think funny. No, it can't be easy for her.

A picture of Karen's face elbowed into her head. Christ. She didn't need to question what her sister would think of Finn. Within days she'd have made it her business to know everything about him. She'd know someone in the village who knew him. It was the way she worked. And what she didn't know, she'd make up. Millie pulled off the face cloth, wiping away the drips of itchy sweat tickling her temple.

Stepping out of the bath she felt weary.

She knew the best way to take her mind off everything was work. She'd start to write up her story on Ashmal, like a real journalist.

Gathering her notes, she realised she'd left her iPad charging at Finn's. She didn't want to go back to the cottage, but she had no choice.

It didn't take long to get there, and she found the key under the pot with no trouble. It was attached to a leprechaun keyring and Millie smiled as she clutched it in her hand.

It was strange being there without Finn and she immediately noticed things she hadn't before. The strong smell of turf from the dead fire, a dripping tap in the kitchen, and, as she entered the bedroom, the unmistakable smell of Finn.

A photograph on the far wall caught her eye. It was of Finn's brothers on a boat. They had their arms around each other and were smiling broadly. A huge fish of some type in their arms.

When Millie studied the picture closely, she saw the family resemblance. Both brothers had the same dark hair as Finn, but their skin was golden from the sun. They were as tall as their little brother but carried more weight. Both were wearing polo shirts – like the golfers in the pub. They looked happy.

She lifted her laptop off the shelf by the fire and was surprised to see the stiff white envelope with loopy writing lying on the side. She wondered if Finn had forgotten to take it to Dublin. When she touched it, she saw the postcard was still inside, the gallery name and address formally embossed along the top.

Scanning the note quickly, Millie recognised a name. *Purdy Perrili.* Finn's old art teacher. The one with the wrap dresses. Millie smiled as she read through the first paragraph: '*...running exhibition of rising Irish artists... saw some of his earlier work... keen to talk to him. Got his address from Purdy Perrili.*'

So Finn was still in contact with the teacher he had lusted after in his youth. Again, Millie smiled, liking the fact she was still discovering secrets about him. It excited her.

Chapter 21

Millie walked to the village. She knew she would never go back to the hotel. Not after the pub, the song. She headed to the cafe, hoping their wi-fi worked.

The start of summer had brought life to Ballydunn. It was just before ten, but many of the shops in Main Street were already busy. Passing O'Neils, she saw the old man from before tethering more animal water floats and a few bodyboards to a table outside; a girl in dungarees with lilac hair was admiring them.

As she opened the door of the cafe, an old-fashioned bell tinkled loudly. This new attraction made her start and a few customers stopped talking and glanced up. Millie raised her eyebrows, trying to make a joke of it.

To secure her favourite spot by the window, she had to squeeze past a large table of golfers. They sounded American and were laughing and joking loudly. One kept slapping the back of the man next to him and another was standing, taking pictures of the group on his phone. Most of them were eating breakfast served in what she thought were old mess tins.

There were a few other customers in the cafe including two men sitting at the far corner table. They were wearing fleeces and bright yellow waterproof trousers, just like Ashmal's. Their skin was a warm deep brown and Millie wondered if they lived up at the cottage – or were they new arrivals to the village. She wanted them to look over so she could smile, but they were hunkered over their food, oblivious to the rest of the cafe.

A striking girl with a shaved head served her. She had a big ring in her ear Millie could see straight through. Her accent was very similar to the girl working in the pub kitchen, the one who helped her after the song.

She ordered a cappuccino and a coconut energy ball.

Waiting for the internet to connect, she put on her noise-free earphones, ready to transcribe Ashmal's interview. She found her notebook, a present from Dom, and as she stroked the luxurious leather she promised herself she'd contact him. She was ready to do that.

Millie opened the file of photographs she had taken of the fishermen at the harbour and around the coast, but then, glimpsing the men in the corner, felt uncomfortable and cleared her screen. After fiddling with her earphones to make them fit, a familiar silence encased her and she relaxed.

Listening to Ashmal's voice, she was amazed how calm he was. When he couldn't express himself in English, he had pulled his plastic garden seat close to hers and they had huddled over her phone using the translation app like before. When she read the words '*all dead*', Millie had felt sick but tried not to show it.

Sipping on her cappuccino, she was vaguely aware of the front door opening. Her eyes widened as she watched Cathal stride across the floor, heading straight to the fishermen in the corner. He was leaning down, talking quietly, all the time jabbing his thumb towards the harbour. His face was still on fire and small veins were pumping on the side of his temple.

Both men at the table were nodding furiously and after a second or two stood up, scraping their chairs back on the hard floor. As they rushed out of the cafe, Cathal turned and caught Millie's eye. She shut her laptop quickly and just as he appeared to walk her way, the shaven-headed waitress tapped his shoulder.

Millie's mind raced. Should she scramble her things together and leave? Or should she stand her ground? She decided to stay. Why should she run from this sad little bigot? If he dared come over, she'd be ready for him.

She took a sip of water. Then another. Pressing her wet palms down on her lap, holding them there tightly, she now wanted him to come to her. But instead, he followed the girl to the counter where she leaned over and lifted a brown envelope from under the till.

With a face full of defiance, she waited.

But her anticipation was blunted as she watched him head for the door, only looking over briefly, giving her a soldier's salute with the bulging envelope. Millie returned the best poker face she could muster.

Through the window, she watched him walk down the harbour, his hands stuffed deep in his pockets, the collar of his jacket turned upwards. He was chatting, more calmly now, to the men he had ordered out of the cafe, all the time pointing out to sea.

She wanted to believe Finn's words about Cathal Quinn: '*He's just an old man… living in the past*'. But his presence caused her such disquiet; she felt there had to be more to his story.

Too unsettled to write, she saved her files and went online.

With her fingers hovering, she wasn't sure what to type – so she started with his name. Cathal Quinn, she soon discovered, was a popular search, throwing up pages of entries. There was a Cathal Quinn who was a hurling champion from Louth. Another one was a student at Yale University who had set up an Irish group, and dozens of others with Facebook entries and Twitter feeds. Shifting her shoulders, she added Ballydunn to his name. Again, a number of entries popped up, but this time they were all about the same Cathal Quinn.

She knew she had found him.

The first story she read was from the *Irish Times*, dated 2009. It was a feature commemorating the thirty-year anniversary of the murder of Lord Mountbatten in Mullaghmore harbour. The feature said a Cathal Quinn from Ballydunn had been arrested in connection with the murder in 1979 but was released due to lack of evidence. There were two grainy pictures accompanying the feature. One was of the boat remains being hauled out of the water by a small crane. The other, a picture of a young man, mid-twenties, maybe, with a thick beard, being taken into a Garda station in handcuffs. The smile was unmistakable.

Millie was breathing heavily and her jaw felt locked. Her eyes darted around the cafe. Surely the golfers would sense something was wrong. But she was amazed to see them continuing to laugh and joke. Some were now standing, taking selfies with the shaven-headed waitress.

No one noticed the screaming inside her head.

She clicked on the second entry. Another story about his involvement in the Mountbatten murder.

A familiar metallic taste was rising, and she felt her body tense. Flexing and then spreading her fingers out like a starfish, she sat back in her chair.

She was hot and as she opened the window, a gust of wind blew in and knocked over a small vase holding daisies. As she grabbed her laptop and phone off the table, she could see the waitress staring over. Closing the window quickly, she glimpsed Cathal drive off down Main Street. His dog, standing in the back of the pick-up, barking as usual.

Falling into work mode, she methodically read through pages of entries about Cathal Quinn from Ballydunn. Jotting down notes, she didn't lift her head from her task for over an hour.

A lot of the press stories focused on his connection with the Mountbatten murder. He was always a main suspect but never formally charged.

He got away with it.

Just like the men in Mulloy.

There were other stories, too. His arrest and imprisonment in the early nineties for his involvement in the attempted murder of two off-duty UDR soldiers just far over the border in Strabane. When Millie read this, she had to force herself to look away from the screen.

The most up-to-date entry she could find was in *The Guardian* – he'd made a speech at a New IRA meeting in Dublin, a few years earlier. He had said he and the other men on stage were not members of the organisation (because that would be illegal) *but* they fully supported their goal of a united Ireland by whatever means necessary. There was a picture of him shaking hands with a man in a balaclava. The quote under his picture read, '*It is better to die on your feet than live on your knees*'.

Millie closed her laptop slowly. She was now the only person in the cafe, apart from the waitress, who was busy pouring milk into tiny miniature milk churns for the tables.

'That man that came in earlier. Do you know him?' she asked, trying to sound disinterested, admiring the tray bakes on the counter.

'Sorry?'

'The man you were talking to. Is he the owner?'

The girl shrugged. 'Maybe.' Then, narrowing her eyes, she went on. 'He collect rent. Every week. He smells.'

Millie nodded.

'Why you ask?' the waitress asked, leaning in towards Millie, as if party to a conspiracy.

'Just thought I recognised him. That's all.'

When she got outside, the cold wind pushed into her, and she felt a physical release. She pulled the hood of her parka up over her head and moved quickly along Main Street, longing for the emptiness of the beach.

Walking, then running towards Ardmara, her mind turned in circles. All the time, coming back to the same thought... *she had been sleeping in this man's house.*

When she got into the cottage, she stood with her back against the door.

Surveying the living room she saw everything differently now. She thought how dirty and ugly the sofas were, how sad the empty fire appeared, how tatty and grey the curtains were. In the kitchen, she noticed the washed-out pot she was going to bring home to her mother. And she suddenly hated it all. It reeked of decay.

The Van Morrison album was lying on the ground and she thought about her father rotting in a grave in Dungrillen. His skin long eaten away, his skeleton riddled with bullet holes, slowly crumbling to dust.

The smell of damp was choking and the noise of the sea outside was intense. Moving slowly to the chair by the window, she curled her legs up to her chest and thought about the village behind her. Her father had loved it here. She hated it now. The people were seeped in sectarianism. The pub with its fiddly-dee pretence was a sham. The old Allicadoos singing along with Cathal that night would surely revel in her father's murder. She closed her eyes tight and pulled her hood over her head.

When she woke, she ached all over.

The beach was empty and the Lookout was being splashed with elephant funnels of sea spray. The sky was blue. It was a beautiful day.

Still curled up in a tight ball, she wanted to talk to Finn – tell him what she had found out. But then she sat bolt upright. She didn't need to tell him, did she?

He already knew.

Millie grabbed her phone; she had to speak to him. She had to know. But she had given him her number, not taken his. In anger, she threw the phone down on the floor, watching it clatter across the room.

A seabird pecked violently on the window and as she swung round in the chair an image of Cathal's grimacing smile filled her mind. She pushed her head back into the seat. She didn't want to think about him. Or Finn. Not even her father. She didn't want to remember the clinic or her dead baby or Dom and the drugs.

She didn't want to think at all.

After a shower, she changed clothes and made herself put on some make-up. If she acted normal, she would feel normal. The therapist liked telling her that.

Sitting at her mother's old dressing table, she knew she had to leave this place. There were too many ghosts in the walls. Just like her mother had said.

She packed quickly, then emptied the fridge, deciding to take the two bottles of wine she had bought in Letterkenny with her. She turned off the heating and hot water at the mains, closed all the windows as best she could, and after checking she had her computer and chargers, she left Ardmara for the last time.

She drove down the lane at speed, feeling every pothole as she went. Pulling up at Mrs McClarnan's house, and with the engine running, she jumped out and quietly pushed the keys of the cottage through her letter box.

Back in the car, she paused, not sure where to go next. Deciding to turn right towards Letterkenny and the north, she saw the small tourist sign for the Atlantic Drive. She swerved quickly and soon she was rising high, up over Black Mountain.

Still driving at speed, she passed the entrance to the lane where Ashmal lived, and a twinge of guilt pulled at her. A sign for Mullaghmore appeared and she was certain she was on the same road Finn had taken her that day on his bike.

She tried not to think about how happy she had been then.

When she got to the village, she pulled into a car-parking space close to the water. It was lunchtime and the harbour was busy. A fishing boat was hoisted out of the water, being painted by two men. Some walkers with backpacks were dangling their legs over the pier; their shoes were off and they were eating takeaway fish and chips.

In the harbour mouth, the water was calm. The sky was still empty of cloud and the sun was beating through the car window. She lifted her face into the heat and leaned back on her headrest. A glint to the right caught her attention and, squinting, she glimpsed a small plaque attached to the harbour wall, just beside the steps. Drawn by its glare, she got out of the car. Shading her eyes with her hand, she read the inscription.

In memory of all those who lost their lives here on 27th August, 1979
Taken too soon

The plaque then listed all those who had died that day and their ages. Millie now remembered the children. Nicholas, a grandson of the royals, and a local boy, Paul Maxwell, who had been out fishing with the party.

Feeling her chest tighten, she looked away. When she saw the Harbour Hotel behind her, she knew what to do next.

She asked for a room facing the front. The girl who had smiled at Finn and glared at her when they had lunch there was nowhere to be seen. Another not-so-pretty teenager showed her to Room 1 on the first floor. It was right in the middle of the building, centred over the small harbour.

The room was simply decorated with heavy patterned curtains and matching pelmet. The bed was old-fashioned and made up with sheets and a wool blanket. Just like home. A pretty patterned eiderdown lay folded at the bottom of the bed.

There was a small en suite to the back of the room, housing a tiny, plastic bath. Millie ordered a prawn open sandwich from reception, telling them to leave it outside her door. Then she called again and asked them to add a large glass of ice and a bottle of sparkling water.

She opened one of the screw-top bottles of wine she had brought and carried it into the bathroom. As she ran a bath, she poured herself a glass of wine, using the small water glass from the sink. She drained the glass, then poured herself another.

She locked the bathroom door and turned off the light. Lying in the water, her knees nearly up to her chest, she thought of all the baths she had enjoyed around the world. At that moment, none of them compared to the warmth and sanctuary she was embracing right now.

Chapter 22

Millie woke with a jolt. Men were shouting outside. She jumped off the bed and rushed to the window, adrenaline flooding her system.

She was still in the robe she had put on after her bath and her face was flushed from the heat of the room. She stood to the side of the window, peeking around the curtain like a nosy neighbour. She relaxed when she saw the men had pints in their hands. They'd left the downstairs bar to have a cigarette and were milling around outside the hotel entrance.

The old-fashioned radio alarm on the bedside table told her she'd been asleep for over three hours. It was still light outside, but the sun had left the sky and a grey rain mist was beginning to cling to the sea.

The water was choppier now and a wind was gathering. The small boats inside the harbour wall were tugging against their ropes and orange buoys were disappearing in and out of water swells. It felt more like winter than early summer.

Millie's head was pounding and her mouth felt dry. In the bathroom, the empty bottle of wine was upside down in the rose-patterned bin. She went to the sink and threw cold water over her face. She caught her reflection in the mirror and saw her eyes were swollen. The wine had left a spider's web of angry veins on her cheeks and her hair was matted from being slept on wet.

Listening to her stomach rumble, she remembered her room service order from earlier. Opening the door an inch, the tray of food was still there and she stuck out a hand to pull it in quickly. Devouring the sandwich, she only stopped briefly, to worry about how long the prawns had been sitting in the heat of the hotel corridor.

Hot under her robe, she tried to turn the radiator down, but the thermostat had been painted over and was stuck on high. She clambered back up onto the bed and put two pillows behind her head, drinking the sparkling water quickly, straight from the bottle.

She scrambled for her phone. Missed calls from Sasha and her mother and a text from Finn.

'*All went well. I love you.*

'*See you tomorrow. Finn x*'

Millie smiled when she saw he had written his name on the text, but then she thought about his cottage and Cathal and her stomach ached.

Now she had his mobile, she could phone him. Ask him exactly how much he knew about his landlord. But just as she retrieved his number, she dropped the phone on the bed and lay back.

She'd wait to see him in person.

Settling down with her laptop, she rested her fingers on the keyboard. Holding her breath, she did what she didn't want to do. She typed in his name.

The wi-fi was slow and at one point she didn't think it would connect. Slowly, an array of entries came up for Finn McFall: two Gaelic footballers, a solicitor, a builder in Letterkenny and an actor from Dublin. She quickly ran through the pages. Nothing. She typed in Ballydunn after his name, then artist. Still nothing.

As much relieved as frustrated, she typed in the only other name she knew had a connection with Finn – Purdy Perrili.

The first entry that appeared for the name included a picture. This Purdy Perrili was attractive. Dark, busty, in her late fifties maybe. Millie enlarged the picture. She was wearing a wrap dress. Millie felt her breath quicken. When she read the accompanying caption, her eyes narrowed: '*Purdy Perrili, Director of Arts, Scottish Prison Service*'.

She clicked on the link. Now on the website for the Scottish prison service, her fingers once again hovered. Finding the search tab, she typed in the name again.

This time, a more formal picture of the same woman came up. Millie's eyes strained. *Click*. Her employment history appeared in a box on the right of the screen.

Using her finger, she carefully traced each line of the CV.

Director of Arts, Scottish Prison Service (2010–Present)
Director of Arts, HMP Barlinnie, Glasgow (2000–2010)
Creative Arts Teacher, Maze, Lisburn (1993–2000)

Millie dropped her finger, confused. How was this woman teaching at both the art college in Belfast and the prison?

She stared at the screen intently, then suddenly snapped the laptop shut. She started to pace the room, letting her mind go through everything. She was sure Finn had said he was at the art college, or had he just said she was his teacher? She was trying to remember, but her head was full of fog. A hangover was creeping over her and she was feeling a panic starting to build.

She sat on the end of the bed. *Think. Think.*

He said he'd just had a big birthday. So he wasn't much over forty. If he had gone to art college it would have been in the mid-nineties. She opened the screen again, checking the dates. Purdy Perrili was definitely teaching in the Maze then.

The second bottle of wine she had brought from the cottage was warm. Using the large glass room service had provided, she filled it up and gulped it down quickly.

Dragging a wicker chair to the window, she flopped into it. It was dark outside now, but there were stars in the sky and a near-full moon lit up the harbour. It was so perfect. Like a stage set. She leaned over and pushed the old-fashioned windows out and secured them. A rush of air hit her face and she closed her eyes, breathing deeply.

She remembered the first time she had heard about The Maze, or Long Kesh, as some people called it. Aunt Lizzie had come to the house for a meal, and she and her mother were watching the news. There was a story about the anniversary of the *Hunger Strikers.*

She could almost hear her mother's voice, low and soft… '*Nothing in life is worth dying for. Their poor mothers.*'

After Dad, when they drove past the prison on their way to Belfast for Christmas shopping or to watch one of the boys play rugby at Ravenhill, her mother always repeated her words.

There had been talk of making it a Peace Centre – but both sides couldn't agree on its purpose.

This made Millie laugh out loud.

The more she drank the better she felt.

She found some music on her phone and put on her earphones. She danced around the room, laughing and singing. After spinning around a few times, she felt dizzy and fell on the bed. As soon as she shut her eyes, everything blurred. Pulling off her earphones, she sat up. Breathing heavily, she grabbed her phone and quickly texted Finn.

'*Something's come up. I'm at the Harbour Hotel.*

'*Come here when you get back.*'

No initial. No kiss.

Sitting in silence, she started to hear noises. The water lapping around the boats in the water; the creaking timbers of their hulls. And there was a soft tinkling. A boat's bell ringing in the wind.

She moved back to the chair by the window and saw the moon's light shining on the water.

She imagined the far harbour wall. The plaque would be plunged under the icy Atlantic by now. Just as those young boys on the Mountbatten boat would have been all those years ago.

She fell back on the bed and closed her eyes, trying to stop more tears. When she knew it was hopeless, she turned her face deep into a pillow to muffle her big, drunken gulps.

***

It was a Friday when her father was shot. He was leaving the house after lunch, on his way back to work. People still did that then. Went home for lunch.

Just as he got into his car, the killers drew up beside him and a man with a long automatic gun leaned out of the passenger window and pumped him with bullets. Well, that's what the people in the car behind told the police. There were ten bullets in his body and more in the car.

The last time she had seen her father alive was a week before.

She had watched him stagger down the pavement, inebriated. The result, she discovered later, of his name and address being found on a local IRA 'list'. An ominous sign of what was to follow.

On that last day, as Millie prayed for no one else to see him, their Presbyterian neighbour, Dr Henley, appeared and helped him up the steps to the house – handing him over to her mother like a sack of potatoes.

A week later it was Dr Henley who tried to save her father's life on the same, now blood-soaked pavement.

Millie was told the news by Ms Dowd of the boarding department. They were standing by her bed in Blue Dorm. The assistant matron, normally so dour, fussed around her, tidying her up, all the time avoiding her eyes. She never said if her father was alive or dead and Millie was too scared to ask.

Standing by the big front door of the dormitory house, with a bag she hadn't packed, Millie had thought about her friend, Stephanie Beggs. Her father had been shot a few months earlier. It was also on a Friday. He had died. Her friend was off school for a week.

When older cousins Millie barely knew came to collect her, she was embarrassed because she couldn't recall one of their names. During the journey there was a palpable silence in the car, but nobody could find the right words to fill it.

When she finally plucked up the courage to ask if her daddy was alive, they said they didn't know. It was only when she got out of the car at Ashbourne, her father's childhood home, and her mother came to her, arms outstretched, she knew.

She'd be off school for a week.

Chapter 23

The village was full of weather. The wind was howling through the harbour mouth making the boats heave in the swell and there was a symphony of noise coming from the tethered fishing boats. Sheets of rain came from nowhere. They fell fast and hard, stopping as quickly as they started. Millie lifted her face, waiting for the next downpour to smack hard against her hot cheeks.

There were few people around and anyone who was out had their waterproof jackets pulled right over their heads. A couple of tourists ventured out from the front of the hotel, then, laughing, ran back in again. They were all wearing plastic ponchos. The type Millie was given at Niagara Falls when she was there with Dom.

Two men in heavy waterproof suits, a different colour from Ashmal's, were lifting lobster pots from a boat and tying them up to a large red bollard close to the far harbour wall.

Millie searched for the Mountbatten plaque again, but the tide was too high.

She walked to the steps leading up to the pier wall and, after pausing, started to climb. As soon as she reached the top, she lost her footing in the wind. She grabbed at the rusty railing that ran the full length of the pier and, leaning forward slightly, held on to the hood of her parka with her other hand.

She was almost hugging the railing as she pushed forward, and every few steps, she used the red anchor bollards to steady herself. As she neared the end, she got soaked by a wave that came from her left, exploding over the top of her.

More invigorated than scared, she took one more step and used the last bollard as a seat, all the time holding on to the railing. Her hood fell away from her head, and she felt the wind whistle past her ears. Sea spray continued to lash around her and she closed her eyes, again lifting her face high into the air. It was cooling, and her mind was finally starting to calm.

She didn't know how long she had been sitting there before she was aware of someone behind her. She turned her head and saw Finn, standing at the top of the steps, holding on to the railing. She looked away and closed her eyes.

She knew he would come to her.

'Jesus, Millie. Are you mad? You'll be blown away.'

Millie opened her eyes but didn't turn or answer him. She watched a seagull struggle against the wind, then give up. Diving low towards the waves for sanctuary.

'What are you doing?'

She felt Finn's hand rest on her shoulder and twisted around.

'Were you in prison?' She heard her own voice hoarse and raspy. 'Is that where you learnt to paint?'

'*What?*'

'You heard.'

Finn opened his mouth to speak, then shut it again quickly. He wiped away sea spray from his face.

Millie turned back to face the sea, not bothering to pull away the strands of hair that were sticking to her cracked lips and catching her eyelashes. A small pool of seawater had gathered in a crease of her parka and she could smell salt in her nostrils.

'Come inside, will you? You're foundered.'

Millie didn't move.

'Please, Millie. We'll talk inside.' Millie noted a more desperate tone to his voice now.

She turned slightly on her bollard and peered into the water below. It was so dark. So deep. For a moment she thought how soothing it would be on her parched skin. How lovely it would be to put her head under it – swimming like a mermaid through the harbour mouth into the open sea.

Another wave crashed over them.

'For God's sake, Millie. We'll get washed away.'

'I said, were you in prison? Tell me!' She only knew she was shouting when she saw Finn's head push back from her.

'I'll explain… I can explain… Millie. Come inside. Let me explain.'

She held his gaze and saw his eyes: wide and alert. She felt a rage rising in her, but she would have to control it. Her mouth was clamped so tight she could feel her back teeth hard against each other. She stood up and leaned in towards Finn's face. A gust of wind pushed her, and Finn quickly grabbed her arm. Shaking it off, she put her freezing hand on the railing next to his.

'Were you in the Maze?' she asked. Then, unable to stop herself, she went on. 'With that man?' Staring at Finn, Millie suddenly felt faint. Everything around her seemed pale and in slow motion.

She was holding on to the railing as tightly as she could, but her grip was slipping. In that moment she wouldn't have cared if a wave had come overhead and take her away.

'Cathal? Is that who you mean?' Finn's eyes were wilder now and his voice was shaking. Millie had never seen him like this.

Thinking she was going to pass out, she pushed past him towards the steps, but he grabbed her arm. Millie didn't resist; she didn't have the strength.

'I love you, Millie. That's all that matters.'

She turned her head sharply.

'Is it?' she asked, finally allowing their eyes to meet.

Back in the room, Millie studied Finn. She decided he was different from before. His leather jacket was grubby and his boots were scuffed. He had the look of a man who had been up all night. Maybe he had.

'God, it's freezing in here,' he said, moving to close the window. She watched as he busied himself, boiling the small kettle – placing the last of the instant coffee into mugs. Millie sat in the wicker chair staring at him, then out towards the wall with the plaque. Finn eventually sat on the end of the unmade bed.

'I was in prison.' His voice was low, his tone slow and deliberate. 'It was a lifetime ago. Over twenty years.'

Millie didn't look at him. She cupped her coffee to her mouth, letting the strong, harsh warmth hit the back of her throat.

'I should have told you. I would have.'

Millie could feel how much effort he was putting into his words.

Turning around she saw his head was down, like an old dog, staring at the floor.

'Is that where you met…' Millie felt her throat tighten. 'Is that where you met… *him*?'

When Finn didn't speak, Millie shouted, 'Is it?'

Finn sat up quickly. 'Yes. Yes. I met Cathal there.'

She studied his face, trying to decide if he would have told her, or would he have kept his nasty little secret forever?

She turned back to the window and for a moment thought she saw the plaque on the far wall, but then it disappeared again. She swallowed hard. 'Why were you there?'

'I can't hear you, Millie?'

Millie cleared her throat. 'Why were you in prison?'

Her hands were shaking, and some coffee had spilt onto her coat, so she set her cup down on the floor beside her.

'Millie. Look at me. Please.'

'I've read all about your friend, you know. Here…' said Millie, quickly leaning over and grabbing her notebook from the table, throwing it at him on the bed. 'About what he did, right here in the village. Right there,' she said, throwing her hand back towards the window. 'But of course, you know all about that.'

When Finn didn't answer, she went on. 'I couldn't find anything about you, mind. Funny that. Not one single entry about Finn McFall the painter. Finn McFall the poet. Why's that, Finn? Or is Finn not your real name?'

Millie could feel all her muscles tensing. She placed her clenched fists under her thighs. Just as she had the night Cathal started to sing in the pub.

'Course Finn's my name. Course it is,' he said, with hurt eyes. Touching the notebook, he went on. 'McFall's my mother's name. I took it after prison.'

Millie closed her eyes and sighed, 'Finally. Thank you.' Swallowing, she took a breath. 'Were you… were you involved?'

'Jesus, Millie. No. No. It wasn't like that.' Finn was now standing up, running his hand through his hair. His cheeks were flushed and his forehead was shiny where a light sweat had started to settle.

'What was it like, Finn? Tell me.' Millie was using all her strength to control her voice. She could feel pins and needles in her fists but didn't dare take them out from under her.

'It was a terrible time, Millie. You've no idea.'

Millie bit her lip and looked past him.

'We lived in the middle of it all. There was no escape.'

'Escape? From what?'

'From what? From them.'

'Who?'

'All of them. IRA. Soldiers. Police.'

Finn was now pacing around the bedroom, manically running his hands through his hair. 'If one didn't get you, the other did.' He had stopped by the door and was leaning up against it, his arms crossed. 'Dad was dead. Blinded by a rubber bullet. Got caught up in a riot on his way home from work.' Finn paused, then went on. 'He gave up after that.'

Millie felt some of her anger drain away.

'My mother was trying to get us out. She hated it all…' His voice was now more conversational than confessional. 'Her mother was a Protestant, you know that. My grandmother. Imagine.'

A small, forced laugh left his mouth. 'If they had known that. God knows.' He was shaking his head now, his mind in the past. 'She got my brothers out alright. But not me. I was too young to go.'

'Go on,' she said, leaning towards him, her tone a little softer.

'You come from a lovely wee house down the country, Millie. You've no idea what it was like up around us. The beatings, the knee-cappings. You had to do what they said. You had no choice.'

Millie wanted to stop him talking. She wanted to go to him, put her hands over his mouth. Tell him about her father. Her story. But she was exhausted and didn't know where to even begin.

'Anyway, they came for me. My brothers got out, so they came for me.'

Millie forced the word out: 'IRA?'

Finn nodded. 'It started with nothing. Taking a package across the city on my bike. Letting a man into the house to sleep the odd night. No questions asked.'

'What did your mother say?'

'Say? You didn't say anything, Millie. You just did.' Finn paused, then went to the sink in the bathroom and threw water over his face.

Millie's eyes followed him closely. She was trying to match the man in front of her, the man she knew, with the words she was hearing.

'I think she thought she'd get me away when I was sixteen.'

'What age were you then?'

'Fifteen.'

Millie tried to remember what she was like at that age. A few years after Dad. All she remembered was devastation. Her mother's sadness, her sister's anger. Her own loneliness.

'And if it wasn't them knocking on our door, it was the army. The Brits.' Finn came into the bedroom drying his hands on a small towel.

Millie stayed silent. Desperate not to hear what he was going to say.

'*Out of your beds, you Fenian bastards.*' Finn was now leaning against the frame of the bathroom door, imitating an English accent. Millie was as ashamed as she was annoyed.

'They spat that in our faces, my mother's face, on more nights than I remember. You've no idea. The things they did.'

'Well, maybe they knew you had been doing things. Bad things.'

Finn let out a short, hollow laugh. 'They came way before that, Millie. Way before.'

Millie felt her scalp was on fire. She caught a glimpse of herself in the mirror and was shocked at the face staring back at her. It was pale, puffy, but there were large red blotches of anger all over it.

Finding her voice, she went on. 'You wouldn't go to prison for that, Finn. Not just for that.'

She could tell he was thinking. Preparing his next words.

'Towards the end there was more.'

'More?'

'Driving.'

'But you were only fifteen.'

'That didn't matter. I could drive since I was a cub. We all could. Joy-riding through the estate. Racing ponies. There wasn't much else to do.'

Millie remembered the pictures on the news.

'Where did you drive?'

'Down the motorways mostly. Fermanagh, Tyrone. Always out of the city.'

Millie felt her stomach churn and she had to swallow some bile that had come into her mouth.

'Tyrone?' She was almost choking.

'Omagh, Strabane.'

'Dungrillen? Where I'm from.'

'Yes. Dungrillen, too.' Finn was making an effort with his words again.

'What were you doing there?'

Finn's eyes creased, as if he was trying to remember. 'Moving things. You know. Dropping lads.'

'You never asked questions?'

Finn didn't speak. Just shook his head sharply.

Millie was now hugging her knees up to her chin. The fur on her parka was matted and there was a strong smell of salt in her hair. She was shivering.

'What did you do in Dungrillen, Finn?'

Finn looked down at her. 'I didn't know what they were planning. I swear to you, Millie. You have to believe me.' He was staring hard at her. His eyes were wide and pleading again.

'I believe you.' And she did.

'I only drove through the town once. It must have been Christmas. I remember there was a big Christmas tree with lights on it in the square. Carols were playing out of a loudspeaker. It was freezing. I remember thinking how stupid it was to have the lights on during the day.'

'What did you do, Finn?'

Finn swallowed. 'I drove outside the town. Way outside. Near the water. The lough. The others were picked up.'

'What others?'

'The lads I had in the car.'

'Picked up?'

'By another car.'

'Then what?' Millie rested the side of her face on her knees.

'I waited. I remember it started to snow. I remember the snow.'

'Waited?'

'Yes.'

'And?'

'They came back.'

She could see Finn struggling to swallow again. He wasn't saying everything he was thinking.

'I drove them back to the city. Dropped them off at a house. Took the car on and burnt it out.' Finn turned away. 'Like I was told to do.'

'What had they done, Finn?' She spoke slowly, knowing what he was going to say before he said it.

'They shot a man.'

Millie closed her eyes and hugged her knees more tightly, rocking slightly in her chair. Back and forth, back and forth.

Then, looking up at him, she went on. 'What year?'

'Ninety-four, I think.'

'You think?'

'Yes, ninety-four. The end of ninety-four.'

The same year as Dad.

Millie knew there was no Christmas tree up in the square when her father was killed, but there was a few months later when Kenny Shaw, her father's best friend, was shot.

Millie turned her head away from him and began to sob.

'You're just as bad as them. Did anyone ever tell you that, Finn?' Millie spun back to look at him quickly. 'Jesus, Finn… for what? A united fucking Ireland? It's pathetic.' Millie knew she was screaming, and she could feel small balls of spit gathering at the edges of her mouth.

'I didn't know they were going to kill someone. I swear it, Millie. I was only a lad.'

Finn had his head in his hands.

Then, lifting his head up, he went on, 'There's not a day goes past that I don't think about what they did. About what I did.'

Feeling she had finally got the truth, she moved to the bed and stood perfectly still. Her face was wet with tears and she had to sniff to get rid of the bubbles of ooze dripping from her nose.

Just as she was about to speak, a ray of light burst into the room. Millie saw patches of a clear blue sky streaming through the window.

'It's in here every day, Millie,' said Finn, as she turned back, watching him thump his temple with his fist. His eyes creasing in the harsh sunlight.

She threw back her shoulders. 'I need to tell you something, Finn, and I don't want you to speak until I've finished. Okay?'

Finn kept his face still and in the burst of light Millie was shocked how haggard it was.

The face of a terrorist.

'My father was killed, Finn. Shot. Shot to pieces by the type of men you drove. Maybe even the same men.' She sniffed and wiped her nose across the back of her hand. '…Men like you, Finn.' Millie heard her voice low and calm.

'*What?*' Finn dropped his hand from his brow, and she could see his eyes, dancing wildly.

'So, yes, Finn. I do know what it felt like back then. I was there. Even younger than you. The car bombs, the shootings, the explosions – I saw it all. And just like you, it's in my shadow, my mother's shadow, my family's shadow every day. *Every. Fucking. Day.*'

Millie thought she was finished, but words kept coming. 'But you know what? There's one big difference between you and me, Finn. One difference. I'm not a murderer.'

Finn stood up. He was shaking. 'Why didn't you say something to me? Why didn't you tell me? Why? Oh my God, Millie. I'm so sorry. Sorry for all of it.' Finn's voice was breaking and tears were now rolling down his cheeks.

With effort Millie glanced away. 'You need to leave me now, Finn. You need to get out.'

'Millie, please... please don't say that.' Finn was now facing her. He tried to stroke her face, but she grabbed his wrist.

'Don't.'

He tried to pull her towards him, but she shook him off roughly.

Finn let out a noise. 'Listen, Millie. I told you, didn't I? Good people can do bad things. It happens. I hated myself for what I did.' He went on, almost whispering. 'I still do.'

For a moment, she wanted to reach out and touch him. Let him pull her into his arms. Tell him she understood that none of this was his fault. But then the face of her dead father lying in the morgue filled her mind and her forgiveness faded away.

'I'm leaving this place now. Going home. To where I belong.' Millie started to move around the room quickly, lifting her suitcase and bag up onto the bed.

'You belong with me... you know that. I love you.'

Millie stopped what she was doing and closed her eyes. 'People like you don't deserve love.'

'You don't mean that.'

'You lost the right to it, when you...' She looked away, disgusted.

'I know you love me,' he said, almost defiantly, 'You can't change that.'

With this, Millie's voice broke. She went to him and took his face hard in her hands. 'I did love you, Finn. You're right. But I am going to stop doing that now. *Do. You. Understand?* Millie's face was so close to his, she could feel his hot breath on her skin.

'I was a lad, Millie. Fifteen. I didn't have any choice.'

'Don't. Don't you dare do that,' said Millie, pointing her finger close to his mouth. She tried to think of something more to silence him.

Finn slumped down on the edge of the bed again.

Millie walked to the window and leaned against the open curtain. The wind had eased off and she could hear the seagulls cawing again as they flicked down over the water.

'The wind has passed. It's calmer now.' Her voice was soft. 'I'm going to forget we ever met. You need to do the same.'

Finn stumbled off the bed and came to her. He raised his hand as if trying to get her to stop talking. 'We can't do that. It will destroy us.' His voice was full of tears.

'We're already destroyed.'

Finn pushed her hair away from her forehead, the way he had done since she met him, and for a moment she wanted to take his hand, hold it to her face.

'We could leave here together. Go away. Canada. Forget about Ireland. The Troubles…'

'Forget about Ireland? The Troubles?' Millie tried to laugh. 'We are the Troubles, Finn.'

His face was so close to hers she could feel the heat from his burning cheeks and smell the sweat sitting on his flushed neck.

'If you go, if you walk through that door, they have won. You know that? They all have.' Finn's eyes were blinking more tears away.

Millie thought about what he said. Then, shaking her head hard, a hollow laugh left her lips. 'Finn. Don't you know? They won a long time ago.'

London

Eighteen months later

Millie's feet throbbed, even with the gel insoles Sasha had told her about. She leaned against the kitchen door and took off her stilettos, throwing them across the hall into the tidy-up basket by the front door. She should have worn wedges, but Sasha had persuaded her heels were the only option for an awards dinner.

She slumped into a chair at her small kitchen table. Smoothing out creases from her too-tight dress, she saw a ladder in her tights, just above the knee. When she touched it, the cracked skin on her thumb made it worse. She frowned, hoping she hadn't left the flat that way.

She looked at the statue on the table. Running her fingers over the smooth glass, she thought about where to put it. Unlike Oscar winners, she didn't have a downstairs loo. Her small flat in Battersea had a single bathroom, which these days was more like a Chinese laundry. It could be a door stop, but that could be dangerous. No, she'd put it on the mantelpiece in the living room or on her bedside table – if she could find an inch of space there. She lifted the award in her hands. It was heavy. The engraved inscription made her hold her breath.

'*Best Human-Interest Feature (National Newspaper)*'.

Running her fingers through her hair, pulling out numerous hairclips the hairdresser had used, she went over the night in her mind. The ceremony itself was a blur. She was nervous. When they called out her name, she thought it was some terrible mistake, like the big awards a few years before. She flushed as she remembered Tom having to physically lift her from her chair and push her towards the stage.

It was nearly a year on from the publication of her feature. After leaving Ballydunn she wasn't sure if she would ever write it – but Ashmal had persuaded her to. He said it was important for people to know how war destroys the lives of ordinary people, like him, and in a different way, her. He trusted her with his story and she in turn made sure identities and locations were never revealed.

The last time she had spoken to Ashmal, she had offered to source other accommodation for him and the men, but he had declined politely, saying their stay in Ballydunn was always temporary.

A moment in time.

Like her visit had been.

Since then, life had then become so unexpectedly full for Millie, contact had dwindled, and as she lifted the award, the heat of guilt flushed her neck.

She would call him in the morning, share the win with him.

She went to the fridge and fought through the tupperware and various bottles to find the mini snipe of champagne Sasha had sent her. She read the heart-shaped post-it Sellotaped to the small bottle: '*You're amazing. Good luck with everything. Sx*'

Millie popped the bottle and took a swig, then sent her friend a picture of the award.

Back at the table, her legs up on another chair, she flipped through her phone. The paper's online edition was already running a banner about her success, and she'd had a text, a drunken one, from Robert Donaldson, the photographer whose powerful pictures were mostly used for her winning piece in the end. Blotches of colour grafting on wild seas and the bleakness of Ashmal's cottage had all been captured beautifully by the talented Glaswegian.

Twirling the small bottle rhythmically around her fingers, her earlier elation faded. Her mind, once again, was full of Ireland.

Hitting a wall of exhaustion, she heaved herself up from the table and moved around the flat slowly, locking the front door and turning off the lights. She tip-toed down the corridor to the bathroom, but just as she pushed the door, two boxes of files she had temporarily stacked up on top of the clothes basket crashed to the ground – the metal handles clanging against the tiled floor.

Millie squeezed her eyes tight and winced, waiting.

Nothing.

Relieved, she washed her face and teeth and peeled off her dress, then fell over trying to get out of her Spanx cycling shorts. Giggling, she wrapped a towel around her middle and continued tiptoeing towards the bedroom. Just as she passed the box room, she heard a noise. Stopping mid-stride, she held her breath. Another sound, this time more of a gurgle.

She opened the door a crack and even though the new blackout blinds were down, the plug-in light gave enough of a glow for Millie to see the source of the noise. There, gazing at her through the bars of his cot, was her son. All nine months of him.

Millie wanted to go to him but fought the urge. He needed to sleep. She needed to sleep. But when the gurgling grew louder, she couldn't resist and gently padded across the floor to his cot. When the boy found her eyes, his legs kicked wildly inside his sleep bag and Millie took a sharp intake of breath. She lifted him up and let his already curly hair tickle her cheek. Using the opportunity to nuzzle him, she breathed his smell as deeply as she could, before laying him back in his cot.

Letting him hold one of her fingers, Millie told him all about her night, emphasising how clever his mummy was for winning an award, for a story he would love to hear when he was older.

Only when he had fallen into a deep slumber did Millie wriggle her finger out of his tiny grip.

When she got to her bedroom, the sight of her bed made her shoulders drop. Most of her wardrobe was on her bed, the result of a panicked trying-on session at six o'clock that evening. Too exhausted to do anything else, she pushed everything off the bed and threw herself on top of it, not even bothering to get under the duvet. Before sleep found her, she went over what she had to do the next morning to get out of the house. She'd take an Uber to work. She deserved it. She was an award-winning journalist after all.

Millie hiccupped, then fell asleep smiling.

Finlay woke just before seven. Later than usual. Mercy, the babysitter, had told her she'd held off until midnight to feed him the milk Millie had expressed. Feeling every muscle in her body ache, she now thanked God for Mercy, or sister Mercy, as she and Sasha had secretly named her.

Mercy Faith McIvor, a Nigerian-born maternity nurse with outstanding references, came as a gift from Finlay's godfather. She had stayed with Millie for three weeks after the birth and the two single mothers had bonded over the new-born. If free, Mercy now babysat on the rare occasion Millie went out without her son.

Struggling to get out of bed, the anticipation of lifting the boy for his morning feed replaced the pain of her hangover. As Finlay fed hungrily, she spotted a cushion lying on the floor. The cover was printed with a picture taken at Finlay's small christening. The image was grainy and Millie couldn't believe how awful she looked, but she smiled when she saw Finlay with his two godparents: Dom and Sasha. Never imagining two such different people could have the same job title. She remembered how Dom, who, after the initial shock of somehow thinking the baby might be his, said he was delighted to take on the role of godparent. It was the least he could do.

Millie had made contact with him when she came back to London. She couldn't bear not to. Not after all they had been through. It helped that an email he had sent her from Singapore was an open sore of an apology. He said he now understood he had bullied her into the termination and asked for forgiveness. He then went on to thank her for saving his life, as he was close to the edge when she left for Ireland.

Very measured. Very Dom.

At the time, she had thought about replying. She wanted him to know that what they had wasn't love. She had thought it was, but she now knew it wasn't. But that would be cruel. You only want to hurt someone when you still love them. When the love has gone, it all doesn't matter anymore.

Dom had a new addiction. Exercise. He was an Iron Man and was dating an Iron Woman. An investment banker from New York called Megan. She had dogs. He was happy.

Since Finlay's birth, his behaviour towards Millie had been faultless. He had insisted on helping her invest her share of the cottage sale – which turned out to be substantial. Her portfolio, his words, appeared to be doing well. Too well, she suspected. He opened an account in Finlay's name. A school fund was set up.

Millie let him do it all.

Sasha had asked to be godmother and Millie was happy to oblige. Pushing Finlay's dark hair gently over to the side of his face, she thought about how her old friend had saved her sanity over the last eighteen months.

Millie was three months pregnant when the nurse at work confirmed her suspicion. She didn't know what to do. She had to tell someone, and Sasha was the first person she thought about.

Millie was careful how she delivered the news to her friend. She said it was a mistake, but a happy one. She said it was impossible to be with the father and asked Sasha to respect her privacy. Amazingly, she had. Choosing instead to come and stay with Millie for weekends of hand-holding. On that first visit, Sasha had slept on the sofa, got up early to clean the flat, found an antenatal class for Millie to join, wrote lists of things that needed to be done. She made terrible Irish stew and ran baths for Millie, who slept most of the time.

On one weekend visit, when Millie was particularly subdued, Sasha made her march across Albert bridge to Knightsbridge, where they had lunch in Harvey Nichols. Millie had felt bloated and awkward, but her friend loved it, even getting a spray tan and blow dry before they left the store. When Millie questioned the cost, Sasha said there were no pockets in a shroud, adding there had to be some benefits to your car always smelling of chicken feed. They had linked arms on the escalator and laughed like hyenas the whole way back to Battersea.

During these trips, which were more often than five children should allow, David cared for the brood. A fact that brought the girls endless amount of pleasure.

Millie knew Sasha suspected Dom was the father and as the pregnancy progressed, her friend became more daring with her questions.

Did she love the father?

Could she ever see a time when she could be with the father?

Millie eventually confided in her friend that Dom was *not* the father but still did not say who was. And again, Sasha never asked. Millie suspected she enjoyed the collusion.

The mother of five took the role of birthing partner in her stride. When Finlay was finally born after a forty-two-hour labour on a Sunday morning at 5am, it was Sasha who took the pictures and sent them to all the family.

She couldn't have asked for a better friend.

Finlay let out a cry. He was refusing her breast and Millie beamed, loving this little game they played every morning. She was certain he was teasing her, as eventually he went back for more, but only once she had tickled his toes and blew raspberries on his cheeks.

Her family were divided over the birth. Karen said it was embarrassing. A woman of her age having a baby with no husband. What would people think? Colin had sent her a text saying how pleased he was for her.

Jamie and Eimear had been suitably conservative in their approval, sending her a White Company hamper of candles and baby clothes and a very '*Catholic-looking*' (Sasha's words) christening card, but never suggesting a visit. Kate and her flatmate Amanda had come over. They had brought Veda bread and Tayto crisps for Millie and cuddled Finlay incessantly. They were a couple.

The others in America had been delighted. For the first time in years, Millie had regular contact, Zooming some or sometimes all of them on Sundays at bath time. Finlay's cousins, who were all older, sang and danced for him, and his giggles whipped them all into a frenzy of love.

Her mother was openly sceptical but privately delighted. She sent Millie a letter, reminding her of what she had said to her that Sunday morning before she left for the cottage. '*You will be a mother one day. God works in mysterious ways.*' Millie now kept the letter inside a Bible Sasha's mother had sent over with a Union Jack bookmark tucked inside.

Millie knew her family also suspected Dom was the father – but they never said anything. Not even Karen. His generosity silencing any criticism of his apparent lack of commitment.

The creche at the paper was on the ground floor. Huge glass doors opened out onto a walled play area, allowing the toddlers space to roam in the open air. It had only opened a year ago, after the new publisher, a Swede who had four children of her own, declared the organisation pre-historic in its treatment of woman and insisted a creche be set up for all the papers in the group.

It was popular from the start and Millie was lucky to get Finlay a place. She didn't like to think about it, but she was sure her single-mother status helped her climb the waiting list.

When she got out of the lift on the third floor, she initially thought there must be football on one of the screens in the newsroom as there was so much shouting. But she soon understood it was all for her.

On the celebrity desk, her old colleagues were standing on chairs, waving papers in the air. As she walked on to features, she saw her own chair had balloons stuck all over it. Looking over to Tom's office, she saw him leaning up against his door, smiling and clapping with all the others.

Millie dropped her bag by her chair and tried to hide her face with her hair, but it was no good: happy tears were already starting to fall down her cheeks.

Sensing her predicament, Tom took charge. 'Over here, Malone.'

Millie heaved with relief and walked quickly to his office.

'You okay?'

'Just tired.'

Tom gave her a crisp, white handkerchief that smelt of Italy. 'We should follow up on the story. You'll need to go over.'

'Go over?'

'Can you organise Finn okay?'

When anyone shortened Finlay's name her stomach lurched.

'Well… I don't think I need to go over, Tom, surely—'

Tom cut her off. 'No. You do. Catch up with Ashmal and the others. People are invested.'

'I need to think about it—'

'Well, think about it by tomorrow and book your flight. Go…'

Millie stood up but didn't leave.

'What?' Tom asked, in a not-wanting-a-reply way. 'Get outta here… and by the way. Well done.'

Just before lunch, Millie was standing at her desk, taking friendly abuse from her colleagues about her win. The mounted TV screens all around the newsroom were showing CNN, Sky News, and Aljazeera. A breaking news banner on Sky caught her eye. Walking towards the screen her whole body stiffened. Grappling around for the remote, which she found on the floor, she turned the volume up as high as it would go. It was a report about an arrest in the Republic of Ireland. The background picture on screen was of Mullaghmore harbour. She could see the hotel in the background. The place was swarming with Garda. Without taking her eyes off the screen, she grabbed a chair on wheels and sat down. She could feel the edges of her ears burning and her breath had quickened. A few other reporters were now standing by her, following the story.

A new image appeared. It was old footage – she could tell by the cars and the clothes the policemen were wearing. A boat was being pulled from the harbour. To the right of the image a photograph of Lord Mountbatten appeared. Millie ran her hands through her hair and then kept them there, cupping her skull. A young reporter now live on screen was talking to camera. He was rushed, nervous.

> *'Details are few, but what we know so far is that it appears the Garda, acting on information, have intercepted a boat destined for a terrorist attack.'*

Millie could feel tension all around her. Other televisions were being turned up and she could hear a melee of voices talking about the story.

> *'The location, just off the coast here in Mullaghmore, is the same location where Lord Mountbatten was killed by an IRA bomb over forty years ago.'*

The reporter went on, now reading from a piece of paper that had been handed to him.

> *'The Garda has now confirmed a local man on the vessel has been arrested in connection with the find.'*

The camera cut to a new location. Millie recognised it straight away. Letterkenny. A man was being led into the police station in handcuffs. The defiant smile.

It was Cathal.

Millie's stomach twisted. There was a ringing in her ears and she could no longer hear what was being said on screen. She felt a hand on her shoulder and jumped.

'Jesus, that's where you were, right?' asked Tom, not taking his eyes off the screen.

'Yes. Yes, it was. Listen, I don't feel well…'

'Hungover more likely,' a voice boomed from behind. Forced laughter followed and Millie spun round to try and silence the voice, but he had already gone back to the screen.

'I have to go…'

Tom opened his mouth to speak, but Millie didn't wait to listen. She grabbed her bag and, after running towards the lift, decided instead to take the stairs to the creche.

Finlay was out for a walk. After thinking for a moment, she hurriedly told the girl at the desk she was going out on a story. Millie reminded her there was expressed milk in the creche fridge and if there were any problems, any problems at all, they were to call her and she'd be back in forty-five minutes.

She decided against an Uber and hailed a black cab. The driver tried to talk, but she ignored him, eventually saying she had a migraine. She leaned her head against the window and let the condensation drip down the side of her temple, cooling her cheek.

When she got into the flat she kicked off her boots and went straight to her bedroom. Walking over a sea of clothes, she climbed on the bed, leaving her phone by her pillow. Pulling the duvet up over her head she shrouded herself in darkness. Her breath felt warm in the space and she rocked herself gently, trying to make her mind go blank. But all she could think about was what she had seen on the screen. A torrent of questions poured into her head.

How long had he been planning it?

Was he working alone?

What about Finn. Did he know?

She cried out Finn's name.

She hadn't allowed herself to think about him, really think about him, since she left Ireland. She didn't dare. Then within months all she could think about was the baby. That was all that mattered. She pulled the duvet even closer and lifted her knees to her chest.

'Acting on information.'

Millie could feel her fists clenching. She didn't want to think about Mullaghmore or that man. She didn't want to think about Finn. Not like this.

She decided to phone Ashmal.

Sitting up, adrenalin flooded her body. She needed water, and leaned over to grab a bottle lying by the bed. When she found his number she inhaled deeply. Her hands were shaking and her fingers fluttered over the phone before finally pressing the call button hard. Waiting for the connection, she could feel her breaths becoming short and shallow.

Nothing.

Agitated, she called again.

Still nothing.

There was no connection; the phone was dead.

Everything around her stopped; the air was silent, like when snow falls at night.

Ashmal was gone.

Dropping her mobile on the bed, she closed her eyes, remembering his eager face, telling her about his hopes of getting to Europe, to his brother – like a migrating bird in search of a new home. She pulled at the bedside drawer and let her fingers fight their way through the mess of motherhood. Eventually they found what she wanted. Taking the small pebble of soap out from its silk wrapping, Millie inhaled its aroma deeply. Like a hit of Fentanyl, it calmed her mind. Lying back on the bed, she drifted, allowing herself to believe Ashmal was finally on his way to a better life.

Sasha called that night. 'Can you believe it? Jesus, I knew that Quinn man was a real Shinner. But not this.' Millie couldn't help but think Sasha sounded excited.

'Wee bastard,' her friend went on when Millie stayed silent. 'And to think I bought petrol from him at the weekend.'

The following days saw Millie in a trance. She got up, went to work, came home, put Finlay and then herself to bed. It was all she could do. Sasha called several times, but Millie only replied by text, using work as an excuse. What words could she say to her friend? That she already knew about Cathal's past. That in fact his tenant, an ex-Republican prisoner, was her godson's father. No. She couldn't do that. Not to Sasha.

Much to Millie's relief, Tom sent Henry Smyth over to cover the story. The veteran journalist had reported on the Troubles for years and the possibility of the New IRA profiteering from illegal fishermen was now a major news story.

Millie had avoided phone calls from home.

She was sure her mother would want to talk of nothing else. She imagined Karen, full of hate and anger, shouting over her mother's shoulder, into the phone.

When she finally did make the call, she was surprised at how little interest her mother showed in the story. More concerned, it seemed, about the cafe closure in Tesco.

It occurred to Millie the older her mother got, the less she cared about the past. Whereas for Millie, it seemed to matter more.

When she tried to bring her mother back to the arrest, she sensed her agitation.

'I told you, Matilda. They'll never stop.' After sighing, she went on. 'It's Ireland. Those boys would fight their own shadow.' Millie's chest tightened when she thought of the only other person who had ever said that to her.

Millie now imagined her mother sitting by the Aga, rocking gently, smoothing out her favourite blanket as she spoke. 'Anyway, how's Finlay?' her mother said cheerily. 'Will you be bringing the wee man home for Christmas?'

Two weeks later, she was at her desk, pretending to organise a trip to Aberdeen, following a tip she had received about migrant fishermen trapped in terrible conditions by the docks. It was just after lunch and Antonio, the one remaining post-boy in the company, was throwing packages across the heads of reporters.

These days, there was little of interest in the post, but today her bundle was bulging with something oversized. Colourful. She pinged the elastic band and a card, larger than everything else, fell out. Her eyes were drawn to the image on the front: a watercolour, painted in bright hues of tangerine, yellow and blue. It was a harbour scene with small boats bobbing in the water and there were people scattered all around, sitting at tables, maybe a cafe. The figures weren't developed, just little sticks, the boats mere splodges. But it worked. She studied the picture carefully and her eyes fell on a shop sign, but unable to make out what it said, she lifted the card closer to her desk lamp. She squinted and for a second was confused. The words '*Sooke Harbour Cafe*' had been written in over the paint, to make it more visible.

She stood up abruptly. Her eyes were wide and she could feel a ball of energy gathering through her body. Unnerved, she turned the card over; the stamp mark burned into her eyes: Vancouver Island, Canada. She fell back into her seat, her eyes skittering the room.

Was anyone watching her?

Tom's office was empty. His door shut. The few reporters there were staring at their screens or chatting about what they were doing at the weekend. The white noise of the mounted TVs buzzed loudly in her ears.

There were two lines of writing centred on the card and she instantly recognised the easy, casual hand.

The first line, *'Nolle timere'*, had the letters '*SH*' beside it.

The second line comprised of one word: '*Veni*'.

Her mind was blank. What language was this? It wasn't Irish; she was sure of it.

She tried to shout out the words, '*Nolle timere,* anyone?'

But her voice was dry. Nobody heard.

She cleared her throat and repeated the words, loudly this time.

A few of the reporters glanced over, shaking their heads, not really interested.

'Not a Latin speaker then?' asked James Hoare, the paper's veteran law reporter and the most conceited man Millie had ever encountered.

'What does it mean?'

'Don't be afraid, my dear. Do. Not. Be. Afraid.'

Millie frowned. She grabbed her phone and typed the term into google. Several posts came up. All referencing the same fact. They were the last words Seamus Heaney said to his wife before he died.

SH. Seamus Heaney.

She typed the word 'Veni' into her phone: '*Come*' in Latin.

Millie threw her phone on the desk. Intense heat was rising up over her neck and face.

But there was something else: a feeling was rising up through her, engulfing her.

It was joy.

Finlay was lying on her bed after his bath. He was wrapped in a Mickey Mouse baby-grow his American cousins had posted over. She had him between pillows to keep him from rolling off and he was happy, trying to fit his whole fist inside his mouth.

It was Saturday morning, Millie's favourite time with her son.

She lay down beside him and propped herself up on one elbow, studying his small, chubby face: his blue eyes, the colour of cornflowers and long eyelashes so familiar to her. His hair, curling more by the day.

He was the image of his father.

Millie had still not told anyone who that was. Not one living soul.

She reached for the postcard under her pillow.

So… He'd gone back to Canada… To the big glass house by the sea. She thought of the girl with the good hair, but she knew he hadn't gone back to her.

He wanted a new life. With Millie in it.

For a moment, she dared to let her mind go to a place where she imagined Finn was responsible for foiling the attack in Mullaghmore. She imagined him finding out about Cathal and going straight to the police. She saw him leaving the village. Not looking back. Glad to be away from it all.

Twirling Finlay's tiny curls in her fingers, she pictured herself arriving on Vancouver Island, finding Sooke Harbour and the cafe, the one on the card. She would lift the boy over into Finn's arms. She imagined his face, full of surprise and love for his son.

The noise of an overhead plane broke her thoughts. She saw Finlay's face crumple a little, so she stroked his cheek, all the time smiling as his eyelids flickered and finally closed. Watching him sleep, she thought about the day she left the Harbour Hotel. She had driven at speed, desperate to get over the border into the north. But there had been a moment when she pulled up into a wooded lay-by near the Lough, and thought not about what she had found out, but rather what she had lost.

Turning the car, she became acutely aware of her surroundings. The hills around her were thick with fir trees, and then, without warning, all she could see was the Christmas tree in Dungrillen town square. The one Finn said he had passed. Millie then remembered how she and her mother used the tree as shelter from the icy rain the morning Kenny Shaw's funeral passed by.

Millie didn't turn the car that day. She went straight to Dungrillen, gripping the steering wheel as hard as she had gripped her mother's hand on that freezing morning, all those years ago.

When she got home, she feigned illness and went straight to her old room. Lying on her bed, she came to the conclusion that their pasts were too big for either of them to endure. She had fallen in love and now, to survive, she had to try and crawl her way out of it. And just like the night before she left for college, she waited for morning, when a plane would once again, take her away from it all.

Curling her legs around Finlay's makeshift bed, she ran her fingers over Finn's words. He still loved her. Still wanted her. Her body fizzed with emotion: a heady mix of fear and exhilaration, just like the day she found out she was pregnant. Then, she was certain she didn't want to be with the Finn she had discovered, but she did want his baby. What he had done couldn't be undone – but the child was an innocent part of him she could love without shame. But as the months went by and her belly grew, Millie began to realise that you can't unlove someone. It's impossible. You have to learn to live with that love. No matter how sad and empty it makes you feel.

'*Sometimes good people do bad things.*' Finn's words tumbled around in her head, and she sat up quickly, unsettled. His life had been haunted by what had happened in the past, just as much as hers. Maybe the Troubles did unite rather than divide them.

Pushing Finlay's hair to the side, Millie knew she didn't want him to live the way she had. Part of a family ripped apart, with only a ghost, a shadow for a father. Why should his future be sullied by their pasts?

A familiar heaviness settled over her.

If she went, she could never tell anyone about Finn's past. It would be a secret she would have to take to her grave. She sank back on the bed, thinking what a terrible way to live a life.

But if she stayed, would regret destroy her?

She rubbed her hot cheeks, knowing whatever decision she made would be laden with consequence.

Moving to the end of the bed, she leaned forward, staring hard into the mirror. Her eyes were aching and as she closed them, she again felt her mind drifting.

She was on a beach in Donegal. The sky was a particular shade of blue and the only noise around was the sound of the sea gently lapping over the shingle. The beach was empty, except for a man who turned round and smiled as she reached out to touch his cheek.

A distant noise from Battersea Park brought her back. Crawling up the bed quietly, she again lay by her son. Feeling the warmth of the morning sun on her body, a calmness Millie had never felt before came over her.

And then she knew. She knew what she would do.

Acknowledgements

I would like to thank Jeremy from the Book Guild for believing in me and my story. Also, his colleagues Joe, Fern, Meera and Jack for helping me bring my manuscript to life. And thank you to Ellie @Elspells, my ever-patient editor, without whom I don't actually think I would have finished the book.

Neil Taylor, the best writer I know who also happens to be the best mentor, friend and all-round hand-holder a girl could wish for. I met Neil on the Faber 'Writing a Novel' course and I would like to thank our superb tutor there Shelley Weiner, a sometimes smiling assassin who above all taught me to cut copy until it bleeds. Also, my fellow Faberites from the Class of 2018 (yes, that's how long it can take to write a novel!).

Tara Loden for her early honesty and insider intel.

Grania McFadden for her 'vibe check' and wise words regarding respect and balance in a manuscript.

Eamonn Mallie, who will never know just how important that coffee was.

Richard, my long-suffering husband, who graciously read and re-read my drafts before anyone else, when all he really wanted to read was the *Burlington* magazine, and my darling daughter Charlotte, who always told me to stop writing (and come and watch Harry Potter) just at the right time.

All my family and friends (you know who you are) for listening and always asking me how the book was going.

And finally, my mother. The other 'Millie' in my life, whose courage and tenacity inspire me every single day, and who, despite everything, still believes life is a gift.

For writing and publishing news, or
recommendations of new titles to read,
sign up to the Book Guild newsletter: